A Gift In The Boonies

By Jan M. Hill

Sharijol Press

DEDICATION

Dedicated to all the imaginative magic users in my life.

THANKS

May thanks to my friends who listened to the story while in development, and to those who encouraged me to finish it; Thanks to Tyler who was my bouncing board. I hope everyone enjoys it.

A special thanks to my friend Kim Gravell for all her proofreading expertise. She caught all my errors.

OTHER BOOKS BY THIS AUTHOR

Asteria Series
Asteria: The Discovery
Annese Does It Again
Rescuing Deavereaux
Like Father, Like Son

Boonies Series
A Gift in the Boonies
Denizens in the Boonies
The Rise of the Seth Drinel

Table of Contents

1 – No Man's Land

I stepped off the train onto an old, weathered platform. Several column beams held up a wooden and copper roof, although the copper had long turned green. Other than a small brick lobby and a few benches, there was nothing. Not even a vending machine! Really? The only other person on the platform was an older man with graying black hair and a tan raincoat buttoned too tightly around his rather round girth. He had gotten off the same train I did. He glanced nervously at me, nodded, and walked towards a dirt parking area.

Walking away from the train as the horn sounded, I glanced around this... rather... quaint... village. From where I stood, I could see what was probably the center of town—if you lived in the 1800s. A large white building with green trim and a wide porch held a sign marked "General Store". It had a Post Office sign in the window, so I guess it doubled as the post office. A few trees lined the walkway to the porch. Next to that was an extensive building that looked like a saloon from the old west. Based on the dirty-looking guy that came out with a brown paper bag and a six-pack, I'm guessing I'm probably right. An old white building with peeling paint stood next to that one with a small alleyway between the two. I couldn't see what that one was.

Turning, I watched the train pull away. Several large bushes on the other side of the tracks greeted me. A dirt road was just beside it. I could see a pale-yellow house that had a large pair of wooden glasses hanging from the porch roof. Ah, the optometrist. Across the road from that was a rather new, or at least newer, brick building that said McCall Veterinary Hospital. A tan storefront with stonework around the bottom had a pharmacy sign. I couldn't see past that.

There were a few people on the streets. They all seemed to dress pretty normally; well, normal for most people. Jeans, t-shirts, sneakers. A bunch of young boys ran past the train station on the other side of the bushes in overalls and T-shirts. They were chasing something I couldn't see, and a brown and white dog chased them with an exuberant bark. I tossed back my jet-black hair and dropped my duffle bag on the platform. I sat on one bench to wait.

OK, so my mother sent me back in time to No Man's Land to spend the summer with an aunt I'd never met all because she didn't want me to be home alone the whole summer. I wouldn't be alone! Well, maybe I would be. Back home, I had only one friend, Marissa. Marissa was about as carefree as you can get. She didn't really care what you were into, or whether your likes and dislikes agreed with hers. She liked you for whatever you were. In my case, that was the biggest outcast in the school. I wore hand-me-down jeans, old shirts from a thrift store, and my sneakers were about to need to be replaced. My hair and eyebrows were black against pale, but not quite pasty, skin. My large blue eyes stuck out so badly that everyone immediately noticed them. A really high metabolism meant I was so skinny that people had called the authorities on my mother three times in the last two years. I ate; really, I did. I just couldn't put on weight. Interests were another issue since I really wasn't into any of the things the other girls were into, or the boys either. I was kinda shy and sensitive, but I wouldn't admit it. And I always had a book in my hand. Not reading wasn't an option!

What made a difference was the dreams I'd been having lately. They were really strange. So strange I wouldn't even tell my mother the details. Then one morning two weeks ago, I woke up to find out the dream I had was real. My bedroom was white with pink curtains. Gosh, I hated those stupid curtains! My four-poster bed had a matching pink canopy. My mother loved pink. Luckily, I had somehow convinced my mother to get me a comforter with horses on it. It was the best I could do. No pink! Anyway, I had this dream that I was waving a pen around and it turned all the pink into spring green. Why spring green? No clue. I didn't like green either. I was actually a blue person; dark blue - or black. When I woke up from the dream, I stretched, looked around, and screamed. The curtains were green. The canopy was green. Even the pink flower on the wall was green! Oddly, my mother didn't seem too surprised by all this, but I was sure I was freaking out!

A horn honked behind me. I turned towards the dirt parking lot to see a red pickup parked facing the station. It had a large cab. The bed was piled high with bags and hay. I didn't recognize it. A gray-haired lady poked her head out the side window with a twinkling smile on her round face.

"Hey, there, lazybones! Are ya coming?"

My eyes widened with excitement as I stood up and grabbed my duffle bag. "Granma?" I started moving towards the truck as the older woman got out. I broke into a big grin and ran. "Granma!"

Grandma was a short woman. I already passed her in height. She was wearing a pair of sweatpants and a blue pullover. Her skin was as pale as mine and her eyes weren't quite as blue. They stood out more since her hair turned gray a few years back. Still, the woman was active, sharp, and strong! She wrapped me in a big bear hug, then planted a kiss on my cheek.

"Come on, now. It'll be dinnertime by the time we get home."

I swung my bag behind my seat and climbed into the cab. "What are you doing here?" I asked, snapped the seat belt in place. "Mom said I was spending the summer with Aunt Eva."

Granma nodded. "Yep. You are. I figured I'd come hang out for a couple of weeks and ease you both in the introductory period."

"The what?"

"The introductory period. You've never met your aunt; well, not that you remember, and she's not used to having kids around. She's excited to have you here, but she's not sure what a young person your age would be into. There's a lot for you to see and do, and you'll have your assigned chores, but what to do with a teenager Eva does not know! So, I figured I'd come help."

"How come Aunt Eva lives in the Boonies anyway?" I asked. I was already feeling lost looking out at the trees and quaint houses that lined the road.

Granma chuckled. "It's a quiet place for her—most of the time. It gives her the freedom she prefers," Granma tried to explained. "My sister was the same way."

"So, what do people do out here?"

"Same things you do at home. Watch TV, play on the internet, go to dances and church, shop, play baseball. Everything is all here."

"You have the internet up here? How?"

"It's called modern technology," Grandma teased. "Not everything is limited to the city." I just rolled my eyes. No duh!

"How come Aunt Eva doesn't come visit mom? Don't they get along?"

"Whatever made you think that?" Grandma seemed surprised.

"Well, I've never met her before; well, not since I was a baby. Doesn't that say something?"

"Does your mother talk about her?"

"Now and again. Sometimes she'll tell me stories from when they were kids."

"Your mother and your aunt get along quite well, actually. They're just different people. Your mother's life and your aunt's life couldn't be farther apart. But they love each other and would do anything for each other. Just remember that."

I nodded. Got it. I went quiet as we traveled along one dusty dirt road after another. The scenery was so strange! I saw horses and cattle, dogs and cats, sheep and chickens. At one point, we stopped for a fox in the middle of the road. A real fox! All brawny red with white sox and the tip of its tail! Just like the pictures! Granma waited patiently as it took its time crossing the street with a rabbit in its mouth.

"So," Granma interrupted the quiet. "Your mother tells me you're having strange dreams."

My gaze shot to her. How'd she know? "I guess. Just nightmares. It's a phase."

Granma laughed heartily. "Come on. Out with it! Tell me about them."

"They're just crazy teenage dreams." I wasn't ready to share these yet.

"Boys?"

"No," I replied quietly. Boys had definitely not entered these dreams.

"Other girls?"

I scowled as I thought. "No, not really."

"What do you mean 'not really'?"

"They're just dreams, Granma! Jeesh!"

Granma nodded with a smile. "Anything strange happen in these dreams?"

"Why are you so interested in my dreams?" I asked defensively. "You suddenly discover how to interpret them or something?"

Granma chuckled. "You'll tell me about them sooner or later. And it's okay. I won't laugh."

Realization struck me like a brick. "Did Mom tell you what happened?" I asked with wide-eyed horror.

"About what?" Granma asked knowingly.

"She did!" I cried. I buried my face in my hands as my entire face reddened.

Granma reached out and patted my shoulder consolingly. "It's ok. It's only the beginning."

"The beginning of what?" I cried. "I'm already a freak!"

I expected Grandma to chastise me for the way I viewed myself. Instead, she laughed a joyful, humorous laugh. My blank expression stared at her. What was so funny about her granddaughter not fitting in with anyone?

"Know this, Kelly," Grandma still chuckled. "Your visit here is more than it appears. You're going to learn a lot about yourself this summer, and Eva is just the person to teach you. Trust her."

"You say that like I don't trust her already," I moped.

"You don't. You're scared and uncertain and skeptical. I already know that. That's one reason I came to help for a bit. It will ease the tension between you both."

Granma pulled off the road onto what looked like an inclining dirt path. There were tire tracks on it, so I guessed it was something more. It twisted and turned and tucked around trees and bushes. Would have been a fantastic toboggan course if it didn't have so many trees to crash into. Neatly cut grass spread outward, but the trees were so thick the sunlight couldn't get through. After nearly five minutes, the pathway leveled out, then opened up into a wide yard. My jaw dropped.

The path was a driveway that led to a huge farmhouse. They painted it a pale blue with white and magenta trim. The railed porch went all the way around the house. A tower stood tall attached to one side, and I could see a glass room at the top. The truck pulled around in front of a three-car garage. There was a shed attached to it with a separate door. The garage was opposite the house with some trees behind it. Peering past Granma, I saw more woods on the far side of the front lawn. The pathway went back even farther. I could see a barn and some other buildings in the distance.

"What's out there?"

"We'll show you around after dinner. Come on! Let's go!"

A tall, broad man with brown hair, muddy eyes, and a scruffy beard came walking over with a long lanky stride. One strap on his overalls was broken, so the bib folded over, revealing a chest full of brown curls and muscle. He looked like something from the backwoods of some southern town.

"Thanks tons, Livy," the man drawled to Granma as she held out the keys.

"Thank you. It was a great way to pick up my granddaughter. Oh, Kelly, this is Mac. He's Aunt Eva's foreman and sees to the running of the farm. Mac, this is Kelly."

"How do, Miss?" he nodded. "It's a pleasure. Hope ya enjoy yer stay here. If I can do anythin' to help, just let me know." I nodded shyly as I crept closer to Grandma. "Don't talk much, do she?" Mac teased.

"Just let her get settled, and she won't stop!" Granma chuckled, taking a few grocery bags from the bed of the truck. "I hope I got it all."

"I'll know when I unload it," Mac said, readjusting the seat in the cab. "See y'all later."

"Now I'm sure I've gone back in time," I muttered.

"Oh, stop!" Granma laughed. "We're still in the 21st century!"

2 – Aunt Eva's Farm

Granma led the way into a wide, airy kitchen. A table set for four stood in front of a large bay window. Delicious aromas wafted through the air. By the stove was a woman who looked an awful lot like my mother. She stood about five-foot-five with hair exactly like mine, only shoulder length. My mother kept hers cut short. She wasn't as thin as me, but thinner than my mother. Her skin was just as pale as mine. Amazing. Must be hereditary.

"Oh, good! You're home!" Aunt Eva cried as she stood up. Potholders covered her hands as she carried a casserole to the table and set it in the middle. She dropped the pot holders and came to hug me. Wow! Her eyes were bluer than mine! "I'm so glad you're here! I haven't seen you since you were 18 months old! Oh, my, how you've grown!" She giggled nervously. "That sounds pretty dumb, doesn't it? You're thirteen! Of course, you've grown!"

"Eva, you're babbling!" Granma grumbled the obvious firmly as she moved to put some things into the refrigerator. "Okay, Kelly. I got you peach slices, string cheese, oranges, Kool Ade, Chex Mix bars, and Cocoa Puffs cereal. That's the list your mother sent. If there's anything else, write it on this small pad here," Granma pointed to a notepad on the fridge door, "and we'll see about getting it when we go into town next."

"What would you like to drink with dinner?" Aunt Eva asked.

"Do you have any milk?" I asked.

"Of course! It's fresh," Eva smiled. "Mac milks the cows each morning." She crossed to a door, opened it, and yelled "Dinner!" into it. She came back smiling. "You can leave your bag over by that doorway. We'll move it up to your bedroom later. Where are your other bags?"

I shrugged. "This is all I've got."

"What?" Aunt Eva snapped up to look at me in surprise.

"It's all I've got. How much do I need?"

"We'll get her some things at the end of the week," Granma said, putting a salad on the table with some dressings. "It looks like her shoes need replacing as well."

I squirmed with embarrassment. Did I look like that much of a charity case? Mom did the best she could.

The soft thump of the other door closing interrupted the tense moment. I glanced towards it, then raised my eyebrows. A teenage boy about sixteen or seventeen came from wherever the door led to. His shaggy brown hair was in disarray. A dirty white, torn t-shirt covered in cobwebs adorned his chest. His jeans were filthy. He looked like he had the coal dust from a fireplace dumped all over him.

"All done," he said to Aunt Eva. He looked down at himself. "I'm, um, gonna clean up before dinner."

I found his tenor voice soft and soothing. It was so different from what I'd expected. He seemed a bit timid, too. I shouldn't judge. That's what everyone else did to me. I was pretty timid myself.

"Take your time, Jasper," Aunt Eva smiled. "We'll wait." The young man disappeared around the corner with a nod.

"Who's Jasper?" I scowled. "Mom said you didn't have any kids."

"I don't," Aunt Eva replied, placing water and milk on the table. "Jasper needed a place to live. I have more than enough room. So, we made a deal. He could live here, but he had to work around the house and the farm and get good grades in school. He must have thought that was a good idea, because he's been working hard ever since, and he's in the top 5% of his class."

"Oh," was all I could say. My grades were nowhere near that. Not that they couldn't be; I just didn't get into schoolwork.

Jasper had washed up and combed his hair and changed his clothes before he came to the table. I gotta admit. He looked tons better. Aunt Eva introduced me before we got started. Talk about the table focused on some things that needed doing around the farm and the house. I ate quietly as I listened to the babble of the others; playing with my food was more like it. I noted Jasper didn't talk much unless they asked a question or he was reporting about something he did.

I fell right into my role at home and started clearing away the table as everyone finished. Aunt Eva stopped me, though.

"Leave those things tonight, Kelly. I'll tend to them. Why don't you go on up to your room and get settled while us old folks do the dishes? Then we'll show you around," Aunt Eva smiled warmly.

"Um, ok. Except, I don't know where my room is," I stated the obvious.

"Oh, gracious! How clumsy of me! Jasper, would you please take Kelly's bags up to the room we prepared for her and show her about upstairs?"

Jasper smiled a shy grin. "Yes, 'um," he replied and downed the last of his milk. "This way, miss."

My eyes pled with Granma silently for support. It didn't help. She just smiled and nodded. With a sigh, I followed Jasper out of the room. He grasped my duffle bag and slung it over his shoulder like it was a feather. He led me down a short, dim hallway, then up some steep, narrow stairs. Behind me, I could hear Granma mentioning that I only had a single duffle bag for an entire summer, and I probably filled with electronics. I grinned to myself at Granma's voice. True; I had my laptop, my phone, my tablet, and my Switch along with some essential clothing. Still, the old lady had a way of making the simple sound so horrific.

Upstairs, Jasper showed me Aunt Eva's room, Granma's room, two other guest rooms, the bathroom, and finally my room. He placed the duffle on the double bed and stepped back for me to look around. It was on the second floor of the tower. The room was pretty; painted in a pale blue with bright white trim. The ceiling was blue as well, with wispy clouds painted across it. The bed had a pretty blue, white, and rose comforter with a matching sham. Below the comforter was a white bed skirt. One side of the room held a beautiful bay window with a sitting bench that looked out over the yard and off into the woods. The other side had three pictures of ballerinas. Under the ballerinas sat a high chest of drawers. A desk and some shelves were in the corner next to the bed. The nightstand for the bed was a side unit to the desk. A small touch lamp with a pretty rose-colored shade sat on it. The other side of the bed had another corner piece with a vanity. A tall, silver, gilded mirror hung on the wall above it. Opposite the bed was a large closet with sliding doors. In the corner, next to the closet, was a corner shelf unit. Several DVDs rested on the shelves below a seventeen-inch TV and DVD player. I had seen the remote on the nightstand next to the bed.

"It's pretty," I commented for something to say. "Not too plain, and not too frilly." Truth be told, I never had a room like this in my life! It was like a princess room.

"Glad you like it. We weren't sure what colors you'd prefer, so Eva went with this," Jasper explained.

"Where's your room?" I asked.

"Upstairs," Jasper replied. "There's two more rooms and a storage area up there. Eva thought I'd like my privacy."

"And do you?" I looked at the boy. A single nod was his reply. "I'll try to remember that." I looked out the window at the wide lawn. "Where's the dome?"

"The dome?" Jasper obviously didn't know what I meant.

"From outside, it looks like there's a room in glass at the top of the tower."

"Oh, upstairs. There's a small stairway that leads up to it. But it's hard to see out of. The glass is so old it's bowed in the middle."

"Why does Aunt Eva have such a big house if it's just her and you?" I needed to know.

"Dunno," Jasper replied. "I'm just glad she took me in. I'll do anything for her."

I glanced over my shoulder at him. That kind of loyalty was rarely seen in anyone. What did Aunt Eva save him from?

"Some things you should know," Jasper began. "It gets really dark unless the moon is out. The light switch here also has one over there behind the headboard. That way, you don't have to get out of bed to turn off the light. Also, the floors get cold during the night. Don't be surprised by the cold when you get up in the morning. It gets pretty chilly here at night, even in the summer. You may just want to keep a warm robe nearby for when you get up during the night. Keep the windows closed after dark. It keeps out the... bugs. You can pull closed the drapes on either side of the window if you want privacy at night. Probably a good idea. Sometimes the men from the farm go past to go hunting. Otherwise, you're welcome to whatever you can find. There's some puzzles in the closet in the hall, and Eva put some of these DVDs in here for you to watch if you want. There's a library in the basement full of all kinds of books if you like to read and more DVDs if you want different ones. The cat goes in and out as she pleases. That's about it. Just ask if I can help you with anything." He turned to leave.

"Um, thanks," I said, turning towards him. My head snapped quickly towards the corner, only to see myself standing in the mirror.

"Something wrong? You see a mouse?"

"No," I mumbled. "I thought I saw something move in the mirror. Just side vision, I guess."

Aunt Eva called from the bottom of the stairs. If anything else in the room had been on, we'd have missed it.

"Coming," I called. Jasper excused himself at the bottom of the stairs to finish his chores, then he had homework to do. The women nodded and called good night.

The walk about the farm was... different. Coming from the city, this stuff was like something out of a storybook to me. There were hens in a chicken coop. The rooster strut about the enclosure. Aunt Eva promised to show me how to collect the eggs in the morning. There were a few goats in a corral. They simply munched on the hay and looked up at us. A pair of sheep also shared the enclosure. Aunt Eva explained they make cheese from the goat's milk and used the wool from the sheep for sweaters and leggings. Mac also had a way of lining slippers with the wool making nice, warm footwear. Down at the barn were three horses and two cows. They used the cows for milk, of course. Calves were born in the spring and sold as soon as they were old enough to leave their mothers, usually when they started eating grass more than nursing. The horses were for getting around the property. They had a small herd of beef cattle in a field behind the barn. Some would go to slaughter later in the season, the others would stick it out through the winter until next year. They used a field in the way back for hay, wheat, corn, pumpkins, squash, and other grains to feed the animals and themselves.

The walk took us to the edge of the woods. It was getting dark in there. I could hear the skittering of small animals getting ready to settle down for the night. Even though I knew they were staying in the woods, it seemed creepy.

The walk back took us through an orchard surrounded by a large fence to the north of the house.

Inside were several types of trees. There were a few apple trees, two peach trees, two sweet cherry trees, a walnut tree, two pear trees, two apricot trees, and a plum tree. The fencing around the outside had blackberries, raspberries, and three different types of grapes. Closer to the house was a Service tree. The berries on this tree were already ripe to eat. Aunt Eva pulled some down and handed them to me.

"Try them. They're delicious! We'll be harvesting them this weekend."

"Joy," I replied unenthusiastically, but popped the berries in my mouth anyway. My eyes flew open in surprise as the mixed-berry flavor burst in my mouth.

We walked around to the side of the house under my bedroom. I wasn't aware of it from my room, but a sizeable garden grew beneath my window. Tomatoes, broccoli, zucchini, summer squash, string beans, carrots, cucumbers, and a host of other plants I didn't recognize grew in this area. Chicken wire surrounded it to keep the rabbits out.

"Is there anything you don't grow here?"

Granma and Aunt Eva laughed. "Oh, yes! There's plenty we don't grow," Aunt Eva explained. "You see, we spend a lot of time harvesting and canning here. Come winter, it's hard to get into town for supplies, so we use what we have stored. I'll only venture into town once a month or so come snowfall. Around the end of September, we'll take some of our wares to town and trade them for other supplies like blankets, extra hay, chicken feed, flour, and other things we can't grow. I'll stock up on shampoo, soap, paper supplies, and the like. We'll get in an extra supply of coal and fill the extra shed full of firewood. I'll even splurge and get a couple of hams and some bacon."

"That's splurging?" I asked.

"It is around here," Granma laughed as we moved indoors.

"Now, something else you should know," Aunt Eva's voice took on a warning tone. "Once the sun goes down, you are to be indoors. There are other things that circulate around the farm at night, dangerous things."

"Like wolves and stuff?" I asked.

Granma and Eva exchanged glances. "Yes," Aunt Eva said after the exchange. "Like wolves and coyotes and stuff. They're dangerous and have no qualms about attacking you. So don't venture out at night, not even to the porch."

"Jasper already told me about the windows and the bugs," I informed my aunt.

She looked startled for a moment, then nodded. "Good. Anything else you'd like to know?"

"Do you get cable here?" I asked hesitantly.

"Yes," Aunt Eva laughed heartily. "Channel 106 gives you the TV listing. It's satellite, so it ends up going out on us during heavy storms, but it's pretty good. We get internet here as well. When you're ready, I'll show you how to hook up your electronics to the router. Your mom said that was the first thing you packed."

"Awesome!" I smiled. I could watch my anime shows and stay in touch with Marissa, and keeping up with my team on the internet game I played would still work.

"There are also some games in the basement outside the library. Stay in the finished areas, please. It could be dangerous beyond that. There's the library and the game room downstairs and the laundry."

The three of us sat in silence for a moment until the kettle Aunt Eva had put on the stove squealed as it boiled. Aunt Eva took down two mugs and some tea bags. "Tea, Kelly?"

"No, thanks. Do you have hot chocolate?"

"Yes, I do," she smiled. "Would you like some?"

"Yes, please," I replied.

"Marshmallows or whipped cream?"

"Marshmallows, please."

I waited until Aunt Eva handed me a mug of hot cocoa and marshmallows. My stomach hurt and my anxiety started to rise as I tried to get brave enough to ask a question. I mean, I really didn't know this lady. I'd heard of her, but that was all. "Can I ask a stupid question?" I squeaked.

"There are no stupid questions," Aunt Eva began, "And yes, you may."

"Why do you have such a large house when it's only you and Jasper that live here?"

"I like this child," Granma said to Eva. "Straight and to the point—just like you."

"Yes, she is," Aunt Eva chuckled. "I have a large home because (1) I had hoped to fill it with more than just me, (2) it gives lots of room for when others come to visit, and (3) I grew up here."

"Who else comes up here?" I scowled.

"Uncle Cliff comes up with his family every summer. In fact, they should be here in about three weeks. Then the quiet ends!!!" she said spookily.

I laughed at Aunt Eva's remark. Yes, my five cousins were always on the run. They were lots of fun, and Uncle Cliff was anything but quiet. They'd have fun. "How long are they staying?"

"They come up for two weeks every summer. Aunt Chrissy likes to help me can the fruit. The apricots, the peaches, and the plums should be ready about then."

"Can I take this into the other room and watch TV?" I suddenly changed the subject, holding up my mug.

"Sure! Make yourself at home. Just remember: You make the mess; you clean it up."

"I'll remember," I smiled and moved into the family room on the other side of the kitchen.

There they go again. I found it strange that Granma and Aunt Eva always went into a hushed conversation as I left the room. Curious, I paused to eavesdrop this time.

"When are you going to ask her?" Granma urged.

"Not now, Mother!" Aunt Eva replied quietly. "She hardly knows me. Let her get used to things here first."

"Marie sent her to you because she's showing the signs."

"I know that. Please, don't push! It could all go very wrong. Just let me handle it!"

"Eva, you only have the summer before she has to go back to school."

"I know, but this is not something you can rush! Just let me take care of the girl, will you?" Aunt Eva sounded frustrated.

The conversation was getting tense, so I moved into the Family Room without listening further. So, my mother sent me here for some other reason than what she'd said.

What could it be? I was showing signs. Signs of what? Was I sick? Was I going to die? What could be wrong? Granted, I didn't know Aunt Eva and wasn't sure just how far to trust her, but I didn't believe Aunt Eva would hurt me. My mind raced with different ideas as I got comfortable in the overstuffed chair with the remote control. A buzzing from my pocket told me my phone was ringing.

Pulling out my cell phone, I was surprised to find I had full bars. The number showing was Mom.

"Hi, Mom!" I answered calmly.

"Hello, darling. Got there ok, I guess," Mom greeted me.

"Yes."

"How're things going?"

"I'm wondering why you sent me to No Man's Land," my cool reply came. "There is *Nothing* up here!"

Mom's joyful laughter came over the airway. "I know. I thought about that when I decided to send you up there. But I'm sure you'll make friends, and I know Uncle Cliff's crowd is due up there sometime soon. You and Abby can spend some time together."

"That'll be fun. I don't get to spend enough time with her."

"Exactly! And it's only eight weeks. You'll be home before you know it."

"I guess. Granma's here, too."

"I heard. She thought she needed to smooth things over between you two for a few days. She'll be back up with Uncle Cliff and Aunt Chrissy. I'm thinking I might take a few days off and come up over a long weekend myself."

"A regular family reunion," I chuckled. "Haven't had one of those in forever."

"So true. So, what have you seen already?"

"Nothing. It's a big farm in the middle of nowhere, surrounded by forests. My room is real pretty, though. It's baby blue and white. I've got a big bay window with a reading bench that overlooks the yard. It's really nice."

"I'm glad." There was a pause in the conversation. It was as if Mom wanted to say something else but didn't dare. The pause grew longer. "Is Jasper still there?"

"Yes. He showed me my room. You knew about him?"

"Yes. Aunt Eva told me she let him live there. She didn't tell me much about him, though."

"Well, he's around 16. Kinda mousy. He works for her around the farm and has really good grades in school, and he's shier than I am. I didn't think there was anyone more shy than me."

My mother chuckled. "There's a few."

I could hear the land line ringing in the background. Mom paused, then let out a superlative under her breath. I hid the chuckle as she answered the other phone and put the person on hold. "I've got to run, sweetheart. It's the boss."

"Yuk! This late at night?"

"Yep. We've got a big presentation in the morning. I'm willing to bet he's double nervous and just wants to go over everything - again! Tell Aunt Eva I'll call her tomorrow. I miss you!"

"You could come here," I tried. I'd be much more comfortable with my mother nearby.

"No. You'll have much more fun up there without me. I'll talk to you soon. Love you!"

"Love you, too, Mom." I pressed the off button and sighed. Work again. It was always work. Mom rarely did anything with me anymore since Dad died because she was always working. Sometimes I'd see her in the den piled high with bills trying to figure out which ones were getting paid. I didn't like the worry that would play over Mom's face. It was just the two of us, but apparently, things weren't too good. I often wondered if it would be easier for her without me. I mean, I knew Mom loved me tons, but sometimes I felt like such a burden. Well, time would tell.

I flipped through the channels on the TV, trying to find something decent. I watched a little of one of my favorite shows, but I'd seen it so many times I could quote it! None of the movies looked any good. Finally, I turned off the TV, finished my cocoa, and went back into the kitchen to wash my mug. Aunt Eva and Granma weren't there. The door to the basement was open. The light at the bottom was on, but I couldn't hear anything. Quietly, I crept downstairs. The stairs opened into the game room. She wasn't kidding—A Game Room. The place was huge. A pool table lay in the middle with a Ping-pong cover over it. Three different arcade games were along one side. A race car and model train set combined against another wall. A dart board hung on another wall. The door to a closet was slightly ajar, showing me shelves upon shelves of games and puzzles. An archway opposite the stair landing showed the library.

I wandered over to look at it. I liked to read, but seldom found anything that caught my interest. Silently, I flipped on the light. I stared in awe at the room. A polished wooden table sat in the middle with four wooden chairs around it. Three large overstuffed chairs were scattered around the room with reading lamps next to them. The rest of the octagonal room was floor to ceiling shelves with four bookshelves in the middle framing a support post.

I stared in awe as I skirted the shelves. Children's picture books, beginning readers, middle school books, and Young Adult novels; many of them fairly new. Biographies, cookbooks, How-To books, fiction, Romance, history, theology, genealogy, diaries, and many, many more. There were even technology books on computers, the Web, and programming. Several shelves were dedicated to herbology and natural medicines. Reference books comprised an entire wall. Another wall held some pretty strange books. Metaphysics, Atmospheric Energies, Combining DNA, Witch hunts, and a host of other really strange topics made my skin crawl; then I was back to the normal books. I could easily spend my entire summer down here and still not read all the books I wanted to.

A door closing in the other room made me look out through the archway. Jasper had come in from another room.

"What's back there?" I asked. I tried to hide my chuckle when the guy jumped six feet in the air.

"Sorry," he mumbled. "Didn't know you were there."

"I'm sorry," I replied, still smirking. "So, what's back there?"

"That goes into the utility room," Jasper explained about the door he came through. "Nothing in there 'cept the furnace, the water heater, and the generator. That door," he pointed to one next to the stairs, "leads to the laundry."

"Thanks." I leaned against the archway.

Jasper appeared awkward. "I'm going to do my homework."

I nodded an acknowledgement. "I think I'm gonna find a book to read."

"Good luck," Jasper said, then climbed the stairs.

Wow. And I thought I was a duck out of water. I returned to a set of shelves in the library to pick out a book. Aunt Eva had a series that I had started at the end of the school year, so I thought it would be good to move on to the next book. Picking it off the shelf, I looked around for some way to mark where it came from. I spotted a set of eight cardboard pieces on the table. Each one was bound on one side with a different colored cloth. I picked up the black one and slid it into the spot where I took the book from. That should work.

As I moved to go upstairs, I heard a growl come from behind the door that Jasper had come out of. I paused at the bottom of the stairs. That was weird. It didn't sound like a dog growl. It was more like the kind of growl you'd hear from a bear or a beast. I started towards the door slowly. What was back there? I got half-way across the room when the door opened. Aunt Eva came into the room wiping dirt off her pants. She started when she looked up and saw me.

"Oh, Kelly! I'm sorry, darling," Aunt Eva caught herself. "You startled me."

"Jasper said there was a library down here. I came to look at the books. That's okay, isn't it?"

"Of course, honey!" Aunt Eva closed the door. "Did you find one you liked?"

I held up the book to my aunt. "I started this series just before school let out. I thought I'd pick it up again."

"Oh, I liked that one!" Aunt Eva smiled. "Lots of adventure in it. You'll love the twist at the end."

I had to smile at my aunt's enthusiasm, then looked at the floor. "What's back there?" I asked.

"Just the utility room. Furnace and stuff."

"I heard a growl."

"Oh, that's just the furnace. It's not on during the day, but it kicks in at night when it starts getting cold. It sounds like a wild beast when it gets started. Jasper was having trouble with it, so I came down to help."

Something in her tone made me think Aunt Eva was hiding something, but I nodded and led the way upstairs. I asked where Granma had gone.

"She said she wanted a nice, long, hot bath," Aunt Eva chuckled. "So, I sent her to my room to use the jets in my tub. I thought she'd like the spa treatment."

I looked curiously at my aunt at the top of the stairs. To look at the woman, you wouldn't think she had much money, yet the size of the property and the things she had in the house said something much more. Even at thirteen, I knew how much things cost.

"What's wrong?" Aunt Eva asked.

"I don't know. I wouldn't have thought you had a spa tub."

Aunt Eva laughed and wrapped her arm around my shoulders. "Sweetheart, just because we live in the boonies doesn't mean we're stuck in the 1800s. We have all the amenities here that you had in the city, just less people and traffic."

I chuckled at her analogy. "What do you do for work?"

"Oh, a little of this, and a little of that," Aunt Eva replied with a wave of her hand. "I'm going to wash the kitchen floor and head to bed," she announced. "Sunrise comes awfully early."

I nodded and headed for the stairs to go to my room. Something was definitely really weird around here.

3 – Nightmares and Animals

The darkness of the woods was closing in. I searched around, trying to find the path out. A moist, hazy fog was rising from the floor beneath my feet. A branch snapped behind me, echoing off the trees. I turned to see who was there, but I still couldn't see anything. Another branch snapped.

"Who's there?" I asked. I could hear the shakiness in my voice.

No answer.

I continued to move forward, trying to figure out which way I came. The fog was getting thicker, the dim light was slowly getting snuffed out. In the distance, I could hear a low growl. Something brushed past my leg. I shrieked and jumped. I searched but couldn't see what it was.

"Granma?" I called softly.

Suddenly, something hard grasped me from behind. Screams echoed off the surrounding woods. A hard, scratchy, thorny hand covered my mouth, but I screamed anyway. The darkness closed in altogether.

"Kelly!" Something was shaking me. That thing was calling my name. "Kelly, wake up." The voice sounded familiar. It shook me again. "Kelly! Come on, sweetheart." The voice called again. "Wake up, honey. It's just a bad dream."

I forced my eyes open. I didn't want to see that thing! My whole body was shaking. Instead, the lamp on my nightstand coated my bedroom in a soothing glow. My eyes darted around in a panic. Aunt Eva's concerned face greeted me, followed by Granma's peering over her shoulder.

"Come on, sweetheart. Sit up," Aunt Eva dragged me up. "It's just a bad dream. You okay?"

I glanced down at my nightgown, then at my arms. Nothing. No rips, tears, or scratches. My heart settled from the fast staccato in my ears as I tried to catch my breath. My arm went up to wipe the sweat off my forehead. Someone offered me a glass of cold water. I looked up to see Jasper and took the glass gratefully, thanking him for it. Man, I felt like I'd been in a desert instead of a forest.

"I'm... sorry," I blurted out, embarrassed. "I didn't mean to wake everyone."

"It's alright," Aunt Eva said softly. "Want to talk about it?" I shook my head.

"Come along, Jasper. Let's go back to bed," Granma suggested. "You sure you're alright, darling?" she asked me again. I nodded silently.

Aunt Eva sat on the edge of my bed. "What happened in your dream?" she asked.

I looked up slowly. "I thought I said I didn't want to talk about it."

"You did," Aunt Eva said more sternly, yet with understanding in her voice. "Your mother tells me you've been having nightmares every night for the last two months. Do you remember what happens in them?"

"Sometimes." I put the now empty glass on my nightstand.

"Are they always the same thing?" Aunt Eva asked. "You know, like the same dream over and over?"

"No." I shook my head. "They're always different."

"Anything familiar about them? Similar?"

I shook my head, trying to figure out what Aunt Eva was getting at.

"Are the places always familiar ones, or are they always strange?"

"Sometimes one, sometimes the other."

"Hmmm," Eva said, thinking. "I think you're farther along than you mother thought."

I froze. A fear of dread raced up my spine. I slowly looked up to meet my aunt's thoughtful eyes. "Am... am... am I gonna die?"

"What?" Aunt Eva snapped up, then realized she'd spoken out loud. "Oh, no, darling!" she chuckled. "There's nothing wrong with you. I promise!"

"Then why does Mom think there is?"

"No, honey. There's a... trait... that comes to some people in our family as they go through puberty. Some of us have it, some of us don't. I have it, but your mother doesn't. Apparently, you also have it."

"Does Granma have it?"

"No, but Granpa did. That's where we get it from. His side of the family."

"Is it dangerous?"

"It can be, if you aren't trained right. Granpa trained me. Unfortunately, we don't have him anymore, so I've become the next best thing we have to a trainer. But we have plenty of time for that. Sit tight." Aunt Eva moved towards the hallway. "Do you still have some water?"

"No."

Aunt Eva came back for the glass, then disappeared down the hall.

I glanced around my room to reassure myself nothing from the dream was there. No trees. No leaves on the floor. No dirt. Okay. So, this time, nothing appeared in my room from my dream. I let out a sigh of relief; then snapped my attention back up to a movement I thought I saw in the mirror. Nothing there. Must have been my reflection. I'm gonna have to cover that mirror. I saw Aunt Eva returning down the hallway.

"Here we go!" Aunt Eva handed me a bottle of purple pills. "I want you to take two of these every night before you go to sleep. They'll chase away the nightmares."

"They'll what?" I had never heard of anything so ridiculous. I read the label on the bottle. Presimonium. "What's Presimonium?"

"They're a small flower specially grown in the Arctic. Very expensive, but very effective. They're dried, crushed into pulp, mixed with honey, and hardened into those small purple pills. Their entire purpose is to relax the body and balance the chemicals in the brain to create a restful, pleasant sleep."

"Mom takes Melatonin for that."

"These are better."

"You're sure?" I wasn't sure about this at all. How the heck do you grow flowers in the Arctic?

"I'm sure. These got me through puberty, and they'll get you through it as well. Come on, now. Two only. We don't want you to sleep the week away!" Aunt Eva chuckled. She watched me take two of the tablets and drink them down with the water.

"Mmm! Leaves a honey flavor in your mouth," I smirked.

"Yep. Real nice. Now," she sat down again. "Where was this nightmare?"

"Somewhere in the woods," I replied. "It was really dark and foggy."

"Thorny?" I nodded. "Kind of wet?"

"Moisture in the air, I guess, and there was fog."

"The bog. OK. Someone knows you're here. You'll need to stay away from the bog until we figure out what's going on."

"What are you talking about?" I asked, confused.

Aunt Eva smiled and pat my leg. "Not tonight. We'll start tomorrow. I just needed to know that piece of information. You feeling drowsy yet?"

"Yes, actually; now that the adrenaline has settled."

"Good. Settle in! Come on!" Aunt Eva covered me with the blankets like I was a little girl, leaned over and gave me a kiss on my forehead. "You are to relax. Rest, and know that everything is alright. I won't let anything happen to you. Okay?"

"Okay," I replied, already feeling like I was drifting off to sleep on a cloud of nothingness.

A soft voice filtered into my haze. "Is the young lady alright, Eva?" the feminine voice asked in a gentle whisper.

"She's fine, Alex," Aunt Eva's voice whispered back. "Now go hide!"

I woke the next morning with the sun shining in behind the curtains of the window. I moaned while I stretched, rolled over, and glanced at the clock. 11:00.

Eleven o'clock!!! I slept that late? And everyone let me? How weird was that!?

Forcing myself out of bed, I found my duffle and pulled out a pair of jeans, some underwear, and a blue t-shirt. Grasping my toiletries and some socks, I headed for the bathroom for a shower. After a short time of making myself presentable, I moved down to the kitchen for something to eat. Strange, no one was around. With a shrug, I opened the fridge, pulled out some left-overs and some milk, and sat down to eat something before I figured out what I'd do today.

My mind wandered to my dream last night. Was it a sign? Was it a warning? Was it just a nightmare? That was probably it. I probably was just spooked by all the woods around the house. After all, there's no real forests in the city. Still, I'd think someone would have come to check on me this morning. I cleaned up my dishes and went outside.

The sun was glowing in a clear blue sky. The warmth of the rays made me smile. I always felt better in the sunshine. Glancing around, I still didn't see anyone. OK. Let's see what's really here.

Moving around the house to the orchard, I grasped a peach off the peach tree and looked about. Acres and acres of hillsides and mountains surrounded the house. Okay. Nature walks. Wonderful. I saw some movement over by the garden area, so I went to check it out.

Granma looked up from picking string beans when she saw me. She sat back on her heels and smiled.

"Good to see you about, sleepyhead!" she teased.

I smirked at Grandma's attempt at humor. She never was very good. Carefully, I stepped over the fencing and kneeled down next to the older woman.

"Whatcha doin'?"

Granma showed me the woven basket with the string beans in it. "We're picking greens. Want to help?"

I shrugged. "I don't know how."

"No better time to learn. See here?" Granma pulled some leaves aside so I could see the string beans. "These skinny ones aren't ready yet. And these big, bulky ones are overdone. Aunt Eva will use those to seed next year. These middle, straight-sided ones are the ones we want. Got it?"

"Sounds pretty simple."

I spent the next half hour picking vegetables with Grandma. Oddly enough, with all the things we talked about, Granma never mentioned my nightmare. Mom would have been grilling me over it. Eventually, Aunt Eva came over.

"You guys ready to see something sweet?" she asked.

I wiggled my head. "Sure. You baking cookies?"

"Better!"

The two of us wiped our hands off on our jeans, then followed Aunt Eva to the barn. Mac was leaning over a stall door, watching something with a tender smile on his face. Aunt Eva nodded towards the large man.

"Go see!"

"What do we have?" Granma asked Mac with an excited grin. She peered over the stall door. I followed not sure what I was going to find in a barn. My curiosity turned into a grin as big as Grandma's as I looked at a newborn foal being washed down by its mother.

"We got us a colt," Mac said so proudly you'd have thought he was the father. "Really pretty little thing he is. Nice and strong."

"Excellent!" Granma smiled, looking down at the little brown and black foal. The mare, all brown with black boots and a black mane, continued to lick every little spot on the tiny tike clean, then went over it again. The little foal looked like all he wanted to do was sleep.

"He's cute," I smiled. "I've never seen a baby horse before."

"Stick around, sweetheart," Mac suggested. "You'll see more than a foal. Come spring, we get lambs, chicks, foals, calves, and more."

"Oh, yes," Aunt Eva teased. "You'll love the bear cubs, especially after Mama roars in your face!"

My eyes widened in fear. "I'll pass on that one, please." Everyone laughed as Aunt Eva rubbed my back.

"What about lunch?" Aunt Eva suggested.

"I already ate. I grabbed some left-overs just before I began helping Granma," I explained.

"Okay," Aunt Eva smiled. "Good to see you making yourself at home. Mac? Mom?"

"Yes, ma'am," Mac agreed. "Birthin' is a tiring business!" We all laughed at his joke.

"The mare did all the work!" Granma teased back. "You just watched!"

"Well," Mac struggled for a retort. "Waiting can be work, too! What if she'd have had trouble? I'd've had to step in!"

"OK, Mac," Granma conceded. "We'll give you that one!" She still chuckled. "I'd love lunch, Eva."

I followed the others back to the house. I really didn't know what else to do. A movement caught my eye as I scanned the yard a bit more. I stopped a moment to stare at it but couldn't figure it out. It was next to the woods on the far side of the property. From what I could see, a human-type shadow stood in the shade almost half the size of the trees there.

"Coming, Kelly?" Aunt Eva asked me. She glanced in the direction I was staring. The sight made her face go firm. "Come on, honey. Let's see what we can whip up for these people. I'm sure Jasper will be looking for something to eat as well." Aunt Eva grasped my arm and led me towards the house.

"What's that?" I asked, nodding towards the woods.

"What's what?" Aunt Eva asked, pretending she didn't know what I was talking about.

"That shadow near the woods. Is it an animal?"

"Maybe. A bear, probably. Or it could just be a shadow from the sun. A cloud block or maybe the leaves blowing in the breeze."

"What breeze?" I asked. There wasn't a breeze. There was practically no wind at all.

"Sometimes there can be a breeze further up in the air," Granma explained. "Down here on the ground, we don't feel it; but the trees will move because they grow higher."

I looked at Grandma as if I didn't trust her anymore as she followed my aunt. After all, I understood what Grandma had said. I'd seen it before, but this wasn't a shadow played by leaves blowing in a breeze. The tops of the trees weren't moving. And Aunt Eva's reaction wasn't one of interest but of defense. I let the subject drop and went to help with lunch, but I was definitely going to check this out.

A bit later, I saw Jasper come in from downstairs as I did the dishes. The other two women were back picking vegetables in the garden. He gave me a polite, shy smile. "Feeling better?" he asked.

I started a moment, then realized he was talking about my waking the entire house last night. I nodded. "Yea. Sorry about that."

"It's alright. You had a nightmare. Sometimes they can seem awful real."

I nodded again. I put the last pot on the counter to dry and turned off the water. "Jasper, you been around here a while, haven't you?"

Jasper nodded. "Almost three years."

"Anything strange happen here?"

Jasper looked me in the eye this time. "Strange? Whaddaya mean, strange?"

"Strange. Like things moving, and Aunt Eva trying to make up explanations for things you see."

Jasper thought for a moment. "No, can't say those things have happened to me. Maybe you should talk to your aunt—heart to heart. Let her know what you think. She'll respect you for it."

"Yea. Maybe I will."

"What are you thinking now?" Jasper asked suspiciously.

"I thought I'd go exploring," I replied.

"Not a good idea."

"Why not? Don't think I can handle things out here in the Boonies?"

"The wild parts of the property can get pretty tough. Unless we're hunting for food, we stay away from the woods. Bears, wolves, elk, and the like can be pretty nasty when you come up on them. Best stay near the house. They won't bother you here.

"Why don't you hit the porch swing and read some of that book you found last night?" Jasper suggested. "It's good reading time."

I got the distinct impression Jasper was hiding something, but before I could respond, Aunt Eva came into the kitchen carrying something in her hand.

"Whatcha got?" I recovered quickly.

Aunt Eva noticed Jasper and me on either side of the counter. "Everything ok?"

Jasper raised his eyebrows and turned. "Yep!" he answered and went towards the bathroom.

Aunt Eva held whatever was in her hands close to her and pulled a dishtowel out of the drawer. She went over and spread it on the kitchen table. Slowly, she moved whatever she was carrying onto the table. I heard a peep come from that direction and went to see what was up.

Aunt Eva held a tiny sparrow still on the table. Several feathers were missing and one wing hung down. "Now stay still so I can check this," she spoke softly to the bird.

"He can't understand you," I chuckled.

"Maybe not, but it's easier on me when I talk to them."

I glanced up at my aunt. "Okay. Sure."

The bird tried to hop away, so I put my hand in front of it. Aunt Eva carefully examined the wing.

"What happened?" I asked.

"Oh, Rascal got at the bird while it was eating," Aunt Eva replied in a frustrated voice.

"Who's Rascal?"

"One of the barn cats." She found the break and lined up the bones with her fingers. "Tabby is too well fed," she referred to the cat in the house.

I watched my aunt and the bird. Aunt Eva held the wing still. She seemed like she was concentrating on something.

"What are you doing?" I asked. "Are we gonna call the vet?"

Suddenly, Aunt Eva moved her hand. The bird instantly pulled the wing back against its body. It hopped up onto my hand and pushed off, flying around the room. I jumped back in surprise. What the......?

4 – There's a Girl in my Mirror

"How....?" I pointed into the air.

"Come on now, little one," Aunt Eva called the bird. She held out her hand. The bird flew down and landed on the outstretched palm. "You be careful of that cat, now, you hear?" she warned the little sparrow as she walked over to the back door. She let the bird loose outside and watched it fly away.

Aunt Eva glanced in my direction as she closed the door. I was still sitting at the table with my mouth open and my eyes wide in surprise.

"Close your mouth, darling," Aunt Eva smiled and rolled up the dish towel.

"But, the bird's wing? Wasn't it broken?"

"Yes."

"Then how...?" I pointed towards the door.

Aunt Eva sat in the chair next to me. "It's part of the Gift," she explained softly.

"The what? What gift?" I asked, totally confused. What did a present have to do with what Aunt Eva did for the bird?

"The Gift. It's what we call the abilities we have – you and I."

"Me? Huh? I can't do that. What are you talking about?" I sat back.

"Do you remember your nightmare last night?"

"All too well, thank you," I replied darkly, crossing my arms.

"Do you remember I told you that there's a trait that runs through our family that brings on the nightmares?"

"Vaguely."

Aunt Eva nodded. "There is a very special trait that our family has. It's called the Gift. It starts to show itself in dreams around the age of thirteen or fourteen years old. The chemical changes in your brain bring it to the surface. It's dormant until then."

"Dormant? Like hibernation?"

Aunt Eva chuckled. "Yes, kind of like that. So far, you and I are the only ones in the family that show any signs of it. That's one reason your mother wanted you to come here; so I can start helping you to control it."

"Is it something dangerous?" I asked, not liking the seriousness in my aunt's voice.

Aunt Eva thought a moment. "It can be. It's controlled by your emotions, wills, and thoughts. So, I suppose, if you were untrained and angry, yes, it could be dangerous."

"Is it going to kill me?" I asked nervously.

"Ya know, that's the second time you've asked about your own death. There something you want to share with me? A dream you had, perhaps?"

I shook my head. "I..." I looked down at the table. "I just don't want to end up like my father."

My voice was so soft I didn't think Aunt Eva even heard me. Gently, the woman laid a hand on mine. "Kelly, The Gift will not kill you, nor will it hurt you. However, untrained, you can hurt other people, or possibly yourself, inadvertently. As for ending up like your father, that was an accident, pure and simple. You are not going to be like your father. He was in the wrong place at the wrong time with the wrong people. You have better judgments than that from what I hear. Okay? You are an individual. Your choices will determine who you are and what you become. Understand?"

I gave a short nod and thought quietly for a moment. "What's this Gift do – I mean, besides healing bird wings?"

Aunt Eva laughed heartily, getting up from the table. "Oh, no. Not yet! There's something you'll need to read before we get started with that." She waved for me to follow.

"Something I need to read?" That's weird. I followed Aunt Eva to the basement.

"This Gift, as best we can figure out, was first recorded by your great, great, great, great, great grandmother. She had a daughter, Tessa, who also had The Gift. Tessa kept a diary about everything she went through. Before we get started with you, I want you to read the first part of it. I think you'll find that the same things that have been happening to you happened to her—and to me. I think you'll be able to identify with Tessa."

Aunt Eva went over to the section of the library that had a bunch of stuff about genealogy. Her eyes and forefinger skimmed the books on the shelves until she came to an ancient, brown, leather diary. She opened it to check something, flipping the pages carefully until she came to a page about a third of the way through the book. Walking to the table where some bookmarks with ribbons on them were, she picked one up, placed the bookmark in the page and closed it.

"I want you to read up to the bookmark, but no further. Once you've done that, we'll start working with you and The Gift. And be careful with it. It's kind of fragile."

"What about the rest of the book?" I asked, taking the outstretched book from my aunt. It was definitely old and felt like it would fall apart in my hands.

"I'll let you read pieces as we work this summer," Aunt Eva smiled. "Don't read on ahead. It will only confuse you. I know. I've read that book at least a dozen times."

"Will I?" I looked skeptically at the diary. I really wasn't into biographies.

"Maybe. We'll see." Aunt Eva smiled. "Oh, one more thing. Stay away from the woods – for now. It's pretty dangerous in there."

"Dangerous because of the Gift or dangerous in general?"

Eva shook her head from side to side. Her eyes were closed, and she had a small smile on her lips. "Both."

I sat back in the quiet of the Family Room with a bowl of dry cereal and a tall glass of ice water. I settled myself in the overstuffed chair near the window. Plenty of light to read by as everyone else went about their chores. I looked over the old, musty diary. The brown leather cover was faded and peeling. The spine looked like it was ready to break. Still, it felt soft and comfortable. Maybe I'd look up how to restore a book like this. A diary, huh? Joy. (Not!) Oh, well! If I had to read it, I might as well get it over with.

Opening the cover, fading, fancy script of an era long gone by greeted me. I remembered hearing that at one time, this is how people wrote. I didn't believe it until we had to do some transcribing in history class. This writing was very similar to that. Oddly enough, I didn't have a hard time figuring it out. The girl who wrote it had beautiful penmanship.

The Diary of Tessa Ann MacClure
1843 –

June 1st –

I'm writing this journal because Father says it will help me understand what is happening. He says this will bring everything into focus. I am uncertain he is correct. I'd better start from the beginning. Everything was fine as I was a child, but since the middle of last year, I have grown rather solitary. I feel like I do not fit in with my classmates any longer. I began having these dreams. Very strange dreams. Sometimes they were nonsense. Other times they were horrible. I feel like something is trying to crawl into my head. Often, I have these horrible headaches. Mother has had me to the doctor twice. He says I am fine—nothing wrong. Father says it is part of growing up. I sense he is holding something back from me. Really wish I could make sense of it all. I haven't had a decent night's sleep in weeks.

June 23rd –

My worst nightmare occurred last evening. I was taking a short nap. "Short" being operative. It was cut terribly by the nightmare. I was walking in the field, picking daisies. I thought Mother would enjoy a basketful for the table. I reached down to pick one, but something moved

*behind the daisy. It was thick and green. I looked up to see
who it was. A giant daisy, almost as tall as Father with
angry black eyes, was staring down at me. As it reached for
me, I fell backwards. Screaming, I jumped up and starting to
run, but I couldn't get anywhere. Looking back, the daisy
held my jumper in its... leaf. Thank heavens Mother woke
me.*

I noticed the next several entries were about her
dreams. Oddly enough, many of her dreams were like the
ones I had had. She had changed the color of her bedroom.
Tessa had cut vegetables in her dream, and thus, in the
kitchen. She had dreamed about an allergy to ragweed and
filled her room with it. Then one caught my attention.

Feb 22nd –
*Oh, am I in trouble now! It's all those stupid dreams! I
cannot take them any longer! I'm actually afraid to go to
sleep. Last night was terrible. I was dreaming again, of
course, but I was dreaming about fire. I was outside burning
dead branches for Father, in my dream. I reached into the
fire and picked up some flames. It was strange because it
didn't burn my hand. In fact, it was sitting just an inch or so
above it, burning brightly. I wondered if I could throw it, and
I did - right into the outhouse! The small flame from my hand
had latched on to the old wood of the outhouse and began to
glow in earnest. I grasped the water bucket from the pump
and ran back, but the little water from the bucket only
sizzled against the intense flame of the outhouse. Then I
heard laughter. It was coming from the flames. It grew louder
as the fire pit flames joined in. The fire was laughing at me -*

a cold, mocking laugh. I awoke with a start and looked about my room, thankful that there was no fire in here. I took a drink from the glass on my night table and froze. I could see a flickering glow outside my window. I got up and went to see what it was. To my horror, the outhouse was in full blaze. Of course, I quickly woke Father. He, Lars, and I began soaking down the small building from the water pump. It was cold and snowy and the pump did not wish to work well, but we did manage to put out the flames. At length, we went inside where Mother had hot cocoa ready for us. Father merely looked at me and sighed. He did not say anything, but I could tell I was in trouble. Even though he sent us back to bed, I could not go to sleep again. What will happen next?

March 3rd –
Mother and I went into town today to gather some supplies. It was the first time all winter that the roads were open. Spring should be here soon. Hurray! We stopped to gather the mail. There was a package addressed to Father from Uncle William. I wondered what it was. When we got home, Father opened the package and read a long letter. He said Uncle William sent his best wishes and had sent some items that will help me. Me? Father said they were from Grandfather's storage room. One was a large bottle of small purple pills. I was to take two every night before bed. It would help control my nightmares. Father said I would find out about the other items in time.

March 4th –

Hurray! I went an entire night without any nightmares. I had the best sleep I've had in almost a year! Thank you so much, Uncle William.

April 19th –
   Something very strange has begun. I've been seeing things moving from the corner of my eyes, but when I turn to look at them, there is nothing there. Yesterday, I noticed some shadows near the woods across the street. They appeared to be moving just inside the woods. With the pitchfork in my hands, I went to see who was trespassing, but nothing was there. Something else is wrong as well. I keep hearing whisperings. Strange whisperings, but I can't make out what they're saying. Sometimes, I hear my name. I'm scared.

May 15th –
   Well, my 15th birthday has come and gone. It has been nice to sleep without the nightmares. Mother and Father gave me a new dress for church. It's a pretty green with white lace. Lars gave me a new pen and pencil set for my artwork. He said he noticed mine was getting worn out. Lydia gave me a small pillow she had made herself. I'm so proud of my little sister. It was a nice day until after dinner. Father came up to my room with me. He sat on the edge of the bed as we had a talk. He told me we had to discuss some things. His tone frightened me. At first, I thought he was going to send me away. Instead, he told me about what was happening to me. He said that the family had something he called "The Gift". Not everyone in the family has it, only a few of us. He knew I would have it because I have the eyes. It is one of the

traits that every gift owner had—large, bright blue eyes with dark lashes and nearly black hair. Another thing is the nightmares. The Gift becomes active during the early teen years. It begins to take hold through dreams because we are not being distracted by other things during that time. Problem is we can cause great harm unintentionally while we dream because we are not in control. He said that there was more, but that it could wait. I asked Father if that was why I could see moving shadows and hear whispers. He seemed disturbed by that news, but said that was one reason, and I was never to follow the shadows or listen to the whispers. He would not explain why. I simply agreed. He kissed my forehead and said he loved me, but before he left my room, he reminded me that The Gift simply made me special, not strange. Odd way to look at it.

I sighed as I leaned back. So far, this Tessa person was going through the exact same thing I was. Oddly, Tessa's father didn't tell her anything more than Aunt Eva had told me. Was there a reason they were so secretive about this thing? What was so odd about it that no one would be up front and honest?

I got up to refill my water glass. As I put the diary on the table, an old piece of newsprint dropped out of the back. I scowled as I picked it up. It was so old it was yellowed and the type was difficult to read. I turned on a lamp to shine on it so I could read it. It was dated 30 September 1883. The headline read "Woman Charged In Murder of Daughter". I continued reading.

"Tessa Ann Reed, 53, was arrested this morning as the prime suspect in the disappearance of her daughter

Alexandria, 14. The child was last seen on 30 August at a friend's party. Police have investigated the woods and the home. There did not appear to be any clues in the case. The child's friends have not seen her since the party, nor have they had any idea where the girl could be.

"Mrs. Reed insists the child is fine, but would not reveal where she was. The child's bedroom has been untouched in all that time.

"'During interrogations, Mrs. Reed kept insisting the child was in a mirror,' Police Chief Charles Lennin stated. 'The mumblings were strange and difficult to understand, but the suspect appeared distraught over the disappearance of the child.

"'At this point in time, we are viewing this as a homicide,' the Chief informed reporters. 'This may be difficult to prove as we have no body, no indication of a struggle, and no motive. We are not ruling out a runaway situation, but evidence is not pointing in that direction.'

"Police are asking the assistance of the public in locating the child. Anyone with information is asked to contact the police. A reward is being offered for the child's safe return. Mrs. Reed will be arraigned on the 21st day of November, 1883, in a closed session at the County Court."

How strange! The woman with The Gift was being charged with the murder of her own daughter? I returned the newspaper to the book and went for my drink, but I couldn't get the article out of my mind.

Granma was in the kitchen starting dinner when I got there. I poured myself a glass of juice, then leaned against the counter.

"Granma, do you know anything about this gift thing?" I asked the one woman I knew I could trust.

"Oh, yes. I followed along with it as Eva grew."

"You didn't know about it?"

"No, not until I married your grandfather."

"Granpa had it?"

"Oh, yes," Granma smiled. "He was quite good with it. I'm ever so happy he knew what to expect. As Eva started showing signs of it, I was totally beside myself. Granpa knew just what to expect when and just how to handle it. He was wonderful, and Eva was an excellent pupil."

"Do you know about the lady in this diary Aunt Eva is having me read?"

Granma put the string beans she'd been splitting in a pot of water and moved it to the stove. She smiled as she turned on the flame underneath it.

"Oh, yes! I was fascinated with it. Eva and I read it together. Both a triumph and a tragedy."

"Then you know about the murder?"

Granma laughed. "Yes. I do. Shame."

"Did she do it? The murder?"

"Well, yes, she did it, but she didn't murder Alexandria," Grandmother mused.

"Then what happened to the girl?"

Granma looked me square in the eye. "Are you certain you want to know?"

I grew wary. "Why?"

"Come." Granma led me upstairs and back to my room. "She's in here."

I sighed as my shoulders sagged. "Granma, this is my room. There's no one here."

Granma smiled. She sat on the edge of my bed by the vanity. "Alexandria, would you come here, please?"

I rolled my eyes as I sat next to my grandmother. "Gran-ma. Ahhh!" I stumbled backwards as the image of a beautiful girl with long, dark black hair and deep green eyes looked back at me.

5 – My Worst Nightmare

The girl wore a spring green dress with white lace around the bodice. A matching ribbon held back her hair. She was extremely pale and slender.

"Alexandria, this is my granddaughter, Kelly. Kelly, meet Alexandria."

"You mean..."

"Yes. Tessa was telling the truth about Alexandria being in a mirror."

"But how?" I asked, wide-eyed.

Alexandria looked at the floor. "Mother was angry with me because I was primping myself in the mirror so much that evening. I thought I looked particularly pretty. Mother said I was being vain. She said that if I loved looking at myself so much, I should become part of the mirror. Next thing I knew, I was in here with no way out."

"Couldn't your mother get you out again?"

"She tried; really, she did. Then they took her away, and she could not return. The last time I saw her was as the police were dragging her out of my room."

"That's awful!" I said, moving to the vanity.

"So, you see, honey," Granma laid a gentle hand on my shoulder. "The Gift is both a blessing and a danger."

"So how is it that the mirror is still around?" I asked, putting my fingers against the glass.

"We have all watched out for this mirror very carefully. No one knows exactly how Alex was imprisoned in it, and until we have a way of freeing her, we are guarding the mirror."

"So, she doesn't age in the mirror?"

"Nope."

"What about eating?"

"It is a mirror," Alex began. "If you put food on the table, it appears in here. I can eat whatever is there until you take it away. Livvy, here, and Eva have been wonderful in aiding my education as well. We have discovered that if a book should be left on the table, I can read it on this side. "

"Maybe you can help me with *my* homework!" We both broke out giggling together.

"I'm going to leave you girls to get acquainted," Grandma smiled and headed for the door. "I'll call when dinner is ready."

"So, you don't have the gift, do you?" I asked solemnly.

"No, I don't," Alex replied. "Wish I did. Then I could will my way out of here."

"Will your way?"

"Yes." Alex looked at me sitting before her. "Eva hasn't instructed you yet, has she?" It was more of a statement. I shook my head. "Then I shan't say more about the matter until she has. Too much information too soon could become dangerous."

"Dangerous how?"

"Let's see; my mother imprisoned me in a mirror. My brother, who did have the gift, set the entire forest on fire when he tried to light the stove. Elizabeth, my brother's daughter, changed the cat into a tiger."

"I get the picture. I've been pretty tame so far," I giggled.

We talked for a while. I found out that Alex liked adventure books. I promised to bring her up some from the library. The TV was placed in such a way that Alex could see it from the mirror, and Aunt Eva would often put on a movie for her to watch. I remembered the shelves of videos downstairs in the family room. We could watch movies together. Alex reminded me to continue reading the diary. We could talk about that as well.

Soon I heard Granma calling for me.

"I have to go. Dinner's ready. I'll bring you up something to eat."

"Thank you. Eva brought me a small breakfast this morning after you'd left, but I haven't had anything since. I'm starving!"

"No problem. This could be fun."

"I'm glad to have a friend. Although Eva is very nice, it gets lonely in the mirror."

"Can you play board games in there?"

"I don't know," Alex replied with a scowl. "I've never tried."

"I'll bring one up. Do you like to play chess?"

"Yes, I do, but I don't see how we can play that way."

"I think I do. I'll see if there's a chess board in the game closet and bring it up. We can try my idea. It may take a bit, but I think it will work."

"Alright."

I heard my name again with a more strident insistance. "Coming!" I called. To Alex I said, "Gotta go. I'll hurry back."

Aunt Eva poked her head into my room to check on me. I had disappeared right after the dishes were done and hadn't come back down. Her brows went up in surprised when she saw me sitting at the vanity. I had a chessboard in front of me and a plate of half-eaten snacks on my left. Across from me was Alexandria, studying the board.

"What's this?" Eva asked with a smile.

"We're playing chess," I smiled back.

"Tis a bit tricky," Alex replied, "Since we're playing in a mirror."

"I suppose that would be strange." Aunt Eva sat on the bed to watch. "I take it you girls are getting along?"

"Oh, yes!" Alex replied with excitement. "We have even discovered we like many of the same things."

"Mostly," I grinned and made a move. "It'll be nice having someone my age to hang out with. I mean, Jasper's ok, I guess, but he really isn't around much."

"No, and he's not much of a conversationalist," Alex added.

Aunt Eva laughed heartily. Apparently, she found something humorous. "No," she agreed. "He's not, but he's a hard worker."

"Where does he disappear to every day anyway?" I asked as I watched Alex's next move.

"To do his chores," Aunt Eva replied vaguely.

Aunt Eva watched us struggle to play chess in reverse for a short while. Although I was black, the black side was next to the mirror. It was an excellent brain challenge for both of us.

"Don't be up too late," she said with a grin.

"We won't," I replied, capturing Alex's knight.

"What? How?" Alex replied, shocked. "Oh. That's how. This reverse thing is much harder than it looks."

AUNT EVA

I chuckled as I closed the window in Kelly's room, then moved down towards my den. Yes, Alex and Kelly were perfect for each other. It would be a fast, albeit awkward, friendship. I noticed my mother sitting in the overstuffed chair in the Family Room knitting. A talk show was playing on the TV. I sat on the couch near her.

"New scarf?" I asked.

"Kelly's going to need it, isn't she? The chills are the next phase, yes?"

"Yes, those are next, but we have other ways of handling that now."

"Oh," Mom replied, deflated. "Well, she can always use it for winter."

"I'm wondering if Kelly is ready for the first lesson," I mused distractedly.

"Won't know until you try," Mom replied. "She's been having nightmares for several months now. You might want to do something soon."

"Maybe you're right. She needs more information than what she has. I'll begin tomorrow afternoon."

KELLY

Something didn't feel right. The house was unusually dark. The nightlight from the bathroom wasn't on in the hall.

Was that a noise? I turned to go down the stairs. Strange. The stairs seemed narrower than before. What is that scraping noise? It sounded like swords scraping each other. A green light glowed in the kitchen. I didn't remember a green light. Slowly, silently, I moved around the banister and down the foyer. The noise was getting faster. I crept to the corner near the archway. My eyes widened in shock as I peered around the corner into the kitchen.

In the middle of the kitchen was a bright green column of light. Four sets of butcher knives were sharpening themselves around the outside. They slid back and forth in unison, sharpening the blades to a point. Suddenly, they stopped. One set came apart and flung themselves in my direction. I pulled back quickly against the wall. Both knives flew past and stuck in the wall opposite me.

I didn't wait. I raced up the stairs as fast as my legs would carry me and down the hall. Swishing sounds carried through the air behind her. Dodging into my room, I slammed the door shut behind me. Pound, pound, pound, pound, pound! The door shook as each knife buried its blade into the wood. All was quiet for a moment. Slowly, I stepped away from my wall. My entire body was shaking. Tentatively, I reached out and opened the door to peer out into the hall. Eight knives stuck out of the other side of the door. At the far end, the green column of light was ambling down the hall. With a jerk, the knives pulled out of the door.

I slammed the door closed, raced to my bed, and jumped under the covers. The door burst open. With a swirl, the covers flew off me as I clutched my pillow. The knives flew across the room...

"Ahhhhhhh!" the scream echoed in the room.

"Kelly!" the voice urged as I shook on the bed. "Kelly, wake up! Wake up!"

I sat up with a start, breathing hard; hurriedly staring around me. I saw my grandmother, my aunt, and Alex all watching me with worry in their eyes. I closed my eyes and drew in a deep, calming breath, falling back onto my bed. I was still shaking.

"Sorry," I murmured. I opened my eyes to look at Aunt Eva. She had a concerned expression on her face.

"Did you forget to take the medicine I gave you?" she asked firmly.

"I must have fallen asleep during the movie we were watching," I explained, realizing I was still in my jeans and shirt. The screensaver was playing on the TV.

"You're never to forget it again! Understand?" Aunt Eva ordered.

I looked at my aunt. She seemed sincerely scared. "It was only a nightmare, right?" I asked. "That's what you guys are always telling me."

Aunt Eva looked at the wall over my head. I moved my eyes to the wall, screamed, and jumped off the bed.

"Oh, my gosh! Oh, my gosh! How'd... Why'd... Agh!" I jumped as a hand touched my shoulder. I stared wide-eyed at my grandmother and burst into tears.

"Come along now," Granma tried to comfort me. "It's alright. You're awake now."

"But... I mean... those...," I pointed to the wall. Aunt Eva was already pulling the knives out of the dry-wall.

"This one could have been deadly," Aunt Eva said sternly. "Mom, stop babying her!"

"I'm just trying to calm her down," Granma retorted, cuddling me close.

Aunt Eva sighed. "Come with me, Kelly," she instructed. "We need to talk."

I looked at Granma fearfully. Granma hugged me, nodded, and gently directed me towards the door Aunt Eva went out of.

Granma sat on the edge of the bed. She must have looked over at Alex. "Sorry she woke you," I heard her say to Alex.

Alex grinned self-consciously. "She didn't wake me. I don't sleep. I'm in limbo."

"I know," Granma smiled sadly. "I was trying to be polite."

"Oh, sorry. It's ok." Alex continued. "Is Kelly in trouble?"

Granma shrugged. "She sure could be if she doesn't start paying more attention," Granma replied.

"But she doesn't know anything!"

"Don't tell me! I'm on her side." Granma sighed. "I'm going to follow them, sweetheart. Good night."

"Good night, ma'am," Alex replied.

I glanced down the hall to see Grandma coming from my room. She motioned for me to move on ahead. I caught up with Aunt Eva on the stairs.

6 – Gift 101, Or is it a Curse?

Aunt Eva led me down to the den on the other side of the Family Room. She definitely wasn't happy. As we passed the kitchen, I glanced at the clock. 1:47-in the morning. Yuk! No wonder Aunt Eva wasn't happy.

Aunt Eva turned on the light as she entered the den, leaving the door opened. She noticed I had stopped at the door. She put the knives down on her desk. Both of us jumped when one clattered to the floor. Regaining composure, Aunt Eva glanced at the shelves behind her desk. They were full of small trinkets. She picked up a toddler's block and wrapped her hand around it as if it was a memory she remembered well. She looked out the window on the side. I saw her squint as she peered out into the dark.

Turning back towards me, she smiled sadly. She walked around the desk and leaned on the edge.

"Come in, Kelly," she invited. She waved a hand to direct me to the chair in front of the desk.

I did as I was told, tentative and scared. I never took my eyes off her as I approached and sat.

"Am... am I in trouble?" a timid voice came from my throat that I hadn't heard since I was 5. "Are... Are you going to send me back home?"

Aunt Eva gave me a loving smile. "No. I'm not," she reassured me. "Do you remember what I told you about the Gift?"

"You said the Gift could be dangerous to others or me, if I couldn't control it," I began. "You said that what I'm going through you did, too, and Tessa; that lady."

"Correct. Problem is, the chemical changes you are going through bring on nightmares. Nightmares of all kinds, from changing the color of your room to..." she picked up one knife, "accidentally killing someone. If anyone had been in the hall while these were flying through the air, they'd have been skewered."

I looked down at the floor. I tried to hide the tears in my eyes, but one slid down my face as I sniffed and hit the floor. Aunt Eva gently leaned over and pulled my head up to face hers.

"It's going to be alright, Kelly," Aunt Eva reassured gently. "I promise; but you must follow my instructions exactly. Do you understand?" I nodded. "Now, first things first, you must take the medicine I gave you *no matter what!*"

I nodded again. "It was an accident." From the corner of my eye, I saw Grandma sidle silently up to the doorway.

"Yes, and killing someone would have been an accident as well, but how would we explain it? I can't resurrect someone."

I sighed dejectedly. "I'm just a menace," I muttered.

"No, you're not!" Aunt Eva chuckled. "I used to feel like that, too. Now. There are two ways to control the gift. One is willpower; the other is clearing your mind. One makes the Gift do what you want it to do."

"Like when you healed the bird this afternoon?"

"Yes. The other stops it." I looked at her blankly. Aunt Eva laughed. "That's the same expression I had when my father tried to explain it. You'll understand soon enough. First, we're going to train you to control it with your will. It's the easier of the two." She held her hand out flat. The block sat in her palm. "Take the block, Kelly."

"What?" I asked, confused. What did taking the block have to do with the Gift?

"Take the block."

I shrugged, leaned over, reached out, and picked up the block from her palm.

Aunt Eva laughed. "Good thinking, but not what I meant," she chuckled. I got the impression she expected that to be my response. She retrieved the block from my hand and moved back a bit. "Try it again. Without leaving your chair, take the block."

I scowled at my aunt. "I can't reach it."

"Use your willpower. I want you to concentrate on the block and will it to come to you."

I looked warily at my aunt. Had she lost her mind? I looked down at the block; staring at it for a long time, trying to persuade it to come to me. Nothing. I returned my gaze to my aunt. Aunt Eva smiled encouragingly. She handed me the block and backed up.

"Hold out the block like I did," she instructed. I did. "Now. When you do this, you must remove everything else out of your mind. Push away everything you're feeling, everything you're thinking, and everything you're seeing. The only thing you want to do is concentrate on the block. Stare at it. Visualize it. Estimate how much it weighs. Try to feel it in your hand. Concentrate so hard until everything in your mind is about the block. Then force your will on the block and have it come to you." With that said, the block left my hand and floated casually across the room to Eva's. "See?"

I swallowed hard. "You make it look so easy."

"It is... now," Aunt Eva replied. "I had to work long and hard to get it to work every time. Try it again." She held out the block and watched.

I drew in a deep breath and glared at the block. Clear the mind. Push everything away. Feel the block. Think of how heavy it is. See it in your mind. Concentrate. Will the block to come. Block, come. It didn't move. Block, Come, I concentrated harder. Nothing. Block, come! I demanded it. The block wiggled. I thought harder. "Block, come!" she commanded out loud. My hands shot up to cover my face as the block flew across the room right at me. It hurt when it struck my open hands and dropped to the floor.

"Are you alright?" Aunt Eva chuckled as she retrieved the block from the floor.

I looked down at the block. "Did I really do that?" I asked.

"Yep. All by yourself," Aunt Eva smiled proudly at me. "And just for the record? I did the same thing, only the block missed me and went through the window I was sitting in front of. Father wasn't real happy about that."

I cracked a weak smile. "Well, at least I didn't break a window."

"Yet," Aunt Eva smiled. She tossed the block back to me. "Your assignment is to work with that block all day tomorrow until you can not only bring it to you, but control how fast it comes. Understand?" I nodded. "Good. Now go back to bed. Chores in the morning."

"Thanks, Aunt Eva," I replied, rising from the chair. "I... don't know what would happen to me without you."

Aunt Eva smiled. "Your mother would be beside herself and go totally gray before she hit 40," my aunt teased.

My smile saddened. "Does Mom know about all this?"

"Yes, she does. That's why she sent you here. She was awakened any number of nights by my nightmares. Sometimes, my nightmares became her nightmares. My father finally stopped it. She often sat by and watched as Granpa and I would run through exercise after exercise. I think she was a little jealous of the amount of time I got to spend with Father, but I know he always made extra time for her as well. I never did know if she wished she had the Gift, too."

I shook my head. "I don't know. She never mentioned it to me."

"She knew you'd have it. You have the hair and the eyes. She knew what to expect. Now go to bed, and don't forget your medicine."

"Right. I'll grab a bottle of water to take it with."

AUNT EVA

I watched the door for a long time after Kelly left. I listened as the child opened and closed the refrigerator and my mother murmuring to her. The usual ones creaking, I heard Kelly go upstairs. The murmurings between Kelly and Alex came through the floor. Then silence. I leaned against my desk and breathed again in concern.

Mom came into the room sleepily. "Everything alright?"

I sighed. "I suppose it will be," I replied.

"Good thing she's here and not with Marie."

"Yes," I agreed. Even my sister had no idea how to handle this.

Carefully, I picked up a knife from the table. It was a butcher's knife, like the ones for chopping large chunks of meat. Its sharp edge gleamed in the dim light of the den. "I'm going to have to step up her instructions. The forces are already looking for her. I can see some of them by the woods. And she's much farther along than we thought."

"What makes you think so?"

I held up one of the knives. "I don't even *own* a butcher's knife. Now I have eight." I watched the color drain from my mother's face as what I said sunk in.

KELLY

"How long do you have to practice?" Alex asked, watching me continually try to move the block. I'd been able to do it twice. Both times, the block hit me in the head. At this rate, I would be covered in black and blues by morning.

"Aunt Eva said I have to practice until I can not only make the block come to me, but I can control how fast," I reported, thinking about the block again. It was sitting on my bed. I was standing near the closet, so nothing would break. After several minutes, the block flew across the room right at me. I ducked in time for the block to bounce loudly off the closet door. Another dent in the door. I sighed as I picked up the square piece of wood, then sat on the edge of her bed.

"Am I ever going to get this?" I asked Alex. "I mean, it's impossible!"

Alex chuckled. "No, it's not. I've watched family member after family member practice this exercise. It isn't always a block, but it's the same anyway. Try shortening the distance between you and the block. That way, you don't require as much energy to move the block to you. Once you can get it to you at arm's length, you slowly move backwards until you can control how quickly the block comes to you. Think that will work?"

"Possibly," I shrugged. "I'm willing to try anything at this point." I placed the block on the vanity only a foot away from me. Concentrating on the block, I started when it hopped off the vanity and into my hand. "I did it!"

"Very good," Alex praised.

"Kel-ly!" Granma's voice filtered up from downstairs.

I ran to my door. "Yes?"

"Come along! We're going into town to go shopping."

"Coming!" I cried excitedly. Finally, I could look at something besides the farm! I put the block back on the vanity and called, "I'll see you later!" to Alex.

"Have fun!" Alex called after me. I noticed her voice wasn't exactly cheerful as she said it. I wondered if she was jealous that she couldn't go.

7 – Can Trees Move?

The sun beat down on the pickup as Granma drove down the dusty roads. It wasn't such a hot day; only about 80 degrees. The air conditioner, at least, felt better than the dry air outside. One glance showed the dust flying behind us in a cloud. I noticed the dust dropped to the ground almost as quickly as the tires kicked it up.

"Great day," I remarked, almost as dry as the air.

Granma laughed. "It's a beautiful day. Lighten up!"

I sighed. "It's so dry!"

"Yes, it is. We'll need to pick you up some moisturizer."

"What are we going to town for?"

"Aunt Eva needs some food supplies, and I thought we'd get you some fitting clothing."

I scowled and glanced down. I wore my usual style of jeans and a black T-shirt with the picture of a yellow Peep on it. My sneakers were really taking a beating out on the farm. Maybe I could use some new shoes. "What's wrong with my clothing?"

"Let's see. Your t-shirts are too tight on you, your jeans are so worn out I can see your underwear through them, and your shoes look like they're about to fall apart. Besides, you're always in black. Don't you like any other colors?"

"What's wrong with black? I like black."

"So do I, but you'll need to learn to flash it up a bit. Let's see what Alise has in her shop, shall we?"

Granma pulled the truck into a parking spot across from the General Store. I recalled seeing the white clapboard siding with the wide covered porch when I came in on the train. Spring green woodwork accented the white. Pretty. It also looked freshly painted. The walkway up to the porch had a couple of trees on either side, creating a cool canopy over the sidewalk. It had a quaint, royal feel to it.

I smiled to myself as the coolness of the shade hit me when we walked under the canopy of the trees. Suddenly, the trees rustled. I peered up into the trees, expecting to see some street urchin up in the branches, but there wasn't one. Still, the trees rustled, dropping a few dead leaves as I slowly walked below them.

"Kelly?" Granma called from the porch steps. "Something wrong?"

I glanced at my grandmother. I pointed towards the trees with my mouth open, then stopped. What was I going to say? The trees were moving without a breeze? Who's going to believe that? This is the second time it happened to me. The last was in the orchard at the homestead. "Nothing," I replied and sprinted to catch up with the older woman.

The general store was much bigger than it looked. The right side was all groceries. It was sort of like a small supermarket back home. The back on the right was the butcher shop. There was a wide booth in the middle of the store where the cashier was. A "U. S. Post Office" sign hung from the ceiling above it. The left side was more farmer-type items. Hoes, shovels, rakes, feed buckets, etc. A glass case against the far-left wall held several styles of rifles and ammunition. A rack up front held an assortment of riding and work boots.

I was surprised by the amount of grocery supplies Granma had gathered. Some of it seemed a little strange.

"Fruit Loops?" I asked with a questioning expression.

"Uncle Cliff and Aunt Chrissy will be out with the kids day after tomorrow, and your mother is driving in on Friday for the weekend. The Fruit Loops are for the twins. They're Lizzie and Eddie's favorite. We figured we'd have a stock on hand in case they didn't want to eat the rest of the food."

I laughed. The twins were five now, but still at the picky stage. They had two older brothers, Brandon and Devin, and an older sister, Abby. Abby was just a couple of years younger than me.

"We'd better pack a few more of those, then," I replied, still laughing. "Those boys can eat!"

Granma laughed. "Yes, they can! It'll be a pleasant change of pace for a bit."

"Morning, Livy," the man behind the counter greeted. "The halter Mac ordered for the foal came in. Do you want it?"

"Oh, yes!" Granma gleamed. "He's been waiting for that to begin training the little thing." While the man went into the back room, Granma pushed me over to the boots. "Go pick out a pair of riding boots that will fit you. Mac wants to start teaching you to ride."

"He what?" my eyes went wide with fright.

"Go on!"

After finishing up at the General Store, we dropped the bags off at the truck and walked down a few blocks.

Nestled amongst the houses was a single shop. It stood out because it was painted bright pink with blue trim. That's one way not to be missed. The sign over the door read "Alisha's First- and Second-Hand Shop."

"First and Second-Hand Shop?" I asked warily.

"Oh, yes. Alisha is very smart. She has a full supply of new clothes, but also takes in the clothes that the locals have either out-grown or don't wear. The customer then gets store credit towards another purchase."

"Oh! Kinda like the video game stores back home."

"Yep. Just like that. Come along, now. Let's see what she's got."

The store wasn't wide, but it was deep. There were sections similar to what you'd find in any clothing store. Each section had a couple of racks labeled "Consignment". Several people were sifting through the materials to see what they might purchase.

An older woman with salt and pepper hair pulled back into a bun came bustling out of a side compartment. She wore a black dress with a dusty white apron over it. She held a box out to a customer.

"I believe these are what you're looking for, Mrs. Wilson," she smiled, holding open the lid.

"Oh, yes!" the other woman smiled back. She was older, probably older than Granma. Her hair was cut in a short, gray bob. She leaned heavily on a cane and wore a light coat. "That's exactly them. You're just wonderful, Alisha!"

"It's not a problem," the first woman gushed back. "Shall I bag these for you?"

"Please, dear. It's getting harder to get around these days."

"You know, I can deliver them to you if you'd prefer," Alisha suggested as she reached behind a counter for a plastic bag.

The older woman chuckled. "You know, if everyone I get things from delivered them to me like they offer, I'd never get out of the house! Not yet; thanks, dear."

"You have a good day, Mrs. Wilson."

Granma stepped aside for the older woman. "How are you, Hazel?" she asked.

"Oh, Livvy! It's so good to see you! Back in these parts, are we?"

"For another week or so."

The older woman noticed me standing behind Granma. Her eyes twinkled. "And who is this beautiful young woman?" she asked with a grin. "I know she must be related to you. She looks just like your mother, but she has your father's coloring."

Granma smiled proudly at me. "Yes, she does, doesn't she? Hazel, this is my granddaughter, Kelly. Kelly, this is Mrs. Wilson from across town."

"It's a pleasure, ma'am," I said shyly.

"Oh, thank you, darlin'!" Mrs. Wilson chuckled back. "So polite. So pretty. Best watch her, Liv," she warned. "When the boys in this town know she's here, they're all going to be looking for her."

"I know," Granma agreed. "Need help to the car?"

"Oh, no, no!" Mrs. Wilson waved Granma off. "I've got it. You have a good time visiting." She started towards the door. "Nice to meet you, Kelly. Have fun."

"Thank you," I replied in my quiet voice.

"Hi, Livvy!" Alisha greeted. "What can I find for you?"

"My granddaughter needs some new clothing. What do you have in the young teen department?" Granma motioned towards me.

"How are you, honey?" Alisha smiled as she sized me up. "Yep, I think I have just what you'd like. Come with me."

Granma and I spent the next hour going through the many clothes in Alisha's store. Surprisingly, I found several items I liked, and, to Granma's pleasure, they weren't all black. Granma had me pick out 4 pairs of jeans. She insisted on at least eight T-shirts. We even got me a pair of sneakers to add to the riding boots. I had to admit, the newer jeans felt much better than the old ones I had been wearing. Granma got me a new dress, too. Why? Who knows? She thought I might need one. On top of that, she added underwear and socks. Wow! It felt like Christmas!

"Thanks, Granma."

"Not a problem, sweetheart. I'm glad to help you out." Granma pulled out of the parking spot and drove down a bit. She turned left over the railroad tracks.

"Do we have more errands?" I noticed we weren't heading home.

"Nope. Now we get to go for my favorite treat!"

"What's that?" I smiled at Granma's expectant grin.

"Mr. Johnson's homemade ice cream! Talk about *fresh*!" I laughed as my grandmother licked her lips. Homemade ice cream. It did sound good.

8 – Cousins!

You could measure the excitement two days later as Granma, Aunt Eva, and I got several rooms ready for our expected guests. We didn't have to wait long. Around mid-morning, a car came up the long driveway honking happily. I looked out the bedroom window where I was just putting on the finishing touches to the bunk beds for the boys. I grinned as I saw Uncle Cliff's long length peel its way out of the mini-van. His blondish hair shone in the summer sunlight. Aunt Chrissy came out the other side. She was much shorter than Uncle Cliff, with shoulder-length brown tresses. Both were slim in stature.

The kids started piling out of the van. The twins were obvious. Both five-year-olds were dressed alike, but Eddie's mousy-brown curls were much shorter than Lizzie's. Abby came out next. I was surprised to see how much the girl had grown since I'd seen her just six months ago. Her wavy blonde hair was French-braided down her back.

It was Brandon who made me stare. I never realized it before. The nine-year-old had such a different coloring than his siblings; much like Uncle Cliff's coloring was so different from Mom's and Aunt Eva's. His soccer-cut hair was jet-black like my own. As he looked up at Granma, I noticed the blue eyes. They weren't as dark as mine, but the coloring was unmistakable. Did Brandon have The Gift, too?

Pulling myself away from the window, I raced down the stairs, through the house, and bolted out the back door to greet my family.

"Kelly!" Uncle Cliff cried as he pulled me into an enormous bear hug. "How are ya, sweetheart?"

"I'm doing good," I giggled.

"Enjoying the farm?"

I nodded. "Yea."

"Hi, darling," Aunt Chrissy hugged me from behind. I turned and hugged my aunt.

My eyes went to Brandon automatically. He looked at me with a mischievous grin. "What's up?" he asked.

I cocked my head to think. There was a ton "up", just nothing I could tell him. "We've got a new colt in the barn," I tried.

Brandon's face scrunched. "That's it?"

Kelly nodded. "Pretty much. For Pete's sake, Brandon! We're in No Man's Land! What could possibly be interesting?"

"Can I see the new colt?" Lizzie immediately asked.

"Later," Uncle Cliff told her firmly. "We'll take a walk all over the farm so you can see everything. Okay?" The statement must have settled the girl because she said nothing else about it. "And there can be plenty interesting on a farm if you know where to look!" His huge hand landed on my shoulder.

"I hope we get to be roommates," Abby turned to me.

"I don't think so. Aunt Eva said she had a special room just for you," I replied. Actually, I was glad Abby was staying in another room. I didn't know how I'd explain Alex, and I wanted my own space to practice with the block. I was pretty sure that my cousins hadn't been told about the Gift any more than I had been.

"Well, let's get this family inside!" Aunt Eva called from the kitchen door. "Can't enjoy the great outdoors until you're settled."

I helped get the luggage and backpacks into the house. I showed the boys and Lizzie the room they were going to share. Abby was thrilled she didn't have to share a room with Lizzie.

"Aunt Eva felt you'd rather have a room of your own, but Lizzie would be afraid in a strange house," I explained, showing Abby the room across the hall where she'd be staying.

"Where's your room?" Abby asked anxiously.

"Around the corner. I've got the room at the end of the hall."

"Really?" Abby seemed impressed. "Aunt Eva doesn't let anyone stay in that room!"

Probably because Alex has that room, I thought. Instead, I shrugged. "I don't know. That's where she put me."

"Come on, girls," Uncle Cliff called from downstairs. "We're going to look around the farm!"

Both of us grinned and raced down the stairs. I loved being with my cousins. It seemed like they were the only ones who accepted me as I was.

"Hey!" Aunt Eva called. "Can we walk through the house, please? We're not a herd of cattle, ya know?"

"Sorry," I replied sheepishly. We hurried through the house and out the back door to catch up with the others. I wondered how often that phrase had been thrown at my aunt and my mother.

"Kelly should lead us," I heard Uncle Cliff say to his wife. "She's been here a while. She should know all the best spots." My eyes widened with fear. I'd hardly left the house except to gather eggs and go for riding lessons! Quickly, I began shaking my head. "What?" Uncle Cliff teased. "Why not?"

"I... really haven't been here that long," I began searching for another excuse, "And other than the corral where Mac gives me my riding lessons, I really haven't been anywhere."

Uncle Cliff's deep, rumbling laugh seemed to echo around me. I wasn't sure what was so funny. "It's alright, honey," he comforted as he wrapped a loving arm around my shoulder. "I've been here so long I could show *you* some places."

My eyes lit up. "Could you? Really? Aunt Eva doesn't like me roaming the farm alone."

"Sure! Come on."

"Cliff! Don't go getting the kids in trouble!" Aunt Chrissy called after our group as we moved down the path towards the outbuildings. Uncle Cliff merely waved back that he'd heard her. I glanced back to see Aunt Chrissy and Aunt Eva mumbling to each other. I could only guess they were talking about Uncle Cliff.

The walk around the farm was fun with Uncle Cliff. We saw all the animals I saw the first time. I introduced my cousins to Rambo, the chestnut gelding that, despite his name, was as gentle as a lamb. He was the horse that Mac was teaching me to ride. We got to pet the new colt and his mother. We fed the chickens, watered the sheep, and headed out back to show the younger ones the cattle.

Walking along a stream, we came to a small pond. Several mallards were swimming towards the middle, diving for food. Trees filled most of the edges. Birds flew in and out of the trees, dipping into the water, and flying back out. An occasional fish splashed at the surface of the water. I tried to ignore the gently swaying branches above me.

"This is a great place to go swimming," Uncle Cliff told us. "Maybe we can come back here after lunch." We all agreed.

"What's that over there?" Brandon asked, pointing to a faded picket fence across the stream. I had never seen it before.

"That's the old cemetery," my uncle replied.

"Cemetery?" I questioned, instinctively moving towards it. I paused momentarily to look up as the trees above me rustled again, just like the ones in town. Again, there wasn't even a breeze.

"Sure," Uncle Cliff replied as he carried Lizzie over the rocks in the stream, completely unaware of my pause. He led the group up the hillside to an old cemetery gate. A huge oak tree stood in the corner, giving shade to the centuries' old stones. Some stones were hard to read from deterioration. Some were tall, others short. A few had fallen over and were partially covered with grass. The grass was neatly cut, so someone had to come up to take care of the place. Uncle Cliff opened the gate with a loud creak.

"Who's buried here?" Brandon asked excitedly.

"People who used to live on the farm. It was tradition for centuries to be buried on your own land."

I looked over at the stones.

Becca Connolly,
Loving wife,
Nov 14, 1764 – Apr 5, 1843

Alabaster Connolly
Devoted Husband and Father
Jan 4, 1761 – Dec 21, 1842

Renee Ann
Precious Infant
Feb 2 – Feb 4, 1786

"Look at this one," Lizzie exclaimed. "It's crying!"

My eyes shot over at her with a start. I moved to another aisle where Lizzie was staring at a stone. Kneeling next to the small stone, I examined it. A sculpture on one side of a small boy was attached to the headstone.

Alexander Whyatt
Aug 4, 1872 – June 23, 1875

The sculpture looked like a small cherub on the stone, and sure enough, several drops of water appeared to come out of the eyes.

"He wasn't even three years old," I whispered sadly.

"Plague came through," Uncle Cliff replied, just as sadly. "Wiped out most of the children and a good number of adults that year. If you go to the town cemetery, you'll see probably a hundred or more stones with that same ending year, all within a few months of each other."

"How sad," Abby said, looking down.

I reached out to wipe away the water droplets. After all, stones don't cry. I jerked back, however, when the droplet burned my finger. I stared at the stone with my finger in my mouth.

"You alright?" Uncle Cliff asked, surveying me carefully. I nodded as I glanced at my finger. "Let me see." It left a small red mark on my finger where I'd tried to wipe away the tear. "Doesn't look too bad," he noted. "Still, we'll let Aunt Eva look at it when we get back."

"Why'd...?"

"Later," was his only reply.

"This is boring!" Eddie complained.

"Quite right," Uncle Cliff cheered up and looked away from the cemetery. "Let's get going."

A more recent tombstone made me stop short when I glanced at it. It was a larger granite one, a bit more elaborate than its elderly neighbors.

Tessa Ann Reed
Feb 12, 1830 – Jan 22, 1884
May God Rest Her Soul

Tessa Ann Reed. Alex's mother? She was buried here? Wait. The article said she was being arraigned in 1883. What happened that she died just a few months later? A quick assessment of the other stones didn't show one for a husband. There was one for another Reed, an infant name Marcus. And there was one for a George McClure. The starting date was May 13, 1810, but there was no ending date. Perhaps it was an older brother to Tessa. Something didn't sit right. I'll have to ask someone.

"Kelly? You coming?" Uncle Cliff's request broke my thoughts.

Catching my bearings, I turned towards my uncle and cousins. "Coming," I cried and started out of the cemetery. Uncontrollably, I took another quick glance at the tombstones while closing the gate.

It was nearly an hour later when we all came in full of hay dust and weeds, but laughing heartily. The three women in the house looked at us with amused expressions.

"Smack the dust off outside!" Aunt Eva ushered us back out to the driveway. "There's a shop vac in the garage, Cliff!"

"Gotcha!" he waved and motioned towards the garage. It was hilarious getting 'sprayed' by the air from the shop vac, blowing all the dust around the garage. We'd all need a shower tonight.

We came back in a few moments later to get ushered into the bathroom to wash up for lunch. There was more laughter as the kids played with the water. Abby and I helped the little ones reach the water spout. I glanced at the burn on my finger as I put Eddie down. The water hurt the burn.

"It's getting worse." Abby noticed the blister as she glanced at my finger.

"Probably just irritated by all we've been doing. I'll wrap it after lunch," I brushed away the concern.

"So, where'd you go that you were gone so long?" Granma asked. All at once, the kids started talking about all the things they'd seen and did.

"You may want to take a look at Kelly's finger," Uncle Cliff whispered to Aunt Eva behind me. "She got a slight burn."

"Burn? How? What were you playing with?" Aunt Eva threatened her brother with a wooden spoon in her hand. I held in the chuckle brewing in my chest.

"Wasn't playing. She touched a drop of water on the stone in the cemetery," he replied. Aunt Eva's eyes went wide. Uncle Cliff nodded. "It was crying; she went to wipe away the tear."

"Oh, no!" Aunt Eva covered her mouth with her hand. Uncle Cliff just nodded in agreement.

After lunch, Aunt Eva treated my burn and wrapped it. "Be sure to leave this on. I'll re-treat it after your shower."

"I can," I replied. After all, I'd watched her aunt.

"I'll do it," Eva replied. "I need to check for healing or worsening."

"Can't you heal it?"

Aunt Eva smiled grimly. "No. It's a paranormal burn. I can't heal it."

"Oh. Why?"

"It would take too long to explain now," she replied, her eyes motioning towards my cousins in the other room. "Shall we try another lesson after dinner?"

"Can we do that with the crew here?"

"It'll be private enough where I plan to go."

I swallowed. "Ok." I looked at the wrapping on my finger. "Is this going to happen every time I touch something?"

Aunt Eva smiled. "No. It's... just an isolated incident."

"You're not going to tell me what's going on, are you?" I accused softly.

"I promise you will know everything you need and want to know before you leave here," Aunt Eva placed her forehead against mine. "However, I will explain things in steps, not all at once. Needless to say, don't go wiping away tears on tombstones anymore."

I nodded. "Ok. I'm going to go up to spend some time with Alex. Uncle Cliff is taking the others swimming up at the pond."

"That's a good idea. She's missed your company today."

"Me, too."

"Take a plate of lunch up for her, please."

"Will do!"

9 – Family History

I lay on the bed with the diary in my hand. I had read a few more pages. Alex sat opposite me in the mirror reading the adventure book I had gotten her from the library.

"Did you ever go up to the cemetery?" I finally asked Alex.

"When I was young," she replied. "Why?"

"Who are all those people?" I asked. "I mean, how are they related?"

"They're all people who lived here on the farm over the years," Alex replied cautiously.

"So, the farm just went from one person to the next to the next, and they all decided to be buried up there?"

"You *do* realize that this farm has been in our family for centuries, don't you?" Alex asked curiously.

I glanced at my friend in confusion. "No, I didn't." I replied thoughtfully. "So, those people up there are all my relatives?"

"Ancestors from as long as the family has owned the farm," Alex replied. "I think the oldest stone is from the late 1600s."

I thought about that for a moment. "So, all those people had this gift thingy?"

"Not all," Alex replied. "After all, The Gift only passed down to some of the children, not all. I didn't have it, but my brother did."

"I don't think I saw a tombstone for a brother of yours," I replied, "But we didn't look that closely."

"He's there. Willard R. Weston. He's buried closer to the back of the plot."

"Weston? I thought your last name was Reed?"

"It is," Alex replied sadly. "After the incidents with Mother, Will changed his name. He reversed his middle and last names so that he wouldn't be associated with a lunatic."

I waggled my head a bit. "I can understand that. People can be pretty cruel. Who was Marcus?"

"My elder brother. He died a few days after he was born. They had me two years later."

"There was a George McClure there that had a birthdate, but no death date."

Alex looked at the floor. "That was my grandfather," Alex replied solemnly.

"Why isn't there a death date? He can't possibly still be alive."

"They never found him," Alex replied carefully. "He just disappeared one day."

I stared at Alex cautiously. "Did he get stuck in a mirror, too?"

Alex shrugged. "In truth, I don't know. One day he was here, the next, when I returned from school, he was gone. Mother kept muttering to herself. Something about it being his own fault. I truly don't know what happened to him."

"Why was the tombstone of the three-year-old crying?"

"Crying?" Alex asked incredulously.

"Yea. Water was coming from the eyes of the little cherub statue on the tombstone."

"It must have been mist or dew or something," Alex thought out loud. "Rock doesn't cry."

"I know. And when I went to wipe away the tear, it burned my finger. Not a burn like hot water, a burn like an acid!"

"Then don't do that!" Alex chastised me.

"Duh!" I replied. We looked at each other and burst out laughing. As we regained composure, I continued. "Aunt Eva says it's a paranormal burn. I don't know what that means. Problem is, I think there's more to this than they're telling me."

"Read the diary," Alex suggested.

"I am, but I mean, there's more. Tree leaves keep moving when I go underneath them, like a strong breeze is blowing them, but there's no breeze out there."

"Hmm, that's not normally pertaining to the Gift, but I remember Mother saying something about it. Read the diary," Alex repeated.

"I know," I replied, glancing at the pages. "But they're boring!"

Alex smiled shyly. "They are at first. Mother really wasn't much of a writer. But they get much more interesting as it goes on."

I nodded and settled down to read again. "I'll take your word for it."

It was a long time later when Alex's voice penetrated the haze in my brain.

"Kelly! Kelly, wake up!" the voice kept calling. It sounded worried and urgent. "Kelly, wake up! Wake up and close the window!" My brain tried to register the words as my body tried to return to sleep. "Kel-ly! Kelly, wake up, or I'm going to smack you!"

I chuckled in my half-sleep daze. "Can't smack me. You're in a mirror!"

"Kelly! Get the window! *Now!*"

I bolted up from my bed and glanced around the darkening room. "What...?"

"Close the window!" Alex ordered. "Now!"

I instantly looked at the big bay window. The sunlight was drifting away behind the trees, creating dark shadows across the yard. We had opened the side windows to let some air into the stuffy room. I jumped off the bed and ran to the window as dusk was turning into dark. I turned the handle on the bottom that would close the window on the one side. I twisted it tight and went to the other window. As I looked up, I could see some kind of reddish-brown shadow flying towards the house. I slowed down as I tried to see what it was.

"Hurry!" Alex urged from the corner.

I renewed my turning as the shadow approached the window. The shadow suddenly glowed orangy-red. I screamed and jumped back. A terrifying, twisted face grinned back at me. Sharp, pointy teeth glinted from the evil smile. The pug nose sat between two small, wild-looking, dark eyes. Black hair pointed all over the place. Two yellowish horns stuck out from above the eyes and curled back over its head. Its claw-like hands grasped the window edge and the wall and began prying open the window again.

"Kelly! Get up! Close the window! Fast! Hurry!" Alex's cries became panicked.

Regaining my courage, I stumbled towards the window on my hands and knees. I grasped the handle and began turning it again. It became a struggle of wills between me and the horrifying imp outside the window. It screamed at me as I struggled against it, but the opening was too small for it to pass through. Man, was it strong!

A large, masculine hand covered mine and helped close the window further. I sat back with a relieved breath as I heard the bump of the window closing against the frame over the pounding of my heart in my ears. The imp banged on the glass angrily, then flew off.

I looked up into Uncle Cliff's eyes. He looked at me with concern. I smiled lamely, then thanked him.

"Tomorrow, I'm going into town to get an air conditioner for this room," Uncle Cliff announced. "I don't want this problem anymore." He held his hand out to help me up.

"Can't they come in through the air conditioner?" I was shaking.

"Not the one I have in mind. Surprised Eva hasn't thought about it. You okay?"

I nodded. "Yea." Grasping his hand, I got myself up off the floor. "What was that?"

"An imp—of sorts," Uncle Cliff replied. "I see you've met our friend." He pointed towards the mirror. Alex was already out of sight.

"Yea. She's really cool."

"Who's cool?" Abby asked, coming into the room. "And what was all the yelling about?"

"Nightmare," Uncle Cliff remarked. "You know all about those," he chided his daughter. "Come on, ladies. Dinnertime."

The next day, Uncle Cliff returned from town around mid-afternoon. I bolted from the kitchen as my mother came around the van with several packages. She dropped them as she gathered me in an enormous hug!

"I've missed you so much!" she gushed in my ear, rocking me back and forth. "The apartment is so quiet."

"I wish I could say it's been quiet here," I laughed. "Between activities and the kids, it's been anything but! And Aunt Eva says you're just in time. The peaches will be ready to pick tomorrow."

"Oh, joy. Canning." Mom replied unenthusiastically.

"No offense, ladies, but this thing isn't light. One of you want to get the door?" Uncle Cliff grunted, a huge box straining his muscles.

I looked at the box Uncle Cliff had on his shoulder. It said air conditioner, but it looked awfully large. Mom picked up her bags again and moved towards the house.

"Where is everyone?" she asked.

"Here and there. I need to go up to the barn in half an hour. Mac is teaching me to ride."

"That's a wonderful activity for you."

Uncle Cliff opened the basement door and yelled down for Jasper. The youth appeared momentarily and followed Uncle Cliff up to my room. He had a gray toolbox in his hand.

"Mom," I said seriously. "Mom, there's something really strange going on here."

My mother put her bags on the kitchen table. "Like what?" She lifted a bag and handed it to me. "Here; I found some things in your room that you might want here."

"Thanks." Inside the bag were my art pencils, a well-worn sketch pad and a new one, and a book I'd been reading but really wasn't into. There was also an odd book I'd never seen before. I pulled the blue imitation leather book from the bag. It measured about 8 x 10 with an embossed flower on the cover. When I opened it, I found blank, lined pages.

"What's this?"

"It's a journal," Mom explained. "Aunt Eva said you might want to start keeping a record of yourself, so I picked one up for you. Now, what's going on?"

"Well, trees keep moving, and I saw this horrible-looking thing last night outside my bedroom window. Aunt Eva thinks I can move blocks, and she keeps saying something about a gift that I have, but I really don't understand it. And there's a girl my age in the mirror in my bedroom. Supposedly, her mother put her there."

"Yes. Alex has been trapped in that mirror all my life, and probably all of Gran's."

"You know about her?" I seemed surprised.

"Honey, I know all about the things going on around you. I used to live here, remember?" Mom wrapped her arm around me. "There's a reason I sent you here this summer. Aunt Eva is the best person right now to teach you about this gift you have. It can get really strong, and you'll need to learn to control it and limit it. I can't do that because I don't have it. I don't know what you need to do that."

"But why didn't you tell me about it before?" My voice revealed how hurt I was to have been kept in the dark.

"Because you weren't ready to hear it. And I was hoping it would pass you, even though your beautiful blue eyes and lovely black hair told me otherwise."

"Oh."

"Aunt Marie!" Abby came in from outside and ran to my mom. Well, that effectively put an end to that discussion. Maybe later. After a few more moments, I moved up to my room, dropped my things on my bed, and grabbed my riding boots. Mom and Abby walked with me down to the barn.

AUNT EVA

"She's a great kid," I mused to Marie as I leaned against the fence next to my sister. We watched Mac instruct Kelly on the back of Rambo.

"Yes, she is. A bit too timid, though."

"Not so much," I chuckled. "You were worse."

"How's she doing?"

"Just fine. Nothing out of the ordinary. Based on Father's records, she's right on target; maybe a little ahead."

"Can she do this, Eva?" Marie asked worriedly. She knew the repercussions if Kelly didn't.

"I think so. We haven't gotten too far in lessons yet. I'm going to need to set up a schedule for her to work on them every day. Alex has been a bit of a distraction."

"Alex? How so?"

"The two girls have really hit it off. They're like sisters who enjoy the same things. They watch movies together, they read together, they eat their meals together, they even figured out how to play chess backwards so they could play together."

Marie looked blankly at me. "Alex can do that?"

"Oh, yes. Kelly brings breakfast and dinner up to the girl every day without fail. The other day they were sharing Rice Krispies Treats."

Marie snuffed. "This from the girl who couldn't make friends." Marie watched as Kelly moved the horse up to a gallop. "How much have you told her?"

"Not much just yet. I've explained a bit, just enough. She doesn't know the dangers yet."

"Did she tell you about the trees?" Marie asked her sister knowingly.

"No. She hasn't mentioned trees. What about them?"

"They're rustling as she walks underneath them."

My expression fell. "They're what? That's not a trait of the Gift. That's something altogether different."

"Ya think?" Marie returned her attention to Kelly as I thought about this new situation.

10 - George

The next several days were a little crazy. Before everyone came out to help, I practiced getting peaches off the tree just like I moved the block. It had become much easier. I even bit into one particularly juicy, sweet peach as I pulled several more off the tree. Out of the corner of my eye, I saw Jasper watching me. His stiff expression was unreadable, as usual. When I looked right at him, he shook his head no. The back door slamming put an end to the silent conversation.

The whole family picked, peeled, and sliced up peaches. It took most of the day. It was messy and gooey. When we were done, we all piled into the truck and drove back to the pond for a swim. Laughter and squeals echoed off the trees. Aunt Eva got a first-hand view of the trees reacting to me. She didn't say anything, but was very interested in it.

After dinner, Uncle Cliff got a fire going in a fire pit out in the middle of the yard while Aunt Eva and Granma got out the makings for S'mores. Granma brought a handful of fire forks for roasting the marshmallows from the garage. The fire ring was made of stones forming a circle. It was piled high with dead wood, branches, and burnables. Several feet away from that were huge logs to sit on. A ring of marigolds ran just three feet behind that.

We had a great time singing songs, playing games, and enjoying the fire. All the while, I kept feeling like we were being watched, but look as I might, I couldn't see anything around us with the bright light of the fire in my eyes.

"Why don't the imps bother us now?" I whispered to Aunt Eva.

"Because 1. They're afraid of fire, and 2. The marigolds keep them away," Aunt Eva replied in a whisper. "We'll be long in the house before Uncle Cliff puts the fire out."

"Hey! No secrets over there!" Uncle Cliff teased with a grin.

"You just wish we were talking about you!" Aunt Eva teased back.

"Here we go!" Aunt Chrissy giggled, and the teasing banter of siblings began, leaving the rest of the group laughing. It was one comeback after another. Glancing over at Granma, I could see her head drop as the two went at it. Yea. Growing up with these two must have been fun.

Rain hit the next day, but that didn't stop us. Board games, video games, ghost stories, and playing in the rain kept us busy. I took time out to spend with Alex and get caught up on my reading. Late in the day, Mom took me to an open field near the house where we picked a bouquet of bright colorful flowers for the dining room table.

We talked a long time before bed. Mom admired the job Cliff and Jasper did on the window. They had removed one of the windows, put in the air conditioner, and framed some plexi-glass that they nailed to the window frame on the outside. She agreed she couldn't understand why Aunt Eva hadn't thought of that already.

"Probably because it doesn't get that hot out here," I pondered.

"You two girls get some sleep," Mom smiled and kissed me on the forehead. Alex giggled. "I know," she blew a kiss to the face in the mirror. "I'll see you in the morning."

Several hours later, I went down to get drinks for me and Alex. From the kitchen, I could hear the adults talking in the living room.

"Marie, you need to consider this," Aunt Eva was saying urgently.

"But she's only thirteen! She's not ready to leave home yet!" came my mother's upset voice.

"Marie, I know this is a hard decision," Uncle Cliff was saying. "But I've seen what's happening already. She's not safe in the city. She needs Eva's guidance."

"It's going to take years for me to get her to the point of complete control," Aunt Eva tried to explain. "Don't you remember how long it took Father to train me? I was graduating high school and still getting lessons!"

"And Kelly's power is stronger," Uncle Cliff added. "I see the signs. Every time we go outside, she's looking at the woods. She doesn't realize it, but she's hearing them. She's seeing them, but she doesn't know what she's seeing. She's been here what? Two weeks? Already the imps are trying to get to her. Look at her eyes, Marie! They are the darkest shade of blue I've ever seen from anyone in the family line."

"But she's still a child!" Mom countered.

"Yes, she is. That's why she isn't seeing what's really there," Aunt Eva replied. "But they will not stop. They will follow her. They will track her down. And without the training and an anchor, she will be helpless to stop them."

"Anchor?" I could hear the scowl in Mom's voice.

"Anchor," Aunt Eva repeated. "Don't you remember? You were my anchor as we grew up. *You* were the one keeping my feet on the ground and my sight where it should be. *You* were the one that warned me of the dangers I couldn't see, especially at night."

Mom sighed. "I remember."

"Alex is Kelly's anchor."

"So, we can take Alex to the apartment," Mom suggested lamely.

"You know you can't do that," I heard Granma. "Alex is trapped in the mirror, but if the mirror is removed from the property, the dimension she's trapped in ceases to exist, and Alex will be wiped out permanently. You know that."

"Oh, yea." Mom sounded like she was near tears. She was losing this battle, whatever it was. "What about you?" she asked someone. "Would you do this to Brandon?"

"I'm going to have to," Aunt Chrissy replied sympathetically. "Have you looked at him? He's only nine and already the nightmares have started. They aren't consistent yet. One here, one there, but they've started. It's just a matter of time."

There was quiet for a period of time. "I need to be with my daughter," Mom said timidly. "It's my responsibility to raise her. I love her!"

"Eavesdropping is a crime," a male voice whispered in my ear.

I jumped back, drawing in a breath and knocking into the person behind me. He let out an "oof!"

"You scared me!" I breathed as I recognized Jasper. I hadn't heard him come down.

Uncle Cliff suddenly appeared at the intersection. "Apparently, walls have ears," he said in a not so teasing way. He hooked his finger towards me, indicating for me to follow him. He nodded at Jasper with a slight scowl.

"Sorry," Jasper whispered. "Didn't mean to give you away."

I nodded as I followed my uncle. The others watching me enter the room made me nervous. My anxiety began to rise and my hands interlocked through the fingers. Everyone looked worried. My mother's eyes were red with tears, and she clutched at a wad of tissues. With a watery smile, Mom patted the seat next to her on the love seat.

"How long were you there?" Uncle Cliff asked.

I shrugged.

"What did you hear?" Aunt Eva asked.

"Nothin'," I muttered softly, staring at the floor. I knew I was really in trouble.

"Don't lie," Mom whispered gently, putting an arm around me. "You know you're a terrible liar."

Aunt Chrissy leaned over from the armchair next to me and put a gentle hand on mine. "Tell us what you heard or thought you heard. It's gonna be okay."

"Well," I thought about how to phrase things. "It sounded like you guys were talking about locking me away with Alex." My voice shook as I spoke. "Something about too long and too strong. You mentioned the imps, and something I couldn't hear or see."

"No one is going to lock you away," Aunt Eva promised. "We're discussing the best way to protect you."

"Like, how?"

"They want you to move up here permanently," Mom said softly.

I stared at my mother in surprise. "You... mean... like... forever? Without you?" Mom was the only person who really supported me; the only person who really knew me.

"I can't protect you the way you need to be protected, Kelly," Mom finally gave in. "Your gift is too strong."

"But there is a way for both of you to still be together," Granma mentioned with raised brows. All eyes turned to the woman. "Oh, please! Don't tell me none of you thought of it!"

"Are you going to spread the light to the rest of us, Mom?" Uncle Cliff asked.

"Marie can move up here!" Granma exclaimed like it was obvious.

"Up here?" Mom and Aunt Eva said together.

"Mom, I hated it up here," Mom complained. "That's why I moved away! I don't like the isolation!"

"But it's the perfect solution," Aunt Eva joined her mother. "If your company won't let you go remote, you can get a job in one of the towns nearby. If you don't want to live here, get an apartment in one of them. You can still be with Kelly nearly every day. Or you can just live here. We have the room, there's no lack of sustenance, and money is not an issue!"

"It is the best possible solution to everything," Uncle Cliff said to my mother. "After all, we're looking at Kelly's best interest, not yours. When she's grown and gone to college, you can move back to the city. And being up here will help your financial situation."

Mom looked up at me. "What do you think?"

"Me?" I replied, confused. "I don't know. I mean, it's nice up here. Kinda weird, but nice."

Aunt Eva chuckled. "You haven't seen anything yet."

"Would you want to live here for the next, say, six or seven years?" Mom asked me.

"What happens if I say no?" I was shaking visibly.

"You can say no," Uncle Cliff replied. "Thing is, there are things out there that want you. Not for you, but for the power you have. A power you don't even know you have yet. They know you have it. They know you exist. They know where and who you are. Untrained, you don't stand a prayer against them. And right now, your salvation is sitting over there," he said, pointing to Aunt Eva. "She's the only person alive who can train you. This house, your aunt; those are your protections. There are things here that keep the enemy out and at bay. Back in the city, as unskilled as you are, you will be at their mercy, and they have none."

I swallowed hard with eyes wide with fear. "Stop, Cliff! You're scaring the girl!" Granma hit the man on the shoulder.

"I'm just laying out the truth."

"I... I... I think maybe I need more training," I heard myself saying. "Maybe it might be a better idea if I stay here for a while."

"Very well. I'll return home and pack up the house and give my notice at work. I should be back within a month," Mom said behind a brave face.

"You want help with that?" Uncle Cliff asked his sister sympathetically.

"Maybe when it comes time to move," Mom replied shakily.

"Marie," Aunt Eva said softly. She waited for her sister to look at her. "It's going to be okay. I promise."

Mom nodded. She looked over at me with a sympathetic smile. "You'd best get some sleep, sweetheart. Tomorrow's going to be a big day."

"And don't forget your pills," Aunt Eva reminded.

"That's why I came down. Alex and I were thirsty, and I needed to take my medicine, so I came down to get something to drink."

"Go on, honey," Granma urged.

I started to leave the room, but stopped halfway across. I stared at the floor as I bit my lip. Everyone was watching me. I finally turned back to my aunt. "Am I ever going to be normal?" I asked my aunt.

Aunt Eva pursed her lips a moment. "Yes, and no. You are normal now, Kelly. You like the things normal teens like. You do the things normal teens do. Intelligence level is a bit high, but that's not abnormal. You are a typical thirteen-year-old. You'll just have a few added skills that extremely few people around you will have. Is that abnormal? I don't think so. Think of the super jock of the football team. Is he normal? He can't add thirteen and seventeen, but he can score a touchdown every time. Very few football players can claim that. Or the science geek at school. You know the one. Captain of the Debate Team, Captain of the Science Team, President of the Science Club, First Place winner in the Chess club, and a genius at computers. He can quote any equation, identify any chemical, and reproduce any experiment with his eyes closed. Is he not normal? No. He just has his area of expertise. You're going to be the same way; but where you will excel will be in the control of energy. That's just you. No different from anyone else. Okay?"

I smiled. "Yea. I think I can handle that."

"Good. Now off to bed! We're starting regular lessons tomorrow."

"Night, everyone." I smiled as I heard everyone else call their good nights. I grabbed a couple of bottles of water from the fridge as the topic of conversation in the family room switched to Brandon. Upstairs, I spent the next fifteen or twenty minutes explaining what took so long to Alex's question. After a while, when the medicine had taken hold, I nodded off to a quiet, peaceful sleep. Tomorrow was going to be a long day. It was my birthday, and I know Aunt Eva and Granma have plans.

I thought about the last couple of days as I searched. My mother left to go home and start figuring out what would happen. At my urging, Mom decided to live in the house. Aunt Eva began daily lessons with me after she and Granma had come back from the train station. Today, me, Brandon, and Abby were out searching the yard for a particular plant Aunt Eva wanted the leaves from. She called it a Maitrix. It was green with leaves like large dandelions, but they had thin black cross-hatchings on them. The flowers were tiny and purple. She said they were only good one week out of the year, just before the flowers bloomed. I had been searching the enormous yard since early this morning. Uncle Cliff showed us the most effective way cover the entire yard. So far, I had only found one, Abby found two, and Brandon hadn't found one yet.

I started as a breeze gushed past me. I thought I heard mumbling in it. It was only when I looked around at my surroundings that I realized how close to the woods I was. Something flew past my face; some kind of shadow. I thought I heard my name. Gazing into the deep shadows of the woods, I could just make out faces like the imp I saw at my window. They kept beckoning me forward. A wave of cold made me shiver. The trees kept rustling warningly nearby. Something seemed to pull at me from the inside. It made my stomach queasy. Again, I heard my name called from somewhere far away.

What's in there? It's just a bunch of trees, right? The shadows were probably birds flying overhead. There had to be a logical explanation, right? Right.

A slight green flicker caught my attention. There on the floor between two trees just inside the shade of the canopy was a Maitrix. The large leaves were unmistakable. I took a step, then another, towards the plant. Oddly, branches started lowering towards me, like they wanted to stop me.

A vast shadow snatched me up so fast I wasn't aware of the talons around my shoulders until I was thirty or forty feet off the ground. I dropped the bag with the first Matrix in it. When I looked up, I saw a belly of white scales. Huge black wings flapped, carrying me higher and higher.

No noise came out of my mouth when I opened it to scream. Breathing hard, I examined the ground below me. I gazed at the beautiful countryside. From this high up, the entire valley could be seen. I spotted the house off to my right. Brandon and Abby were staring up, pointing towards me. Uncle Cliff was running towards the house.

Disappointment settled in my chest as I realized I would probably never see my family or Alex or Rambo again. The lump in my throat made it hard to breathe.

The creature was flying over the trees; what seemed like miles and miles of trees. The river to the west came into view for a moment. It was a beautiful memory for a last view. Up ahead was a small mountain range. The creature was descending. A large plateau jutted out from one side of a mountain. The creature dropped me gently on the landing, circled overhead, and landed near the cave on the far side.

Heart pounding in my ears, I looked over the creature with the gleam of the sun bouncing off sleek black scales. Long black talons dug into the rock beneath it. Bright blue eyes glared at me. What was he waiting for? I realized of all the ways I could have died, death by dragon wasn't one I had considered.

After what seemed like an eternity, the dragon sighed and sat. "Just what did you think you were doing?" a deep voice asked with strained control.

My mouth dropped open in surprise. "Wh... what?"

"What did you think you were doing? Going to the woods? Surely Eva told you to stay away from them!"

"You can talk!"

"May we stay on the subject, please?" He was getting agitated. "Were you or were you not instructed to stay away from the woods?" The dragon took a step towards me.

I wavered when I stepped back to find the edge of the plateau. My breath caught as I glanced over the edge at the shear drop into the trees.

"Steady," the dragon crouched in preparation. "That's not the best way to go."

"Look, if you're gonna eat me, just get it over with, will ya?"

"What?" the dragon drew up, surprised. The sound began as a low rumble from deep inside the dragon. It grew to a chuckle, then erupted into a full-fledged laugh. His entire body shook. When he looked up at my confused expression, he began laughing again.

"Child," he began when he could talk again, "I have no intention of eating you. There isn't even enough of you for a midnight snack!"

The scowl on my face deepened. "Then why did you take me?"

"Let's go back to our original discussion," he was still chortling. "Were you or were you not told to stay away from the woods?"

I nodded. "I was."

"Then why were you right next to them, about to go into them?" he took another step towards me.

"I just found myself there!" I defended. "My aunt had us looking for Maitrix. My search just took me near the woods. I wasn't gonna go into them. There was a plant just on the edge between two trees I was going to get."

"There are no maitrix in the woods," the dragon replied. "It was a mirage. Maitrix need open space and sixteen hours of full sunlight a day to grow and bloom."

I sat down on the ground as I peered at the dragon. "That would have been nice to know when we started. Who are you? How do you know that?"

"My name is unimportant," the dragon replied. "You, however, are not. As half of the Seth Drinel, you are extremely important!"

"The Seth what?"

"Seth Drinel. You and one other are the saviors of your family; *all* of the family."

I shook my head. This was crazy. "The what? How am I going to save a family? I can't do anything!"

"By yourself, you are limited. When paired with the other half, you will wield incredible power."

"You're kidding me, right?"

"Do I sound like I am joking?"

"No."

"Think of your friend Alex. In the mirror. Would you not like her to be out of the mirror?"

"Of course! Hey!" I realized what he said and scowled. "Wait a minute. How'd you know about Alex? Who are you?"

"Call me George," the dragon replied. "You have great potential, Kelly, but you have much to learn before you can even hope to rescue an entire generation."

"I don't understand."

"I'm assuming your aunt has you reading Tessa's diary."

"Yes."

"Tessa was a wonderful person until she began letting the Gift control her. You must always maintain control of the Gift, not the other way around. Tessa stopped controlling the Gift. As a result, she became very angry and vindictive. She refused to listen to others with more experience. Her anger made her do unspeakable things."

"Like with Alex," I murmured.

"Yes."

"What happened to her? Tessa, I mean."

"The authorities executed her for the murder of her daughter," George said. "The state permitted the family to bury her in the family cemetery."

"I saw." I thought for a moment. "Wait a minute. There was another tombstone there without a death date. Alex said it was her grandfather. He'd just disappeared." I looked up at the dragon and it all clicked. "You're George McClure! You're Tessa's father!"

The dragon seemed to smile. "Very good! You have excellent deductive reasoning. Now tell me why we don't want you near the woods."

"The imps," I replied.

"What about them?"

"I don't know! Aunt Eva said they were dangerous. And Uncle Cliff said they want me."

George nodded. "*Why* would they want you?"

"Because of the Gift?" I took a guess.

"Exactly." George pointed to me with a long, sharp talon. "If they can reach you, especially now when you are just beginning to learn, they can get you to use your power to aid them."

"What would they want?"

"To take over the world. Not just government and places, but every single person."

I swallowed. "How?"

"Another time. There are other entities there that want your power as well, and not for good. For now, you are to obey *ALL* your aunt's instructions; and watch out for your young cousin."

"Which one?"

"Think."

After a few moments, I looked up with a start. "Brandon?"

George nodded. "I like you. You're quick. Brandon is just beginning to start the transition."

"But he's only nine. Granma said the Gift didn't start until the teen years."

"Yes. He's beginning very early, but the two of you are needed quickly. The Gift knows it. Let Eva know." I nodded.

"I think we've educated her enough for now, George."

The two of us turned to the gentle voice to see Eva leaning against a rock. She had her arms crossed over her chest and stood with an upturned lip. Her brows were up as she glanced at George.

"As you wish," the dragon nodded.

"Aunt Eva!" I got up and ran to her. Aunt Eva wrapped an arm around me.

"So, you've met our resident dragon, I guess." Aunt Eva's voice chuckled as she said the sentence.

"Scared the life out of me. I thought I was a gonner!"

"I apologize," George rumbled with suppressed laughter.

"Come on. We've got things to talk about," Aunt Eva directed me down the narrow path that came up the mountain.

"I can fly you back," George offered.

"And my truck?" Aunt Eva smiled. "How do I get that back? And what if someone else sees you? And the last time you carried a vehicle back for me, your claws pierced the body."

"Understood," George conceded.

"We'll be in touch," Aunt Eva informed him. "And thanks for rescuing her."

"My pleasure."

"Bye," I called over my shoulder. George simply nodded, a glint of a smile in his eyes.

11 – Imps and Fae

I woke with a start. I glanced around my room. It was just barely dawn. I could barely see my furniture, other than the nightlight Uncle Cliff put in. The reflection in the mirror showed you could barely see outside. Alex wasn't anywhere in sight, so I guessed she was asleep, even though she said she didn't need it.

I sighed and got out of bed. A big stretch eased my back as I moved to look out the window. In the pre-dawn light, the grass in the yard looked gray. The woods were barely visible. Suddenly, I stopped, staring out the window. Something, no, someone was moving across the yard. I looked harder. It was hard to figure out. It was a smaller body, not full grown, and the pajamas! Pajamas?

I grasped my jeans from the laundry pile and pulled them on. I pulled on a t-shirt as I raced down the hallway, pounded down the stairs, and sped out the front door. I peered over the field of grass. The figure was getting closer to the woods. I could see a series of dim glows just inside the edge of the trees. Pushing, I took off after the figure.

"Bran-don!" I yelled after him. "Brandon, stop!" The figure didn't stop. He continued his hypnotic march towards the woods. Pushing myself as hard as I could, I chased after Brandon. "Bran-don!" Getting closer, I continued to shout. At one point, he paused, but continued his trek.

"Brandon! Stop!" I cried, nearly out of breath as he passed the edge of the woods. I pulled to a stop with a depressed sigh. Now what? Well, I can't let him go in there alone.

"Kelly!" I heard my name being called from behind me. I glanced over the yard but couldn't see anything. Still, the voice sounded urgent. "Kelly!"

One glance at the woods showed me that Brandon was inside. With a firm determination, I ran towards the woods again. I had to find my cousin.

"Kelly! No!" the male voice cried.

The darkness closed over me as I dove into the forest. I pushed in as far as I had seen Brandon go. The sun was coming up. The rays were just coming over the trees at the angle needed to see the ground. It broke up the suffocating feeling of the dark. Brandon's footprints were clear on the ground. It was slow going, but I followed Brandon's trail. It zigged and zagged through the thickening trees. As the morning sun rose, it became harder to see the trail. Shadows covered everything. Eventually, I had to slow down.

A dim glow appeared next to me. Looking swiftly to the new light, I saw a tiny creature. If I had to guess, it was a fairy, but it didn't look like one. It was small and tiny and thin, with a rounded face and shoulder length hair. Large blue eyes, much like my own, stared back at me. A small, knowing smile greeted me. There were no wings, no antennae, nothing that would have made it look like a fairy, but it didn't look like an imp, either. The being motioned me to follow.

I took a deep breath and followed the creature. My instincts told me to retreat. Go back to the house. Brandon was gone. Aunt Eva would know what to do, but my feet followed the fairy-like being of their own volition. I glanced about, noting I was going west-ward. The moss grew on the north side of the trees. Moss and ivy vines covered some trees. It was quiet; eerily quiet. The only sounds were my heartbeat in my ears and the crunch of dead leaves under my feet. No bird calls. No crickets. No trees quivering above me. Nothing.

We traveled for almost fifteen minutes. The woods grew thicker, then thinned. Finally, I saw Brandon up ahead. He seemed to stand there, waiting for me. With a grin, I broke into a run and wrapped my arms around my cousin.

"Thank God you're alright!" I whispered. But Brandon didn't return the hug. I backed away slowly. He was still in a hypnotic state. "Brandon?"

"Brandon is not here," came a deep voice that wasn't my cousin's.

I fought an instant spike of anxiety. I swallowed and asked, "Then who are you?"

"Quaslinik," came the answer.

"What is, are Quaslinik?" I asked slowly. My peripheral vision noted several imps coming from the shadows with more little people.

"We are Quaslinik," came the answer. "We need you."

I suddenly realized there was a small cave built into the ground behind Brandon. It glowed yellow and orange as if the rocks inside were on fire. Several of the small people came from it to see "the show".

"Where is Brandon?" I asked, trying to think of what to do.

"Brandon is not here."

"I don't understand," I cried in frustration. "Where is Brandon?"

"Brandon is not here. We need you. Must..."

A loud roar shook the forest as trees fell around us. The imps and little people took off in every direction. Claws reached down and pulled me off the ground. Once again, I found myself flying above the trees as another roar shook the canopy below me.

"George! Put me down!" I struggled to get free of the dragon's grasp. "Brandon needs my help!" George didn't answer. "George! Please! He's my cousin!"

I could see we were heading back towards the house. Aunt Eva's truck was also heading in that direction. Uncle Cliff and Granma were looking towards the sky. Both came running as George gently set me on the grass near the house, circled, and landed behind me.

I whirled on the dragon. "What did you do? Brandon is in the woods!"

"No, I'm not!" Brandon's voice came from behind me. I whirled to see my cousin running towards us with a wide-eyed, amazed expression. "Whoa! Awesome!" he gazed at George. Much to everyone's disappointment, the kids didn't stay inside as they were told. The girls and Eddie followed Brandon out of the house to look at the real, live dragon.

"But... how... where..." I sputtered as I turned back and forth between the woods and Brandon.

"It was a trap," George informed me. "An imp changed into Brandon to get you to follow."

I palmed my forehead. "That's why they wouldn't tell me where Brandon was!"

"Why did you go to the woods?" Uncle Cliff scolded. "You were clearly told to stay away. And after I called you back, no less!"

"Brandon, or at least, what looked like Brandon, was heading to the woods. I was trying to stop him," I tried to explain. "When he went into the woods, I remembered George saying it was really dangerous, and I didn't want him in there, much less in there alone. I went to get him out!"

"You are just lucky George monitors things." Granma hugged me.

"Stop the hugging, Mother," Uncle Cliff snapped angrily.

"Easy, big boy!" Aunt Eva tried to calm him with a gentle hand on his arm. Aunt Chrissy came up behind them. "Kelly, did you even look into Brandon's room?"

"No. Why would I? I saw him walking across the grass!"

"You should have checked his room to be certain it was him," Aunt Eva instructed gently. "The imps are very good at forging people's identity and playing tricks."

"One thing is certain, however," George stated above us all.

"He can talk!" Brandon and Abby cried together.

George chuckled, then turned back to Eva. "They want her, and they want her badly. Enough to imitate someone she loves; someone they know will have the same power as she does."

"It means we need to start training Brandon - *now*," Aunt Eva whispered.

"What?" Uncle Cliff and Aunt Chrissy cried together.

"But the nightmares aren't even consistent yet!" Uncle Cliff argued.

The sad expression on Aunt Eva's face worried me. "No, they aren't," Aunt Eva said so softly we barely heard her. "But he's only nine and already he's having nightmares. That signal isn't supposed to happen for another three years. The Gift is calling him early. I don't know why; don't ask."

"Me?" Brandon said, wide-eyed. "I get a gift?"

I lightly shoved his shoulder. "It's not a present."

"The ripples are becoming closer together," George informed Aunt Eva. "Whatever is going to happen is going to happen soon."

"What ripples?" I asked.

"We'll just have to prepare," Aunt Eva said, urging me and Brandon inside. "Thanks, George. I've got a lot of explaining to do."

"Can I have a ride?" Brandon called over his shoulder.

"Not today," Aunt Chrissy replied, gathering the other children with Granma. They all watched in awe as George launched up into the sky and flew off. It was an awe-inspiring sight.

"Mom, would you mind getting breakfast started?" Aunt Eva asked as we got back into the house. She let go of me. "Kelly, would you run up and get the block you've been practicing with?"

I nodded as I heard Granma ask who wanted what for breakfast. As I grabbed the block from my desk, I heard Alex.

"Hey! What is all the yelling about?"

I glanced at my friend and dropped into the chair. "I screwed up again," I sighed, sitting opposite Alex.

"What'd you do?"

"I ran into the woods after my cousin, but it wasn't my cousin. It was an imp that changed to look like my cousin."

"Oooh! How much trouble are you in?"

"I don't know yet. Aunt Eva took Brandon to the den and sent me to get the block."

"Brandon? Isn't he the little one?"

"Well, littler," Kelly smirked. "He's around nine, almost ten."

"Who are you talking to?" Abby asked, coming into the room. "Oh, my..."

"Quiet!" I ordered, then sighed. Oh, well. "Abby, this is Alex. Alex, my cousin Abby."

"You have a mirror that talks?" Abby asked, kneeling next to me.

"It's a pleasure to meet you," Alex replied politely. The coolness of the girl's voice told me she wasn't happy about Abby.

"Huh? Oh, sure," Abby replied.

I elbowed the girl's shoulder. "Be polite!"

"It's a mirror!"

"It's a person trapped in a mirror. Be polite!" I growled.

"Oh, all right! Nice to meet you!" Abby spouted off.

"Now get out of my room!" I ordered. I didn't care for her attitude. "And stay out unless you're invited in."

Abby looked at me in surprise. I pointed towards the door. "Ok! Fine!" Abby touted as she stomped from the room. The door slammed behind her.

"You closed the door mentally," Alex beamed at me.

"Huh?" I looked up in surprise and grinned with sudden dawning. "I did, didn't I?" I smiled at the minor accomplishment.

"So, how'd you get out of the woods?"

"A dragon."

"What?" Alex looked surprised.

I squirmed a bit. "How much do you know about your grandfather?"

"Only that he disappeared."

"Well,... it seems your mother turned him into a dragon," I finally revealed.

"A dragon!!!" Alex's jaw dropped. "No!"

"Yes. He's been keeping watch over the estate ever since. He's saved my butt twice now."

"I have a grandfather?" Alex seemed happy with the news. Suddenly, her excitement dimmed as her face dropped. "But how am I ever going to meet him? I'm trapped in a mirror."

Squinting, I thought for a moment. "I don't know. Maybe I can take you out to the lawn and introduce you. We'll see."

A fist pounded on the door. "Kelly! Aunt Eva is calling you!" Abby's insulted voice came through the door.

"Coming!" I said, getting up and grabbing the block again. "I'll see ya later. I'll bring breakfast."

"Thanks."

In the den, I could tell Aunt Eva was just finishing up the "This is what The Gift is" chat I had received. She was already done with the different signs of The Gift and was just beginning into what kind of training would be required. I handed Aunt Eva the block and sat in the chair she pointed to.

"Here's your first assignment, Brandon. I want you to take the block." Aunt Eva held out her hand with the block in it, just like she did for me. Brandon just looked at Aunt Eva. He got up and took the block out of Aunt Eva's hand. Just like before, Aunt Eva chuckled. She took the block from Brandon and held it in her hand again. "Take the block, Kelly."

I found I didn't have to concentrate so hard anymore. I glanced at the block and put my hand out. The block floated easily across the room and into my hand. I grinned as I flipped the block in the air and caught it again.

"Very good!" Aunt Eva beamed. "You've been practicing. See how much better you handled that from the first time?"

"Yea," I grinned and tossed the block back to Aunt Eva. "It's so much easier now. No more black and blues."

"Ok, Brandon. Try it again." She gave Brandon the same instructions I had heard the first time. We waited as Brandon tried to move the block and failed.

"I can't!" the boy whined.

"Keep trying," Aunt Eva encouraged.

"It took me more than a few tries," I encouraged.

After several tries, the block flew across the room, slammed into the wall behind Brandon, and landed on a shelf. Aunt Eva and I chuckled, seeing as how it had

happened before. Aunt Eva easily floated the block back to
her hand. "Ease off of the anger," she instructed. "Try
again."

Again, several tries passed before the block flew at
Brandon. He quickly caught it in mid-air before it hit him in
the head.

"Good!" she praised, telling him about the window
she shattered her first time. "Your job is to practice with
that block until you can move it every time. Learn to control
its speed and direction. When you can do that, come back
to me."

Granma called for breakfast. Aunt Eva let Brandon
go, but kept me in the den. A heavy feeling came over me
instantly. Aunt Eva was leaning against her desk with her
arms crossed. Her blue eyes stared at me authoritatively.
It felt like I was in the principal's office after getting in
trouble.

"I suppose you know why I kept you here?" she asked
matter-of-factly.

"I'm about to be grounded?" I squirmed.

"In a way," Aunt Eva pulled the chair Brandon
abandoned in front of me and sat in it. "I'm not happy you
disobeyed me."

"I really thought it was Brandon," I stared at the
floor. "I wouldn't have gone in there if I didn't think that."

"That's why I'm not punishing you too harshly," Aunt
Eva replied. "Your heart was in the right place, but your
brain had been tricked." She sighed. "The imps know how
to manipulate you. They are going to pull every stunt they
can think of to get control over you. If George hadn't been

so quick, they would have gotten into your mind while you were trying to figure out where Brandon was.

"You must stay away from the woods, Kelly. The imps will try everything to appeal to you emotionally, but they're after only one thing—your power."

"But what do they want with it?" I asked.

"I don't know. It's not something good, I'll give you that. If you think you're seeing Brandon, check around for him. If you think you're hearing your name, identify where it is coming from. If you find yourself in the woods, get out!"

"Have you ever been in the woods?" I wondered aloud.

"Once," Aunt Eva shivered involuntarily. "It was raining, and I thought I saw shelter. I ducked into the woods to stay dry instead of running home in the rain. These little fairy people came floating around me."

"I saw them!" I pointed at my aunt.

"What I thought was shelter turned out to be a prison. The imps and the fairy people tried to tie me up. The fairy people tried to get into my mind. George came through then, too," Aunt Eva reminisced. "He saved my life."

"George is Alex's grandfather," I intoned sadly.

"Yes, I know. I don't have a way to turn him back." She looked up at me. "Have you finished the diary I gave you?"

I squirmed a bit. "No. Alex and I have been doing so much; I forgot about it."

"Ok. Today's 'punishment' is to finish the diary. Yes, finish. The whole thing. You need to read it. It's important."

"Is Brandon going to have to read it, too?"

"Perhaps. He's a little young yet. Maybe in a year or two. He'll need to understand the dangers."

I nodded. We were silent for a moment. "Aunt Eva?" I looked into my aunt's eyes. "What happens to Alex if she's released from the mirror?"

"Why?"

"I don't know," I shrugged. "She's been trapped in there for over a century. It's kinda like suspended animation. But in that you come back as yourself, just like when you left. In the mirror, Alex doesn't age. What happens if she's released from the mirror? Will she stay fourteen, or will time catch up with her?"

Aunt Eva sighed. She stared at the floor as she responded. Obviously, this was a question she pondered as well. "In truth, I don't know. Since we weren't the ones to put her in there, we don't know what was going through the person's mind when they trapped her. It could be a permanent trap. It could be a time bond, where time catches up, as you say, when she's released. It could be just a holding cell where everything stops. I really don't know."

"How do I find out?" I asked, happy to have something else to think about.

"I'm not sure. There might be something in the library about it, but I couldn't tell you which book would have it. I haven't read even an eighth of them. And I didn't have much luck finding an answer."

"Do you mind if I research it?"

"No. I think that might be a good idea. Then we'll know whether Alex is stuck there permanently."

"Thanks," I smiled.

"Go get breakfast," Aunt Eva suggested.

"You, too! Gotta keep up your strength," I teased my aunt.

"Especially if I'm going to be keeping up with you!" Aunt Eva laughed and moved from the room with me.

12 – The Nursery

It was a couple of weeks later when Brandon found me in the library. He looked solemn and his poor body was sagging.

"What's up?" I asked, glancing through a rather thick old volume.

"Homesick," Brandon replied. He dropped into the opposite chair like a rag doll. His parents had left a week ago. Granma had gone home as well. Word had come to me that my mother would be returning by the end of next week. Brandon wished his family would come back.

"Try not to think about it," I suggested. "It's just for a while."

"But I was going to get into soccer this year," Brandon complained. "Now I can't."

"Aunt Eva said she'd get you on a league in town," I reminded him.

"I guess. When does school start? I'm tired of being alone."

"Thanks a lot!" I feigned indignance. "I'm nobody?"

"You know what I mean! You're, like, old!" Brandon tried, then winced at his faux pas. "Ok. Not that old! But you know what I mean!"

"I know," I softened. "You miss your friends and old activities. I felt that way, too, the first couple of weeks I was here. The feeling will go away as you get more and more things to work on."

"What are you working on now?" Brandon asked, looking at the book in my hands. It didn't look very interesting.

"I'm trying to find out how Alex got locked in the mirror."

"Her mother thought her into it."

"Yes, but Aunt Eva says there's different ways she could have been put there. Depending on which one was used depends on if we can even hope to get her out of it."

"How do you know which one was used?"

"I'm not sure. I've searched through two dozen books so far, and not one lists the properties of a mirror prison."

"Wow!" Brandon looked at the book. "What else is in here?" Brandon looked around him.

"Tons!" I smirked. "There are adventure books there, and mysteries over there. Children's books are down there. Sports books in that corner. Old spell books are up near the ceiling. Biographies, cookbooks, reference, all kinds of stuff." I pointed to each topic as I mentioned them.

Brandon laughed. "Aunt Eva could start her own public library!"

"It gets worse. I saw a box of books arrive just yesterday. Stuff that's more current reading for us."

"Cool!"

Once again, Jasper came from the utility room. I watched him cross the archway to go upstairs. "Ya know," I mused out loud. "I always see him come out of there, but I never see him go in."

"Really?" Brandon asked. "What's in there?"

"The Utility Room. You know, where the furnace and water heater are."

"That's all?" Brandon's voice said he didn't believe it. His eyes sparkled as his brows rose.

I glanced at my cousin with a scowl. "Ya know, I'm not sure. Last time I went to check, Aunt Eva came out with some excuse about coal."

Brandon's eyes lit up with glee. "Wanna check it out?"

A slow grin came onto my face. "Sure." I placed the book on the table.

Brandon quickly opened the door to the Utility Room. I had peeked in here before. There was the furnace, and the hot water heater, and a deep two-basin sink. Other than that, there wasn't anything else. We were about to leave when we noticed a muddy footprint near the far wall.

"Bingo!" Brandon muttered in triumph.

I explored the paneling, looking for anything that might trigger a door to open. My balled fist hit the door in frustration.

"What?"

"How does it open?" I asked rhetorically.

"Why not try the knob?" Brandon asked, looking at a knot in the paneling.

"What?"

Sure enough, someone hollowed the knot out and put a bar knob into the hole. Reaching into the hole with two fingers, Brandon turned the handle. The door swung open almost silently, revealing a well-lit, very warm room.

"You're a genius!" I complimented him. I had completely missed it.

"I know," he said conceitedly. His giggle told me he was teasing.

Down the middle of the dirt-floored room sat three rows of tables. Plastic tubs, set approximately one foot apart, were on each table. Heat lamps hung on a truss over the tubs.

We neared the first tub and looked in. Three reddish-brown, furry pups were curled up sound asleep.

"What are those?" Brandon whispered.

"I think they're red fox," I responded. "We had some near the house back home."

Another basin held six small black moles all curled together and asleep. The next bin held three baby opossums. At another table nearly twenty brown winged cat-like creatures hung from a grate placed over a bin.

"What are those?" I asked curiously.

"They're Villibats," came Jasper's voice from the entry.

"You mean like vampire bats?" Brandon asked, taking a step back.

Jasper smirked. "No. These are related to brown bats. They eat vegetation and insects, but right now they drink milk."

"Where're their mothers?" I wanted to know.

"Dead. We think the imps ate her."

"Her? As in one?" I looked in the bin again.

"Yep. Villibats can have as many as thirty in a litter. They're very organized and can tell which young they have fed and which they haven't. We found these in a bat house in the back."

"What about these?" Brandon pointed to the fox.

"Mother got it by a wolf or a coyote. We found traces of her fur."

"And the moles?" I asked.

"They were dug up by accident." Jasper handed each of us a bottle from the bucket he carried. "Actually, I'm glad you found this room. We're quite a bit more full than usual, and I could use some help feeding these guys."

He led us over to yet another table, this one with a cage around the basin. Three small raccoons were climbing all over the cage. One huddled in the rear corner, watching the commotion. Jasper opened the cage door and grasped one. He handed it to Brandon.

"Here," he said. "Feed this one. Just turn him over on his back. He'll hold the bottle till he's done." He reached to the one in the corner and gave that one to me. "Here ya go. She'll enjoy the warmer one."

I marveled at how the tiny hands on the raccoon held the bottle as she gulped down the milk. She seemed content to just lie quietly and drink. Jasper had grasped another one and fed that one.

"What do you do with them?" I asked. I instinctively rocked back and forth with the little one.

"We feed them until they're ready to go back into the wild, then we release them in the woods," Jasper explained. "These guys are just about ready to learn how to forage. I've been slowly weaning them into solid food. The foxes have a few more weeks yet."

I glanced around at the other animals in the room. The little raccoon in my arm finally pushed the bottle away, curled up next to me, and fell asleep. There was an owlet in another cage. Two baby squirrels were curled up and sleeping.

"Here, I'll take her," Jasper said.

"No. She's ok. She is so sweet!"

"Yea, she is. That's probably the best sleep she's had in a while."

"Why?"

"The boys beat up on her. She needs to sleep with one eye open so as not to get pounced on," he explained. "She's probably feeling protected right now."

"I'll hold her a bit more," I offered, "If that's okay."

"Give her back to Jasper," came Aunt Eva's voice from the doorway. I reluctantly gave the raccoon back. "I see you found the nursery."

"This is so cool!" Brandon exclaimed.

"This is such a tremendous responsibility. Jasper is very good with animals, so I put him in charge of it. They adore him. But right now, it's time for practice."

Brandon and I thanked Jasper and followed Aunt Eva upstairs to the den for more lessons. I was finding The Gift easier to handle. Brandon was still going through some difficulties. I'm not sure if it was the difference in age or skill that caused his problem.

It was several hours later that I returned to my room. Alex was eager to hear what I had found as I put a plate of food on the vanity for her, along with a couple of water bottles.

"I don't know. I've found four books that describe the action, but none that tell how to reverse it."

"There has to be something," Alex replied. Disappointment laced her voice and her features.

"Don't give up. I've still got six more books to go through. Your mother didn't write anything about this, did she?"

"No. She stopped keeping a journal after she finished her lessons," Alex thought hard. "She would write in the diary occasionally, but only when it was something important to her."

I sighed. "I'm afraid to try without knowing more."

"Why?"

"There's three different effects that would have put you in the mirror," I explained. "One puts you in stasis. That's where you're just in limbo. You don't age, don't mature, nothing. Pulling you out again will just let you pick up where you left off, just in a different time period. Another effect traps you in the mirror, but when you come out, time catches up with you very quickly. You age, die, and disintegrate in a matter of minutes."

"It would be better to stay in the mirror than go through that one," Alex nodded.

"The third one traps you in the mirror permanently. As best I can tell, there is no way to reverse that one. Trying to reverse it would kill you or worse, scatter you in a void in time where you would have no contact with any time or relation."

"Yuk!"

"Exactly. Without knowing what was going on in your mother's mind when she did this to you, I can't even *begin* to figure out which effect she used."

"She was angry with me for being vain," Alex replied sadly. "But it's such a pretty dress!"

I smirked. Alex was still in the dress she was wearing when all this happened. "Yea, it is. But how would that anger have been used? I'll bet it's the same situation with George."

"George? You mean my grandfather?"

"Yea. Do you remember I told you about the tombstone in the cemetery that had a beginning date, but no death date?"

"Yes. It's my grandfather. He's been missing since shortly before I was imprisoned here. You said he'd been turned into a dragon."

"Yes. She turned him into a black dragon. He's really a nice-looking dragon, but a dragon none the less. He rescued me from the woods twice now. Still, he's limited in his social life, his life would be in danger if anyone else knew about him, and he really can't explore more about the world around him except up high on the wind. Not exactly the life I'd want for my father or grandfather."

"She turned her own father into a dragon?" Alex stared in horror. "But he has The Gift. Why doesn't he turn himself back?"

I shrugged. "I don't know. Maybe he can't."

"I'm beginning to think my mother was a monster instead of a woman," Alex grumbled.

"The diary showed that the Gift was taking control of her instead of the other way around," I reminded my friend. "It's what Aunt Eva has been warning me about. George, too. Problem is, the imps seem to know how to manipulate my mind. And Aunt Eva said there were other things in the woods that want me for my power."

"You'll learn to identify those. I remember reading about my mother's episodes with that, too." I nodded. I did, too. I didn't completely understand it, but I'd read it.

Fatigue was setting in as I stretched and yawned. "I'm beat. I'm going to bed. Do you want to watch a movie?"

13 – The Ghost in the Cemetery

The summer was moving along pretty quick. My mother moved in to her old room, right next to Aunt Eva. Brandon and I got the job of helping Jasper to feed the nursery twice a day. I really enjoyed cuddling and learning to care for the babies. It didn't last long since the animals grew so fast. And Aunt Eva had us practicing just as hard. Some days were techniques. Other days would be actual spells. Still, other days would be learning the different types of magic and what they were used for. Somehow, even with all the practice, it seemed like we weren't getting very far.

Alex and I continued to try to figure a way to get her out of the mirror. Despite all of my efforts, I couldn't find an answer. We were missing too much information.

Today was so hot, humid, and sticky, we were even sweating inside the house. It was difficult to concentrate on our lessons and forget about our rooms. I tried hiding in my room with the air conditioner. It helped a lot, but it was still so muggy it was sapping the energy right out of me. Strange. We weren't near enough to water to create this kind of humidity, and we were at such a high altitude that it should have been much cooler.

AUNT EVA

"Aunt Eva?" Brandon asked in the kitchen.

"Yes?"

"Can Kelly and I go swimming?"

"Out at the pond? Sure. That's a good idea," I replied as I chopped a carrot.

"Great!" Brandon grinned and disappeared upstairs.

"Wait," Marie paused. "Isn't the pond near the cemetery?"

"Yep," I smiled to myself.

"But isn't it...."

"Yep," I agreed. "I think it's time."

Marie shook her head at me. "You're crazy!"

"It's ok. George is making his rounds. Besides, all they're going to see is fog. It's not like they're going to get hurt."

KELLY

Brandon and I walked our way back to the pond. The humidity soaked us through before we got to the barn.

"This is really weird," I said, wiping the sweat from my forehead. "It's been hot before, but not like this." I felt tired from the heat.

"I don't get it," Brandon agreed. "I've never known it to be like this up here."

"The pond is going to feel so good!"

And it did. The water was nice and cool. We had fun splashing around. The laughter echoed off the trees as they swayed above us. We giggled as the fish nibbled on our skin and toes.

"It tickles!" I laughed.

"Hey! What's goin' on at the cemetery?" Brandon asked, looking towards the fence around the cemetery. A strange, thick, white mist was forming in the middle of the cemetery like a white cloud.

I stood up on the bank of the pond and looked towards the cemetery. A chill went up my spine as I noticed the mist spreading out towards the fence. Something seemed to move in it.

"Come on," I said, leaving the water. "Let's check it out."

"You sure we should?" Brandon asked, grasping his towel from the grass. "Aunt Eva may not want us in there."

"She wouldn't have said we could come if it were dangerous."

"Maybe she doesn't know."

The mist was moving out beyond the fence. It left a cold moisture on our bodies as we slowly walked into it. I opened the gate to the cemetery. Brandon followed me in, closing the gate behind him as if it could keep the mist inside the graveyard. We twisted towards the gigantic oak tree. Something had moved over there.

"Probably just a squirrel," I tried to reassure my cousin. Or was I trying to reassure myself?

"Awfully big squirrel," Brandon replied shakily.

We moved further inside the mist. Something seemed to glow towards the outside of the tombstones. A slight glow came from one stone.

"I think that's Tessa's tombstone," I whispered. Brandon had just begun reading the diary since I was done with it.

"What's that?" Brandon asked, pointing towards the glow.

"I'm not sure."

A scream echoed around the cemetery that made us freeze in our tracks. A figure seemed to rise out of the mist; tall and thin. A woman. White curly hair spread in disarray. Her features were delicate and tortured. Suddenly, she whirled about to look at us as if suddenly realizing she wasn't alone. Blank eyes stared at us. No irises, no color, no pupil, just white eyes. Her hand rose and pointed in our direction. The body followed as the ghost glided across the ground towards us.

"Run!" Brandon cried as he whirled around and raced for the gate.

I tried to move my feet but couldn't. They were stuck to the ground. I looked down at them. They seemed fine but wouldn't move. The ghost was getting closer. Panic rose into my throat. Wiggle as much as I could, I couldn't move. I looked up directly into the ghost's tortured face. She was there, right in front of me, less than arm's length.

I didn't dare breathe. The ghost stared at me. My wide, frightened eyes stared into the ghost's blank gaze as my body shook. Still, the ghost didn't move. When she finally opened her mouth, a moan came out. Without warning, both of the ghost's hands came around and clasped the sides of my head. An icy shiver went through my body, and my head ached as I let out a yell.

I found myself in a bedroom. The décor was different: pale yellow with gingham curtains. The bed was made of crude wood, but the multi-colored quilt on it gave the room a happy, comfy feeling. A desk sat in the corner with a large, gilded mirror over it on the wall. Despite the differences in time, I recognized the room. It was mine.

A teenage girl came into the room, making me turn. The girl was a little taller than I was, with long brown tresses pulled back by a large green ribbon. Deep green eyes sparkled in a Victorian-shaped face as she glided to the mirror. She wore a bright green dress with a lace collar.

The lace was also around the ends of the sleeves that came down to the middle of her forearm. A green sash tied around her waist to a bow in the back.

"Oh, Father! It's beautiful!" she cried as she twirled in front of the mirror.

"It's vulgar," a woman's voice grumbled as she came into the room. She placed some folded clothing on the bed.

"It looks lovely," the man at the door complimented. He was really tall. I guessed he must have been over six feet. His hair was light brown. His eyes looked like the girl's. He had a brown beard on his face. His broad figure wore a plaid flannel shirt tucked into worn black pants. He leaned against the doorjamb as he smiled warmly at his daughter. "You'll be the most beautiful girl at the dance."

The woman looked vaguely familiar. She was tall and thin, almost too thin. Her face appeared gaunt, like she hadn't had enough to eat. Her eyes were dark blue, much like mine. She had pulled her dark black tresses back into a bun at her crown. Several curly strands had pulled loose and were hanging down the sides of her head. Thin lips pressed together in a thin line.

"And who says she can go to this dance?" the woman asked angrily. "Certainly not I."

"Nay. I," said the father calmly. "Tis only fittin'. She's fourteen, after all. Tis time."

"Says you," the woman stormed out of the room.

"Best get goin'," the man smiled. "We've a bit of a ride into town."

"I'm coming!" the girl smiled happily as she slipped her stocking feet into black, high-topped shoes. I recognized them as the button shoes girls wore in the early 1900s. As

the girl turned towards me to exit through the door, I
recognized the face and watched as Alex and her father left
the room.

From the window, I could see a horse and carriage
next to the house. Funny. That wasn't the front of the
house. And there wasn't a drive there. Apparently, the
layout of the outside had changed over the years. The man
lifted the girl up into the carriage, then climbed up. With a
quick slap of the reins, the carriage was off down the long
drive.

The woman came back into the room carrying a red
plaid dress with a simple white collar. She hung it on a
hook on the wall.

"I swear! He spoils that girl! She'll never amount to
anything if he keeps this up," she complained as she moved
about the room. A harsh pull opened drawers in the dresser
so she could put the folded clothing in. She slammed them
closed again.

A young boy around the age of ten appeared at the
door. "The fire is ready," he said timidly. I froze. The face,
the eyes, the hair. He could have passed for Brandon's
double. His dark black hair was cut collar length. His bangs
came down just above his eyebrows. The round face, dark
blue eyes, button nose, and thin lips looked exactly like
Brandon's; except this young boy in the flannel shirt and
torn brown pants seemed much less confident than my
cousin. He appeared almost afraid of his mother.

"I'm coming!" the woman snapped. The boy nodded
and left, and the woman muttered something about
impatient fools.

I tried to follow them downstairs, but I was stopped at the doorway. I tried again to move past it. There seemed to be a barrier of some kind keeping me in the room. I didn't need to wait long. The scene seemed to speed up. It grew dark. The woman had come in at some point and put a candle lantern on the dresser.

Alex came in again. She was chatting away happily as her mother followed her.

"It was so much fun, mother!" she exclaimed. "Mr. Fox said we weren't allowed to dance with the same partner twice. And Reverend Mossier kept going around encouraging the boys to ask the girls to dance." She stopped once more in front of the mirror and spun. Her skirt flared as she spun about. "Darrin Payne said I looked real pretty," she remarked dreamily.

"Stop looking at yourself in the mirror. It's vain to stare so!" the woman snapped the comment in irritation.

"What do you think? Is this too much to wear to church on Sunday?"

"I said stop looking in the mirror!"

The girl's shoulders sagged. "I don't think I've ever looked so nice. And I'm not being vain. Why would you say so? I simply asked if I could wear this dress to church." She turned again to look at the bow in the back. It made her waist look tinier than it already was.

The woman growled in anger. "If you are going to continue to stare at your reflection in that mirror, perhaps you should be a part of it!" Her hand flew out towards the girl.

Suddenly, Alex was staring out from the mirror. A look of surprise, then horror, crossed her face. She tried to reach out of the mirror, but the glass stopped her. She pounded on the glass. "Mother!" she hollered.

The woman's eyes grew wide. "Oh, my God!" she screamed in horror. "Alexandria! Alexandria!" She moved towards the mirror and touched the glass.

Heavily pounding feet echoed in the hallway. The man I saw earlier burst into the room. "What's wrong? Is everyone alright?" His eyes widened as he looked at Alex's crying face staring back from the mirror. "Tessa," he said deathly quiet, "What have you done?"

"I don't know! I was angry! I couldn't take her primping and staring and vain prattle about her dress and how pretty she was. Somehow, I threw her into the mirror," the woman cried.

"Get her out of it!" the man ordered.

"I don't know how!"

"Well, try!"

I watched as the woman tried over and over to retrieve Alex from the mirror. Each time, the mirror surface would shimmer, but Alex remained trapped. In the end, the woman sat at the desk and cried herself to sleep.

I opened my eyes again to see the ghost staring at me again, her hands now at her side. "You're Tessa, aren't you?" I asked quietly. The ghost nodded. "That's how Alex became trapped in the mirror. Why did you show me that? Wait! I know. You want me to help her?" Again, a nod. "I don't know if I can." The ghost nodded again. "I can? How?" The ghost pointed to her head. "Think? Think. Think. The library?" Again, the ghost nodded. "But I've checked all those books. Which one do I need to show me how to help Alex?" The ghost wrote in the air with her forefinger. The letters seemed to glow bright orangy-red, as if they were on fire. S—T—Y—X. "Styx?" The ghost seemed to agree. I ran the books through my mind. Styx wasn't a part of any of their titles. "Is that the author?" The ghost seemed to smile. "I'll look again. I promise." The ghost nodded. I felt chilled. "May I go now?" I asked tentatively. The ghost turned and walked back into the mist.

"Kelly?" a deep voice seemed to roar near the cemetery gate.

"Coming!" I called.

As I got to the gate, I saw George and Brandon on the lawn under the trees. I smiled as I closed the gate and ran towards them, the cold slowly leaving my body.

"Are you alright?" George asked, sniffing at me.

"Fine," I replied. "A bit of a headache, though."

"Did the ghost hurt you?" Brandon asked.

"No. It was kinda weird though," I mused. "She showed me how she trapped Alex in the mirror."

"She did what?" George pulled his head up straight.

"Yes. And she said I can find the answer on how to release her in the library."

"And you believe her?" George seemed surprised.

"I think she's serious," I replied. "She seemed really upset that she'd done it in the first place."

"Then she should have released her herself," George huffed.

"What if she wasn't strong enough to?" I asked the dragon.

"What if you're not strong enough?" he asked.

"The thought has crossed my mind." I sat down and agreed.

"Don't sit, young lady. I'm taking you two home."

"Why?" I asked. "We're not in trouble, are we?"

"I don't know, but your aunt will want to know what has happened," the dragon replied.

Brandon was watching me. "I think I've had enough swimming," he replied nervously.

I nodded and glanced back at the cemetery. The mist was already dissipating. "George, did she show up just for me?"

"They come every few months. Each time they arrive, the humidity in the air becomes nearly unbearable," the dragon explained as he hunkered down so we could climb up. "Wait until winter. It is almost as if they have icicles hanging in the air. Freezing cold."

"They? I only saw Tessa," I scowled.

"Oh, there are more people in there than Tessa. The ones that come are the ones who cannot find peace. They are the ones who let the Gift overtake them instead of learning to control it," George informed me.

"So, they're the ones who have done bad things with the Gift?" Brandon asked.

"Yes."

"Will they ever find peace?" he asked.

"I don't know. Do I look like God?"

Back at the house, I explained what had happened to Aunt Eva. Her concerned face worried me. I relayed the story as I remembered it. "It seems the action was more of an emotional response than intentional," I remarked, thinking.

"Which means what?" Brandon asked.

"Well, I'm guessing it means that there is a way to get Alex out of the mirror. In the vision I saw, the mirror would shimmer and swirl when Tessa tried to get Alex out."

"Anger is often a booster to the power of the Gift. You've seen that, Kelly." I nodded. "But it still doesn't explain what happens to her once we get her out."

"She said the answer was in a book by someone named Styx," I explained.

Aunt Eva scowled. "I'm not familiar with that author."

"Me, either. I don't recall looking at any book with that name on it."

"We'll go down after dinner and take another look. Okay?"

I smiled. "That'll be great!"

"Can I come?" Brandon asked.

"Sure!"

AUNT EVA

I stared thoughtfully at the children as they ran upstairs to change. I could feel Marie staring at me from the kitchen table.

"What?" I asked her without turning.

"What are you thinking?"

"I'm trying to figure out what it is in Kelly's future that has all these things happening to her."

"What are you talking about?"

"Marie, you've been with me every step of the way through the development of the Gift. I've been to the cemetery. I'm aware of the crying child. Never did the liquid harm me. It burned Kelly. I've seen the ghosts traversing the mist. Never did any of them try to speak to me. Yet

Tessa spoke to Kelly. The imps were here my whole life. They've been a nuisance, they've tried to gain my power as well, but they never put forth as much effort to get me on their side as they have Kelly. Even nature has taken an interest in her. Kelly is showing signs of so many skill levels, I'm beginning to wonder if I'm qualified to train her."

"You have to!"

"And I will," I nodded. "At some point, however, she's going to have to train herself. Kelly's powers are going to become far more powerful than mine."

14 – Getting Alex Out of the Mirror

I lay on the blanket in the front yard, looking up at the billions of stars that covered the dark sky. A soft breeze blew over me making it a comfortable night. It was a new moon, so the moonlight didn't interfere with the starlight. My fascination with astronomy finally got the best of me. I enjoyed this time to examine the night sky. Problem was, with so many stars visible, it was difficult to spot the normal constellations.

"See that bright ball just over the northern trees?" came George's deep voice. "That'll be Saturn."

I glanced over at the dragon keeping guard next to me. I giggled as I noticed he was lying on his back, giant claws up in the air like a kitten near a fire. He was gazing up at the night sky and pointing out various planets and sights. He was very good at astronomy, and I had already learned more than I had already known. Still, the sight was... well... funny.

"What's that one there?" I pointed to a spot in the sky flickering between green, yellow, and blue. The smaller stars around it seemed fixed as tiny white points.

"Hmmm," George studied the point. "I'm uncertain. I haven't seen that one before."

"Could it be a UFO?"

"Could," he agreed. "It wouldn't be the first time a space ship has hovered above us."

Scowling, I responded, "I was only joking."

"I was not."

"You mean there really are UFOs?"

"That would be correct."

"Why?"

"Why what?"

"Why do UFOs come near Earth?"

"I know not. I have never spoken to an alien. I have just observed their ships." George smiled at me. He seemed to be thinking of a long time ago.

"George, what's that?" I pointed to a star moving across the night sky. "It's too slow to be a comet."

George looked up at the star in question. Quickly, he rolled over and covered me with a wing. "Quickly! Get inside! Now!"

"What? Why?"

"Do I say, child! Move!"

I darted across the lawn to the front door. With a quick look back at George, I glanced up. The star was descending, coming closer. With widened eyes, I darted into the house.

"Aunt Eva! Aunt Eva, come quick!"

Aunt Eva rounded the corner from the family room with concern. She stopped as she saw me looking out the front windows on either side of the door. Mom and Brandon came around right behind her.

"Done with your Astronomy lesson already?" she teased. She knew how much I dreamed of going to the stars one day.

"Something's wrong. I saw a bright white star moving across the sky. When I pointed it out to George, he shooed me inside. I looked back at it. It's coming down out of the sky."

"Where's George now?" Aunt Eva asked calmly. She moved to look out the window.

"He's gone further out into the yard. There," I pointed.

A white glow was filling the open expanse of the yard. It was almost like daylight. Strangely, the black dragon was easy to see in the middle of the night. A figure stepped out of the light and moved towards George.

"Ahh!" Aunt Eva nodded. "Stay here." She opened the door and moved to join George.

Brandon took her place at the window. The figure seemed odd. The glow came from behind the figure. It was humanoid with long white hair, pale skin, and white flowing robes. The sleeves were so long they covered the figure's hands. The light was so bright, we couldn't see its features.

"Is it a guy or a girl?" Brandon asked.

"I can't tell," I replied.

"I'd get away from the window before you're spotted spying," Mom told us.

"What is it, Mom?"

"If I recall correctly, it's the magistrate."

"The what?" both Brandon and I asked together.

"A magistrate is a judge in a small village," I replied.

Mom giggled. "I'm glad to see you've learned your history. Here, the magistrate is the person who oversees all those with The Gift."

"He's got to be old," Brandon exclaimed.

"Older than you can ever imagine," Mom laid a gentle hand on the boy's head. "The magistrate goes back to before the first person with the Gift. In fact, it is believed he was the first person with the Gift. He lives a life in limbo.

He doesn't age and doesn't eat. In fact, he doesn't see—at least, not like we do."

"Why is he here?" Brandon asked tentatively.

"And why was George afraid for me to see him?" I asked.

"I don't know," Mom said softly as she gazed out at the trio on the lawn. There seemed to be some heated debate going on. Each member of the trio kept insisting something.

"I'm going to ask Alex!" I cried and ran up the stairs.

"Wait for me!" Brandon followed.

Mom watched us run upstairs. Concerned, she peered back out into the yard.

"The magistrate?" Alex asked, wide-eyed. "This is bad. This is very bad!"

"Why?"

"The magistrate was the one that sent my mother insane," Alex complained from the mirror. "He generally comes to view the upcoming Gifters. Problem is that he's so powerful, the sheer presence of him can alter your body. He's not from this world," Alex tried to explain. "I don't know exactly what happened. I just know that he came to view my mother. Father said that before the Magistrate came, mother was sweet and kind. After he left, mother slowly became mean and vindictive."

"What's that mean?" Brandon asked.

"She liked revenge," I explained.

"Oh."

"Please, Kelly. If the magistrate calls for you, refuse to meet him! Please!"

"Am I allowed to?"

Alex looked worried. "I don't know," her voice replied softly.

"Kelly? Brandon?" It was Aunt Eva.

"Yes?" I called from the door.

"Come here, please!"

"Looks like the answer is no," Brandon replied from the window. He noticed that both George and The Magistrate were waiting out on the lawn.

Slowly, we made our way down the stairs. We both noticed the two women at the bottom exchanging worried glances. Both of us felt uneasy.

"What is it?" I asked.

"The Magistrate wants to meet you," Aunt Eva replied uncertainly.

"Can we say no?" Brandon's voice shook.

Aunt Eva tried to give us a comforting smile. "No, I'm afraid not. And he will not listen to reason."

"But..." I began.

"Let's get this over with. George assures me he will protect you." With great apprehension, we followed our aunt across the lawn. "Don't go any closer than you have to," Aunt Eva instructed. "And stay out of his direct light. Understand?" We both nodded.

A bright yellow ring glowed just inside the bright white rays. Apparently, that was the edge of the magistrate's glow. Aunt Eva stopped well before the ring with a protective hand on each of our shoulder.

It took a few moments for my vision to peer into the light. It was like looking into the sun. I could see a man with a full beard down to about mid-chest. The robes reminded me of a silk bathrobe. Under those was a tunic

with some kind of dragon design on the front. I couldn't see
the whole thing. He held a staff that he seemed to lean on
heavily. His eyes were blank, still they looked directly at me
and Brandon.

"Magistrate, this is my niece Kelly and my nephew
Brandon," I heard my aunt say. "They are the next
generation of Gifters."

I saw a movement out of the corner of my eye. I
smirked as I saw Brandon duck behind Aunt Eva. With a
grin, I held out my hand to him. He shook his head. I
motioned for him to come to me. Slowly, he took my hand
and moved next to her.

"We're two gifters in the same generation," I
whispered to my cousin. "There's nothing we can't do if we
do it together." I wasn't sure if I believed it, but if it made
Brandon feel braver in front of this stranger, it would
suffice. Brandon looked up at me with a question in his
eyes. I nodded bravely. He broke into a grin and turned to
meet the Magistrate.

"Depart," the deep voice of the magistrate
reverberated around them.

"I'll not," Aunt Eva said sternly. "They are my
children, and I am responsible for them. I'll not leave them
in your care. You may greet them, that is all. They are too
young and inexperienced to handle your power."

"I agree," George interjected.

The light around the Magistrate seemed to brighten
threateningly. Brandon covered his eyes and murmured
something about wishing the guy would dim it down a bit.
Every being within a mile radius would see him.

"Can you dim the glow… please?" I exclaimed. There seemed to be a throbbing about the light that echoed in my head. "It's awfully hard to see."

The Magistrate whirled around on me. "You dare?"

"Yes, sir. I dare," I responded angrily. "You're being incredibly rude, throwing around all that light and power in the presence of a couple of kids." I could hear George chuckle in amusement.

The Magistrate pointed his staff at me. Unable to stop, he drew me into the circle. Face to face with the old magistrate, I fought the pounding from the fluctuating light. I could feel a power trying to get into my mind. The eyes before me starting changing scenes. I could see faces in them. As fast as I would see a face, it would change to another. It went faster and faster and faster. My fists clenched. I fought against the power. A small hand took hold of mine. Suddenly, a burst of power sprang from my chest, knocking down the old magistrate and knocking out his light.

I shook my head to clear it. I looked down at the hand on mine. It was Brandon. He smirked at me.

"We can do anything, right?" he said with a grin.

I hugged him. "Right."

Aunt Eva helped the old man up. Without all the powerful light, he seemed like a normal old man: salt and pepper black hair, deep blue eyes like mine and Brandon's, and pasty pale skin. It reminded me of a ghost. I'd guess he hadn't seen light in a very long time—other than his own. His robes were indeed white, but the tunic was blue with a gold dragon curled about itself on the breast. A black belt and black pants added to the outfit. His feet were bare.

Once on his feet again, he stared over at us. He didn't say anything, just stared at us. He didn't bring back the glow, either. After a long period, the Magistrate turned to Aunt Eva. "These are the two you were worried about?" he asked her. Aunt Eva nodded. The Magistrate chuckled. "Eva, train them hard and train them well. Brandon and Kelly are correct. Together, there isn't anything they cannot do, but they need to know *how* to do it."

He turned back to us and slowly approached like a tired old man. He smiled then. "Very good, children," he breathed. "In my many, many centuries as magistrate, no one has tried to resist my power and beat me. George's bit of magic can protect you from physical harm from my power, but he could not aid you in overthrowing me. Very well done, by the way. I may get to rest yet."

"Sir?" Aunt Eva questioned.

"Kelly? Brandon?" Mom came running across the yard to see if we were alright.

"Marie," the magistrate nodded at my mother. "Eva," he lowered his voice as he approached her. "You must step up their training. They do not have time to be children. The enemy knows they are here and is already planning ways to harness their power. Alone, they are too inexperienced to handle the ones coming for them. Together, they can be unstoppable. I believe the prophecy is true. These are the saviors, and their training lies in your hands."

Aunt Eva looked over at us, securely held in my mother's arms. She glanced at Mom to see if she had heard. I guessed by her expression she hadn't. She returned her attention to the magistrate, a concerned expression on her face.

"You will know," he replied to her unspoken question. He turned and walked back a few steps. "I take my leave of you. I am certain I shall visit again."

The glow began around his waist and spread like a pool of water. His body became encompassed in the light. The fluctuating power thrummed through my head again. Soon it was back up to full power. The Magistrate rose. He glided across the yard as his body rose higher into the night sky. Soon, he was just another star in the heavens.

Aunt Eva raced to me. "Are you alright?" she asked worriedly, taking my face in her hands. "Anything hurting? Your thoughts are clear?"

I laughed. "I'm fine," I grinned. "I was fighting his entry into my mind, like you showed me in practice."

"What did you see?" George asked, coming closer.

"I think he was trying to scare me with the varying scenes of people with the Gift," I replied, thinking of all the faces she'd seen. "Thing is, I've seen all those faces before."

"You have?" Mom asked, confused.

"Yea; they're in the book downstairs with our family history, complete with all the mean and nice things they did."

Aunt Eva laughed heartily. She hugged me tight. "You are amazing!" she complimented. She let go of me and hugged Brandon. "You, too! What made you enter the light?"

"I knew Kelly would have trouble fighting someone that powerful," Brandon revealed. "I figured I could help." His face softened to concern. "I didn't expect the power to be so... strong when we linked hands, though."

"It was pretty awesome," I grinned. "I've never felt it
that strong before."

"Eva..." George began.

"I understand," Aunt Eva replied to the dragon.
"Tomorrow. Let's get these two to bed."

Everyone said goodnight to George as Aunt Eva
directed us all back to the house. George watched the
house for a few moments, then flew off to his mountain.

A short time later, Brandon knocked on my door.
Alex and I had each been reading, so he wasn't interrupting
anything.

"Whatcha got, Brandon?" I sat up in my bed. I
noticed a book in my cousin's hands.

"What was the name of that author you were looking
for?" he asked, staring at the cover of the book. It was old
and dusty with a torn cover.

"Styx," I replied. "But we couldn't find it. Remember?"

"I remember. Would this be the book?" He handed the
volume to me.

I glanced at the cover. "It could be," I replied, flipping
the cover over. The writing was by hand. The second page
had the name *Byron Styx* written on it. "Where'd you find
it?"

"Holding up the broken leg on my bed," he sat on the
edge of mine. "I knocked the leg off it and the bed wasn't
level any more. When I went to see what happened, I
noticed the author of the book."

I immediately began searching pages. There wasn't a
table of contents, just notes about various events and
desires. Alex watched nervously from the mirror. Suddenly,

a grin crossed my face. "This is it!" I cried. "The technique we're looking for!"

"What's it say?" Brandon and Alex asked together.

I read the page, then read it again. I turned the page to be certain there wasn't more. Aunt Eva said you have to understand everything about a technique before trying it. I read the page a third time to be sure I understood. Slowly, I explained the technique to Brandon in terms he'd understand. Alex listened closely.

"It comes down to you, Alex," I finally said. "You have to want to come out. Not part way. Not sort of. Really, really want it." I looked at my friend.

"And you're sure this won't kill me?" Alex replied.

"I'm not sure of anything!" I admitted with a chuckle. "And I'm scared to death to try this, but your mother told me where to find the instructions, so I can only imagine it will work. She seemed really sorry for her actions."

"She's a ghost!" Brandon exclaimed. "Of course, she's sorry. She's stuck walking the Earth instead of resting in paradise!"

"Let's do it!" Alex nodded matter-of-factly. "By the way, if it doesn't work? Thanks for trying."

"That's the spirit of positive thinking," I sarcastically teased. "Ok. Everyone remember what I said? Shall we go over it one more time?" Once more, I reviewed the instructions with Brandon and Alex. Nervously, Brandn and I held hands. "Start wishing, Alex," I instructed. "Good luck."

"Go!" Alex cried, closing her eyes.

Brandon and I started chanting the lines from the book.

"Mirror lost,
Mirror Found,
Once was thine,
Is No Longer Bound!"

Inside, I wished with all my might that Alex would come out of the mirror. I focused my energies on Alex, trying to pull her to me. I could feel Brandon's power mixing with mine. A sucking sound echoed around the room. I opened my eyes in time to catch Alex as the girl flew out of the mirror. We landed heavily on the bed.

Standing up again, we checked Alex over. Brandon's eyes danced.

"How are you feeling?" I asked.

"Great! Tired! Excited!"

"No dizziness?"

"A little, but nothing I'm worried about."

"Fading?"

"I don't think so," Alex said, touching herself everywhere.

We stared at each other for a moment, then at Brandon. All three of us began jumping up and down. "We did it! We did it!"

"What's going on..." Aunt Eva's voice came from the door. Her hand went up and covered her mouth. "Alex?"

Alex smiled a big, wide grin. "I'm free!" she cried. Aunt Eva raced forward and hugged the girl.

"Oh, wait until your grandfather sees you!" she laughed and cried at the same time. "How?" she suddenly asked.

I handed the book to Aunt Eva. "Apparently, Brandon's bed needs fixing."

Aunt Eva looked at the book. "Where'd this come from?" she asked. "Besides Brandon's bed. I don't recall ever seeing this book."

"Someone must have put it under the bed," Brandon remarked.

"It doesn't matter," I laughed. "We found it, and it worked."

"Now wait a moment," Aunt Eva brought things down. "We don't know what repercussions this is going to bring about. Don't go celebrating until morning when we're sure Alex is going to stay with us."

"I have only one request," Alex said solemnly.

"What's that, honey?" Aunt Eva asked.

"Can I *please* take a bath?"

We all broke into laughter. I pulled some underwear and a nightgown from my dresser. Aunt Eva showed her where the bathroom was and how to operate the indoor plumbing. Brandon smiled at me.

"We're a pretty good team, huh?" he said.

"We sure are!" I agreed, high-fiving him. "We're going to need to practice doing things together. I get the impression by all the mumbling and whispering around here that something's about to happen." Brandon simply nodded.

15 – Does My French Teacher have the Gift?

It took several days to get Alex adjusted to real life again. It required getting her clothing and shoes, linens and bedding, toiletries, and an assortment of personal items. We kept sharing the bedroom, so Aunt Eva had the full-sized bed pulled out and a set of bunk beds put in. Jasper fit the extra dresser in there as well. It was a little tight, but it worked. Aunt Eva and Mom laughed a few times as Alex tried to get familiar with electric and gas appliances and indoor plumbing.

Alex asked if she could take piano lessons. Apparently, she was taking them before she was imprisoned. Aunt Eva began looking up piano teachers for her. Alex also tired easily since she hadn't had much exercise in almost a hundred years. I spent time in the library or the garden while Alex napped in the afternoons.

It wasn't too long after that when Mom dropped the bomb!

"School starts next week," she announced happily at dinner.

"What?!" I snapped up.

"School! No!" Brandon cried.

"School?" Alex asked tentatively.

"Come on, now. I suspect all three of you will be well ahead in your studies," Mom chuckled.

"And it will give you the opportunity to meet some of the other kids in town," Aunt Eva supported her sister. "You've been locked away here at the homestead all summer. Besides, Brandon, your soccer league starts next weekend."

"The high school isn't too bad," Jasper tried to encourage us. "I can't speak for the middle school."

"I'm not in middle school this year," Brandon scowled. "I'm still stuck in 5th grade!"

"Out here, fifth grade is in the middle school," Aunt Eva broke to the boy. "There are six villages that all use the same schools. They divide up the costs so that the kids can get a better education."

"What about sports and stuff?" I asked. "How does that work?"

"They have the usuals," Jasper spoke into his plate. "We compete against some other larger towns. We were second in the region last year for football and soccer."

"Do we hafta go to school?" Brandon whined.

"I've never been to school," Alex whispered. "Mother taught us at home."

"That's it!" I brightened. "You guys could teach us at home. Homeschooled. I mean, we're going to have to keep up our Gift studies anyway."

"Oh, no! You three are going to school," Aunt Eva said firmly. "It's vital to your development." She chuckled, amused, as all three of us groaned.

AUNT EVA

"Vital to their development?" Marie asked me later.

"Yes, well, sort of," I nodded.

"Since when? You wanted to be homeschooled, too!" she teased as she put dishes into the dishwasher.

"The opposition is getting stronger. I've felt it outside. As the colder weather comes in, the opposition is going to get stronger as it drains the energy."

"How is this going to affect the kids?" Marie asked, worried about Kelly and Brandon.

"Don't know. They've already fallen prey to the tactics being used by the imps. I can only hope they're strong enough to resist it."

"Solstice isn't too far off."

"We have until December. That gives us three more months to train and strengthen. With luck, we'll be ready."

"Can they..."

"Yes, they can," I cut her off. "That's why I'm pushing the training."

"Heaven help us."

KELLY

Alex tip-toed back down the stairs to the nursery. As she walked back into the room, I glanced up at her. I immediately got a bad feeling in my gut as I saw the worry on her face. She looked directly at me. "Something's up."

"Whadaya mean?" I asked, putting a small fox back under the heat lamps.

Alex relayed what she overheard in the kitchen. She looked at each of us.

"The winter solstice can be rather noisy," Jasper commented absently. He put an injured bat back in its cage.

"Why?" Brandon asked. "What's a solstice?"

"It's when the Earth has reached its farthest point in its elliptical orbit around the sun," I explained. "There's two. One during the winter, and one during the summer."

"So why would it be noisy?" Brandon asked again.

"Well, the creatures in the woods get rather noisy. You'll see various lights flash through the woods. Sometimes their chants will hypnotize you," Jasper continued his explanation.

"And the ghosts?" I asked.

Jasper looked up at me. He seemed to pale as fear crept into his eyes. "They pretty much stay to themselves; though you may see them traveling around the yard."

"Do you get the impression he knows more than he's letting on?" Alex asked her.

"I've had that impression the entire time I've been here," I retorted dryly. "No one wants to tell you the truth!" I put a bottle in another kit's mouth. This one wanted to play with it instead of eat.

"So, when is this Winter Solstice?" Alex asked.

"December, just before Christmas." Jasper seemed to be more interested in the young skunk he switched to than in answering.

"Something wrong?" I asked him.

"Nope. I think he's ready to be released," Jasper replied. "I can feed him near the woods in the morning. He'll be good, then."

Several days later, Mom drove us into town. We stopped at the middle school in the village and registered Brandon. The office allowed us to walk about the school and find his classroom. Luckily, the teacher was decorating, so we stopped to chat a bit. She seemed especially happy to have Brandon in her class. Brandon looked about and realized, like I did, there were only seven desks in the room.

"Where's the other desks?" he asked.

"Other desks? There will be one moved in for you before school on Monday," the teacher smiled.

"No. The other desks? For the other students?"

Mom chuckled. "You'll have to excuse him. He's from the city. The classrooms he's used to have almost 30 students in them."

"Oh!" the teacher suddenly understood. "No, Brandon. Counting you, there are only 8 students in this classroom."

"Eight?" Brandon seemed surprised. Yea. I was, too. No Man's Land.

"Yep. Nice and small. We move along much faster than in the city schools. I think you'll like it."

Brandon sighed. Alex and I read his mind. Eight students. They probably had been together since kindergarten. They probably knew each other very well. Now he's the new kid. Not a good scenario.

As if reading our expressions, the teacher added, "You won't be the only new kid on the block," she smiled. "We get the students from six villages. They all have their own grammar schools. The students arriving might know another person in the classroom, but they won't know everyone. You'll fit in just fine." Brandon smiled at her, an embarrassed blush creeping up his cheeks. He nodded his thanks.

We said goodbye and drove across town and into the next one for the high school. Mom registered me and Alex. She and Aunt Marie had already brought Alex's age closer to mine since, technically, we were the same age. I watched Aunt Eva's not-so-legal skills as she adjusted a birth certificate for Alex and created some papers listing her as Alex's guardian. She even magically created a state seal for it. Luckily, the school didn't try to verify them. Mom registered both of us for freshman year. After a bit of discussion, we turned in our choices for electives. It only took a few moments for the secretary to give us our schedules. Of the seven classes, we had four and lunch together.

Mom had a reminiscent smile as we walked about the old building, finding classrooms and lockers. "You'll find that your classes here are just as small as Brandon's, though you will have different students in most classes."

"Why is everything so small?" I asked as I peered into our biology classroom.

"Because there aren't that many people who live around here. In our village alone, there are only about three dozen children. There are more animals than children. Those that do grow up here usually move out to get better jobs. Those that stay usually take over their parent's farms."

"Like Aunt Eva?" Brandon asked.

"Yes," Mom explained. "Although Aunt Eva dabbles in other financial transactions. You should learn from her. She's very good."

Our French teacher was in his room when we entered. He turned about and smiled. The three of us moved closer together. Only Mom pulled herself together to introduce us. Brandon and I looked at each other in surprised. The teacher was tall and thin, maybe around six feet tall. His shoulders were broad. He had a heart-shaped face with a bright smile. What struck us as strange was his coloring. His skin was paler, like Brandon's, with jet black hair cut just below his ears and along his collar. His eyes were deep blue, just like ours. I swallowed hard as I shook hands with him. Alex seemed genuinely afraid.

"Aunt Marie?" Brandon asked later. "Are there other families with the gift?"

"I suppose there could be. Why?"

"You didn't notice anything strange about Monsieur Broward's features?" I asked.

"No, why?"

"He has black hair and blue eyes," Brandon said warningly. "The same as us."

Mom suddenly realized what she saw. "I hadn't realized that. We'll ask Eva when we get back. But keep in mind, many other cultures have black hair and blue eyes. The Greeks, for example."

"Mr. Broward?" Aunt Eva asked when we brought the subject up. She thought for a moment and shook her head. "No. I don't recall hearing anything about a Broward. Could he have another name?"

"Don't know," I replied. "But his hair and eyes are exactly like ours, and his complexion looks a lot like Brandon's."

"Keep an eye on him. Not everyone with the gift uses it for good." We knew that from Tessa's history.

"He wouldn't try anything at school, would he?" Alex asked fearfully.

"I doubt it," Aunt Eva reassured the child. "There would be too many witnesses."

AUNT EVA

I continued to think about the topic after the kids had gone to bed. Something seemed strange. I'd lived in this area all my life. I was well familiar with the others who held the Gift. No one named Broward was among either set of people. Of course, it was possible that he just happened to be a person with those features and didn't have any inkling as to the Gift at all. Yes, that was probably the case.

16 – Where Are We From?

September seemed to fly as the three of us got used to school and classes. Aunt Eva got Alex piano lessons on Saturday mornings. Brandon got involved with the chess club and the soccer team. Jasper disappeared twice a week, but I didn't ask to where.

"What about you, Kelly?" Aunt Eva asked one evening.

"What about me?" I scowled.

"What would you like to do? Alex is taking piano and Brandon has a few clubs. What would you like to do?"

I shrugged. "I don't know."

"How about art lessons?" Mom piped up as she finished snapping string beans and covered the pot with water.

"Oh, that would be wonderful! Mrs. Taylor in town does art. She's very good. I could inquire about lessons," Aunt Eva became excited. Her twinkling eyes caught mine. "You can't stay with your nose in a book all the time!"

A slight smile crossed my face. "I don't. I play games with Brandon and Alex, and I help with the animals. And George helps me study the stars."

"I saw your art pad." Mom turned from the stove. "You've hardly drawn in it. Back home, you were in it all the time. You're so talented in that area. Why not pursue it?"

I sighed. "I could, I suppose. There's a ton of lessons on YouTube."

"It's not the same as having another artist help you hone your skills," Aunt Eva said. "Kind of like magic. You can try to learn it on your own, but your skills will grow much faster when you have an experienced user guiding your progress."

"Ok. Art lessons, then," I caved. I wasn't going to win the discussion, and I did like drawing.

Late September brought another incident. The last bell of the day rang. The students immediately closed their books and started gathering their things.

"Don't forget—study chapters two and three for the test on Monday," Mr. Broward called above the noise. "Kelly, can I speak with you a moment?"

I spun around and stared at my French teacher like a deer in the headlights. I'd been trying to avoid the teacher all month. Slowly, I swallowed and nodded.

"What do you think he wants?" Alex whispered.

"I don't know. Stay close."

"Remember what Aunt Eva said," my friend reminded.

I nodded as I moved to approach the teacher's desk.

"Is something wrong?" I asked timidly.

"No, no. Your French is coming along nicely. Watch your accents, though. Inflection makes a difference, much like with a spell."

I scowled. "Sir?"

"Where are you from, Kelly?" Mr. Broward asked.

"I live with my mom and aunt just outside Devon's Junction. You should know that from the school records." Alex came up behind me.

"Yes, yes, but where are *you* from?" he asked again.

"I was born in Illinois," I replied again.

Mr. Broward smiled. "Think about what I'm asking, Kelly."

I couldn't think about what he was asking. I was too busy trying to block his mind from infiltrating mine. It was hard to keep an innocent persona and block his magical attempts.

Jasper saved the day by poking his head in the door. "You girls ready?" he asked. "We need to go get Brandon."

"I'm sorry, Mr. Broward. I don't understand what you're asking. I need to go. May I be excused, please?"

Mr. Broward nodded. Alex and I wasted no time getting out of the room. Neither Alex nor Jasper asked questions as I hurried to get as much distance between me and my teacher as possible. We stopped briefly at my and Alex's lockers, then hurried out to Jasper's station wagon.

"What was that all about?" Alex asked once we were in the car.

"I know exactly what he was asking," I replied. "George told me about it just before school started."

"Wanna spread a little light on the subject?" Jasper asked.

"No one knows when the gift started," I went on as Jasper drove out of the parking lot. "But ancient records indicate it was in three locations—Inkton River, Levir Hamlet, and Wik'r Basin. The people in the Hamlet died out—or so we think. The other two ended up in a war, each claiming the right to be the most powerful with the gift. The war basically destroyed both villages. Somehow, one of our ancestors got away and moved here. The gift continued on down the line."

"Could someone from the other village have also survived?" Alex asked.

"I imagine it's possible," I thought.

"Why wouldn't it?" Jasper asked. "If one family got away, why wouldn't someone from the other side also get away? Everyone has the instinct for survival," he explained.

"So you think he was trying to find out which village you're from?" Alex asked.

"I'm sure that's what he wanted to know. He wants to know if I'm an ally or an enemy."

"Do you know which village your family is from?"

"No. George didn't say."

"The village will not determine if you're an ally or enemy," Jasper pointed out. "Which side you take will determine that."

I nodded in agreement as I continued to think about Mr. Broward.

"What's going on down here?" Aunt Eva asked, walking into the library. Jasper was on his laptop, Alex and I were reading, and Brandon was working on math problems.

"Homework," Brandon replied.

"Reading," we said together.

"Research," Jasper responded.

"What are we researching?" Aunt Eva asked, looking over Jasper's shoulder. He was Googling *Levir Hamlet*. Interesting.

"Old villages," came the reply.

"You do realize that depending on how old you're talking about, they may not exist anymore, right? Or they could go by another name."

"I would think it would show up somewhere, though."

"Not necessarily. If it's a tiny village, it could have been overlooked by the cartographers, or lumped in with the larger city it was near."

Jasper nodded and went back to searching the internet. Aunt Eva looked over at us. Alex slouched into a comfortable armchair with an old mystery. She'd come to like those over the years, and she found a whole stash that she hadn't read yet. Aunt Eva would need to go to the bookstore for more books soon.

I, on the other hand, had a rather tall and wide book with decaying pages. Splayed on the armchair with one leg over the arm, I sat comfortably examining the page before me. Aunt Eva lifted the book to look at the title.

"What are you reading?" she asked.

"One of the spell books from the top. I've been going through the entire series."

"You realize you need to practice spells to use them, right?"

"I know," I replied. "I'm just getting an idea of what's available and what they can do."

"You need to be very careful with spells, Kelly," Aunt Eva warned. "The Gift can give you the power to do the incantation, but inexperience can bring about devastating results. Also, that particular series holds some very complicated spells."

"I noticed," I replied lowly. "I read one that had nineteen distinct steps! How are you supposed to remember those?"

"You don't," Aunt Eva advised with a smirk. "Most of the really long ones are more for potions or spells that take time. They're called rituals. While some of them are quite handy, you usually have the spell in front of you as you recite it."

Oh! I got it now; then I paused a moment. "Aunt Eva? Do you know what village our family originated in?"

"Does this have anything to do with Jasper's research?"

"Yes,"

"No, I don't. No one in our family knows which village we came from. It was too long ago. At this phase, I'd think that the villagers were more likely intermingled rather than kept a defunct war going. Why do you want to know?"

I closed my book but kept my finger in the page. "Mr. Broward kept asking me today where I was from. He kept asking the question over and over. I told him here, and that I was born in Illinois. I said I didn't understand the question, but I totally did. All the time, he was trying to infiltrate my mind, like you do at practice. Jasper finally came and got us, stopping the questioning."

"Did Mr. Broward say where he was from?" Aunt Eva asked.

"No. I wouldn't think he would if I were saying I didn't understand."

"Keep up the innocent act," Aunt Eva advised thoughtfully. "I don't like the sound of this. Excuse me. I need to consult with George."

The four of us watched Aunt Eva stride out of the library in a hurry. Obviously, Mr. Broward was starting something.

"Ya know," I commented to no one in particular. "The more I learn about the family and the Gift, the less I seem to know."

"Is it me, or does it always seem like she'll never give us a straight answer?" Brandon asked, staring after his aunt.

"There's safety in ignorance," Jasper commented.

"Not necessarily," Alex replied and went back to her book.

17 – Winter Solstice Disaster

The fall passed quickly. School and practice took most of our time. Aunt Eva was hard on us, but we learned fast that way. We each made a few other friends at school, but no one we'd share our "secrets" with.

True to Jasper's warning, the solstice was noisy. All night long! No one got any sleep. Alex and I finally went down to the kitchen around one in the morning to find something to eat. To my surprise, Mom and Aunt Eva were both sitting around the table with a cup of coffee and some muffins.

"What are you guys doing up?" I yawned as I reached for the fridge door.

"Same thing you are," Aunt Eva smirked.

"What's wrong, honey?" Mom asked, rubbing Alex's back. "Can't sleep?"

Alex shook her head and tried to stifle the yawn that came when she opened her mouth. "The woods are so noisy we can hear them over the hum of the heater. I guess this is one of those times when the mirror was a lot better. It used to dull the sounds from everywhere but in front of me."

I poured two glasses of milk. "The lights from the woods look like fireworks! And the roof sounds like something is trying to hack through it. I won't even mention the horrific screams from near the cemetery."

"It's when the imps have the most magic," Aunt Eva informed me. "Not exactly a safe neighborhood at the moment."

"Can they get into the house?" I asked nervously as I handed Alex one glass. I reached over and grabbed a chocolate chip muffin.

"Only if you open the door," Aunt Eva smiled.

"No way!" both of us responded in unison.

"Where's Brandon?" Mom asked, taking a sip of coffee.

"Sound asleep in his room," Alex responded sleepily. "We checked on him on the way down. He sleeps like a log!"

"At least one of us will be awake tomorrow," I murmured.

Another step was heard in the room. "I figured if everyone else was up, I'd join you," Jasper replied. He walked over to the stove and poured a cup of coffee. He sat at the table next to me. "What's up?"

"Ceiling. Noise. Us. Pick one," I replied, holding my head in my hand.

The five of us sat in exhausted quiet as we each sipped on our drinks and picked on the muffins and crackers Aunt Eva had put out. Outside, the noise was almost unbearable. Forceful winds blew past the house, rattling windows. Pounding on the roof echoed through the house. Screams echoed off the trees. Laughter came through the walls. Knocks continued to come on the doors. Sharp, scratchy music floated in from the woods. Several trees sounded like they were being split in two.

I noticed it first. The noise seemed to subside. I sat up straight and looked at Aunt Eva. Was that my voice I was hearing?

"Aunt Eva, listen."

Aunt Eva looked at me, listening intently. Sure enough, I heard it again. Something was imitating my voice calling Brandon.

"Brandon! Come on! Come play! You hafta see this! Bran-don!"

Everyone toppled their chairs as we heard the lock draw back on the front door. Racing for the hall, I tripped over the others. A small fireball passed my head and hit an imp trying to get into the house. Brandon closed the door behind him. I heard it latch.

Jasper hit the door hard and turned the latch. He glanced at Aunt Eva. She nodded. He swung the door open and the three of us toppled out the door. Mom had grasped Alex and moved to watch from a window. I looked around the yard. In the various fireworks of light, I had a hard time finding Brandon. Jasper picked up a bat from behind a bush.

"George!!" Aunt Eva yelled over the din. She needed the dragon.

"Where is he?" I asked, looking around. I absently batted an imp away with an air shield I'd learned last summer.

"I don't see him," Jasper said next to me.

"George, help!" Aunt Eva yelled again.

The shadow of the dragon made the imps scatter. Several turned in an attempt to attack him. George made quick work of them with a fire blast. In the flame's light, I saw Brandon's image walking slowly towards the woods. A feathery white lady was floating in front of him, coaxing him onward.

I didn't wait. My hand thrust out in front of me and I concentrated. Using all of my strength, I tugged and tugged. It was a struggle against the feathery lady as Brandon continued to walk forward. Closing my eyes tight, I used all the energy I could muster to pull Brandon back towards the house. I didn't see George swallow the lady. I didn't see the imps Jasper knocked out with the bat. I didn't see Aunt Eva place a protective shield around me. I didn't see anything until Brandon slammed into me, knocking me into the house.

Luckily, Aunt Eva was on it. She grasped us both as Jasper knocked another imp out of the ballpark. She dragged us inside. Jasper shut the door tight as three imps slammed into it full force. I grasped Brandon by the shoulders and shook him hard.

"Wake up, you oaf!"

"Oaf! Who you callin' an oaf?" Brandon pushed me back.

"You were sleepwalking!" I yelled back.

"That's enough," Aunt Eva murmured. "Brandon was under a spell. It's not his fault."

"Spell?" Brandon asked. "No, I was following Kelly. She was going to show me something in the woods."

"No," I shook my head. "You were following a ghost." Suddenly, I stood up and scowled. "What ghost was that?" I turned to Aunt Eva. "I haven't seen her before."

"It was probably an imp pretending to be a ghost who was pretending to be you," Aunt Eva directed us back towards the kitchen. "They're getting smarter. We'll have to be on our guard."

"But how'd they get past the medicine?" Alex asked, getting a cup for Brandon. She knew he'd like hot chocolate.

"The medicine only keeps us from casting the spells ourselves," Aunt Eva explained. "It doesn't help with outside influences."

The thought left me wondering. So far, the imps have used the same tricks over and over with slight nuances. Both Brandon and I had fallen for them twice now. If the imps were getting smarter, then we had better work together more often to get stronger. I glanced over at my cousin. The poor kid was falling asleep at the table even though the noise outside had gotten louder.

I rose groggily from the couch. Thank heavens it was Sunday, and I didn't have school. Slowly, I stretched and glanced outside. The sun was already high. I trudged my way to the kitchen. What time was it, anyway? A quick glance at the clock showed it was after 11. Wow!

Alex stood at the stove and grinned at me. She had a spatula in her hand and an apron around her waist. Eggs and milk were on the counter.

"Morning," my friend greeted.

"Sure. We can go with that." I moved to the fridge for some orange juice. "Whatcha making?"

"French toast," Alex replied. "No one else is up except Brandon. He's watching TV in the family room."

"I guess we're not going to church today?" I smirked.

"That would be my guess. Here," Alex handed me a plate. "Bring these to Brandon, please?"

"Sure."

I wandered into the Family Room. Brandon was watching Scooby Doo reruns on the floor. He had a book in front of him.

"Here." I handed him the plate. "Alex made breakfast."

"Huh? Oh, thanks." He took the plate and laid it on the book.

"Look, um," I squirmed a little. I felt guilty inside, but I really didn't know how to apologize. "I'm sorry I yelled at you last night. I suppose I should have thought it out more."

"It's alright. Those guys have duped us both. I just wish I knew how to stop them."

Alex came in with two more plates. "You know," she interrupted, handing one plate to me. "I remember my mother saying the imps weren't always there. Something about a rift."

"A rift?" Brandon asked, sitting up.

"Yea."

"Like a rift in space?" I asked.

"I don't know, but she clearly said the imps just appeared one day. It was right after some kind of storm. I didn't get many details because I rarely listened to her rattling for long."

"Perhaps you should've listened for this one?" Brandon remarked.

"Perhaps," Alex agreed with a grin.

"Wait. If the imps just showed up one day, someone has to know what happened." I knew a gleam crossed my eyes as my mind raced with thoughts.

"Who would know?" Alex shrugged.

"I can think of one," Brandon replied. "George would know the story."

"And I can think of a few more, though they're harder to reach." Both Alex and Brandon looked at me in confusion. "Someone buried in that cemetery knows the entire story."

The three of us cleaned up and let ourselves out. Looking around the front lawn was like looking at the results of a tornado. Splintered wood was everywhere. Shingles from the roof lay scattered across the grass. Several trees from the edge of the woods had been uprooted. We walked around to the side of the building. Two of Aunt Eva's fruit trees were split in half.

"Aunt Eva's not going to like this," I mumbled.

"Well, they tilled the garden area for us," Alex pointed towards the strip on the far side of the orchard where we planted vegetables in the summer. The ground had been turned over and scattered. Holes looked like dogs had been burying bones in there.

"There's one worse," Brandon pointed towards a tree near the shed. Hanging out of the branches was the tail end of the pickup truck. "Wonder how we're gonna get that one down."

As we turned the corner, we found Mom's car turned upside down. "And that one."

"We're gonna need help with this bunch," I mumbled. "Come on."

Carefully, I led the way up towards George's hill. It would be a hike, especially in this cold wind, but I knew exactly where it was. As we climbed up the path to his rocky cave, we could look out over the woods. Destruction was everywhere. At one point, we had to work together to push some rocks off the path so we could get up. Finally, heaving and out of breath, we reached the top. George wasn't on the plateau. I went to look into the cave. It was deeper than I thought. Far in the back, I could see a dark shadow curled up. The snore that reached my ears told me George was still sleeping.

"He's sleeping," I whispered to the others when I came out of the cave. "Should we wake him?"

"It's too early in the day to talk to the ghosts," Alex replied.

"I thought your mother was the only ghost that actually appeared," Brandon commented.

"No," Alex recalled. "Several of them walk the cemetery. They're the ones who lost control of the gift. Some have been there since before I was born."

"They're the ones punished to walk the earth for eternity because of their crimes," George's voice came from inside the cave. His colossal form filled the opening a moment later.

"We're sorry, George," I apologized guiltily. "We didn't mean to wake you."

"Then you shouldn't have been talking outside my entrance," George gently reprimanded. "Now I know you didn't walk all the way up here to thank me for my help last night."

"Oh, yeah," Brandon dipped his head. "Thank you."

"Most welcome. So, what brings you three up here on a cold, windy day?"

"We want to know about the circumstances when the imps showed up," I replied. I was scrunching down inside my winter coat to get out of the wind.

"I see," George settled in his cave entrance. He put out a wing as a windshield. We all ran for it. "Well, I don't really know much. They've been around for centuries. As long as I can remember. It was during an equinox, I believe. Yes. A syzygy and a solar eclipse that occurred at the same time, but I don't know more than that. The circumstances were pretty mysterious."

"What's a syzygy?" Brandon scowled. He'd never heard the term

"A syzygy is when three or more celestial bodies create a straight line, usually with Earth in the line. The more bodies in the line, the greater the gravitational tension is."

"A syzygy and a and a solar eclipse at the same time?" Alex asked. "What are the chances of that happening?"

"If I had to guess, about 4.6 million to 1," George replied.

"Exactly," I replied. "That's why they've been here so long."

"I was only guessing," George reminded the girl.

"No, that's why the imps have been here so long. The chances of a solar eclipse happening at the same time as the height of the equinox is so rare that the imps are trapped here."

"Still, they try to open that... door thing," Brandon replied.

"The rift," I murmured. My mind immediately brought the vision to view. "It looks like a hole with fire behind it. There are voices inside it, like people are trapped."

"I do not know what is inside the doorway," George replied. "I simply keep them away from you."

"They need us to open the doorway," Brandon determined. "Why?"

"Don't know," I replied.

"I would think there is at least one book in the library that will tell you about the rift and the imps," George instructed.

"Yes, but which one? There are *thousands* of books in that room," Brandon countered.

"I'm going to guess one that is handwritten instead of typed."

Alex and I laughed. "Grandpa," Alex chuckled. "*Most* of those books are handwritten."

"Ah, well, that does present a problem, doesn't it?" The dragon had a knowing smile on his face. "Off with you now. You're shivering, and I'm going back to sleep. It was a difficult night."

"You're telling us?" I agreed sarcastically. "By the way, there are a couple of vehicles that could use your help."

"One's in a tree, and one is upside down," Brandon added. "Can you fix those?"

"After my nap," George chuckled.

We thought about the problem as we traveled back towards the house. Snow began falling as we came down to level ground. Alex and I merely looked up at the sky, less than thrilled as we walked. A good day for a fire in the fireplace. Brandon was the only one who appeared happy with the prospect.

"Maybe we'll have the day off tomorrow!" he smiled.

"Don't get your hopes up," I replied, shrugging my coat up higher around my ears.

"We're way up north. People around here know how to get around in deep snow," Alex reminded him.

"Oh. Yea." Brandon sighed and kicked a stone out of the way.

"Books in the library," I muttered out loud.

"We can eliminate the children's books," Alex added.

"Maybe we should talk to Aunt Eva about this," Brandon suggested.

"Yea," we both agreed.

Aunt Eva was sitting at the kitchen table with a plate of French toast when we walked in. She looked up and smiled at us as she put a bite in her mouth. She watched as we hung up coats and kicked off our boots.

"How's the damage?" she asked.

We exchanged glances, as if trying to decide who was going to tell her. "It's… damage," I replied, then sat down across from her. Alex and Brandon each took a seat at the table as well.

"So eager to see it all?" Aunt Eva chided.

"No, actually, we went to talk to Granpa," Alex replied.

"Oh? Was he up?"

"No. We accidentally woke him," Brandon added guiltily.

"Aunt Eva, what do you know about the imps?" I finally blurted out.

Aunt Eva sighed. "Not very much, I'm afraid. They've been there as long as I've been alive. There's some kind of portal they keep trying to open."

"The one with voices behind it," I nodded.

"Yes." Aunt Eva folded her hands under her chin as she thought. "There are two theories about that portal. One is that the imps want it open so they can go home. The other is that they want to open it to let others from their world in to create more havoc."

"I'd like the first one, please," Brandon offered.

Aunt Eva chuckled. "Me, too. As to how they came to be here, I'm not sure. The magistrate may know."

"Grandpa said they came centuries ago," Alex informed her. "And I remember my mother saying they came before she was born, so they came before we lived here."

"George also said they came when a solar eclipse happened at the same time as an equinox," I mused. "If it's a solar eclipse, it would have to have been in the afternoon."

"He also said it was millions to one of happening," Brandon retorted.

"Not necessarily, Kelly," Aunt Eva said, taking another bite. She swallowed before continuing. "Equinoxes happen at different times each year. The movement of the Earth changes the times as it rotates around the sun."

"OK, so that would mean that the time could vary, but when is there going to be another solar eclipse at the same time?" Alex asked.

"That would require a little research on the NASA website," Aunt Eva suggested. "The other question would be that if a solar eclipse brought them, would it return them or bring more? Likewise, how would a lunar eclipse affect the situation? Would it change if the event happened during a solstice instead of an equinox?"

"All excellent questions," I replied. "But where do we find the answers? It's not like we can just conjure one up and try it to find out."

"George suggested the library," Brandon sighed.

"Good place to start."

"But which books?" I whined. "There are hundreds in there!"

"Let's use a process of elimination," Aunt Eva suggested.

"We can eliminate the children's books," Brandon suggested.

"And the dictionaries and encyclopedias," Alex added.

"And the spell books," I thought.

"Not necessarily," Aunt Eva stopped me. "The spell books may have a hint as to what spell was being cast when it happened. That's probably a longshot, but a possibility. Also, I would probably venture to say that someone opened the portal, then tried to close it, but wasn't successful. So, I would begin with the journals."

I thought for a moment. "Would that type of accident be a reason a spirit would have to walk the Earth for eternity?"

"I would think that would depend on if it was done on purpose or by accident," Aunt Eva replied thoughtfully. "Why?"

"We thought maybe a ghost in the cemetery would know what happened," Alex continued. "Grandpa said that

the ghosts in the cemetery are condemned to walk the
Earth for eternity as punishment for their crimes in life."

"So, who are the ghosts in the cemetery?" Brandon
asked, suddenly interested.

"Quite a few," Aunt Eva replied. "I'm not sure I know
them all."

"Looks like we've got a lot of work to do." Alex sighed.

Aunt Eva chuckled. "Yes, it does. I'll see what I can
come up with as well." She got up to put her plate in the
sink. "Practice in an hour."

18 – Oooh! My French Teacher's in Trouble!

Monday was the usual at school. Alex and I were more focused on our equinox problem than the petty problems of the girls our age. It wasn't until French class that we thought of something else.

"Quite a racket the other night, eh, girls?" Mr. Broward greeted us.

Both Alex and I stopped to look at our teacher. "Racket?" I recovered quickly.

"Yes. Saturday night? Lots of noise?"

I paused with a scowl on my face. It almost seemed as if Mr. Broward was talking about the noise from the solstice. Supposedly, however, that little 'racket' was only supposed to be heard at the farm. "Probably just a party up the road," I replied, trying to throw him off.

"Mm, hmm," Mr. Broward observed me a moment. "You're telling me you didn't hear anything?"

Other students began filing into the classroom. "Saturday night?" I looked at the others. "Seemed ok to me. Alex?"

"Huh?" Alex started. "Um, yea. Pretty quiet."

Mr. Broward just nodded. "I see. Well, then. Sorry I brought it up."

"He knows about..." Alex began to whisper.

I waved a hand to hush her. Not here. If Mr. Broward heard the noise from the solstice, it meant he had the gift or lived on our land. Or the imps had more than one portal nearby. Either way, was Mr. Broward on our side or the imps' side?

"Aunt Eva!" I yelled as I slammed through the back door. "Aunt Eva!"

"What's the matter?" Aunt Eva came around from the study. "You sound like its life or death!"

"It might be," Alex replied.

"What is it?"

"Mr. Broward, our French teacher that we asked you about at the beginning of the year? He heard the noise during the solstice."

Her face scrunched up in confusion. It said it all. He shouldn't have. "What?"

"He asked us about the noise during the solstice," Alex told her.

"We just pretended we didn't hear anything, but he directly made a comment to us about it," I informed her.

"Kelly told him it was probably a party up the street," Alex added.

"No. No one without the gift or in a house directly involved can hear the goings-on during the solstice celebration. I've tested that theory."

"Well, he did," I said emphatically.

"I'm going to have to check in on this," Aunt Eva said thoughtfully. "Let me make some phone calls first."

"Can I show you what I found?" Brandon asked, looking up.

"Sure, what?" I asked, grateful to have a different topic running through my head.

Brandon held up a sheet of paper to Aunt Eva. It held several notations of Lunar and Solar eclipses. "I've got the list of the next ten solar and lunar eclipses that occur during an equinox or solstice."

"Good work, Brandon!" Aunt Eva praised, laying a hand on his shoulder. Her expression was one of pride.

"Only two are Lunar eclipses," Brandon replied, pointing at the paper.

"Yea, but look at the top one," Alex said, reading over Aunt Eva's shoulder.

"That's this spring," I replied. "Does the location of the eclipse count?"

"I don't think so," Aunt Eva said thoughtfully, "but until we have more details, I won't know for sure."

"There's not a lot of time," Brandon said out loud.

"There's no real rush, either," Aunt Eva said, handing him the paper. "The imps have been here for centuries. A little longer won't hurt them. Keep that paper safe, Brandon." She turned to move to the study. "We may need it."

"Yea," I muttered lowly. "But will it hurt us?"

Alex and I gathered our things at the end of class when the bell rang.

"Don't forget the take-home quiz," Mr. Broward called above the din. "And practice over the weekend for Monday's verbal quiz! No sloppy pronunciations!"

The kids were bolting out the door. I grabbed the last of my books and got ready to leave. Alex stood next to me waiting.

"Kelly, have the imps been more active at your place?" Mr. Broward asked softly.

"Sir?" I feigned.

"You know. The imps."

"No, she doesn't know," Aunt Eva's voice broke the tension of the room. Alex and I both looked at the door with relief. "Afternoon, Rolf."

"Eva! Look at you! You look wonderful!" the man smiled nervously.

"Thank you. You, too." She walked slowly towards the desk. "I understand you've been harassing my niece."

Mr. Broward took on a defensive stance. "I haven't been harassing her. Simply asking some thought-provoking questions. I mean, if she's living with you, then she must know about... things."

"What she knows and doesn't know is no concern of yours," Aunt Eva became firm. "You teach her French, that's it. I'm the one entrusted with her upbringing."

"Eva, you know what's coming."

"And it doesn't concern you."

"Eva, please. You need to understand..."

"I understand that you're trying to get information from a 14-year-old girl who doesn't have the foggiest clue what you're getting at! Now leave her alone or they'll be looking for a new French teacher! Understood?"

Alex and I watched in amazement that quiet Aunt Eva easily put Mr. Broward in his place. Obviously, they had a history. I wondered what it was.

Mr. Broward sighed defeated. He nodded. "Just be aware that it may come back to bite you," he said to Aunt Eva.

"I know exactly what I'm doing," Aunt Eva said confidently. She turned towards us. "Ready to go home?" We nodded quickly. Aunt Eva motioned towards the door where Jasper stood. "Have a good weekend, Rolf."

"You, too, Eva."

I took a quick look over my shoulder as I left the classroom. Mr. Broward looked defeated and concerned as he watched us leave. I waved lightly.

"What was that all about?" I asked on the way home.

"What?" Aunt Eva replied.

"The exchange between you and Mr. Broward."

"One of my contacts got back to me this morning after you girls left. Mr. Broward's real name is Rolf Bursmith. I went to school with him, and yes, he also has the gift. We did part of our training together. He doesn't have the control over the gift as I do, which is probably why he backed down so easily."

"What's he talking about, something about to happen?" Alex asked.

"Well," Aunt Eva chuckled. "You've been introduced to the Solstace. The Equinox is just the opposite. It seems the imps lose energy during the Equinox. Problem is, other things happen as well. Lights and strange images. Odd reflections. Spirits from unknown realms. But it is much quieter."

"Is there something else we should be aware of?" Brandon asked.

"I think you'll be fine," Aunt Eva said reassuringly as she pulled into the driveway. "Practice in 15 minutes."

"Do you get the feeling she's holding something back? Like there's more to the equinox than she's telling?" Alex asked me.

"She's been holding things back since I got here!" I exclaimed dryly. "Why should that change now?"

Aunt Eva laughed as we got out of the car. Only Brandon scowled with concern as he followed us in.

"All in good time," Aunt Eva muttered as we headed for the house. "All in good time."

19 – A Hint About The Rift

The few weeks before Christmas saw us decorating the house and the yard. Brandon was glad Aunt Eva let us practice our levitation instead of climbing the ladder. She said it would help us with precision. We'd have to get these thin wires to hang on tiny hooks around the house. She was right.

Excitement followed us into Christmas break. Aunt Eva had taken us all into Gallagher's in Heart's Bluff so we could do some Christmas shopping. She gave each of us some money to get gifts. We spent all day at the mall, had dinner there, then went to pick up some groceries for the next two months. Supposedly, they were expecting a lot of snow.

The rest of the family came out for the holiday. It made the house pretty crowded again. Uncle Cliff wrapped each of us in a huge hug. He was delighted to see Alex out of the mirror.

"You adjusting okay?" he asked the girl in concern.

Alex nodded. "Yea. I'm okay. Eva has been watching me pretty close."

"Good! She's the one who can help."

"Actually, Kelly and Brandon have been great at helping me adjust to this era."

"Even better!"

Only Abby wasn't happy about Alex. It was obvious she was jealous of the girl spending so much time with me. I tried to ease her fears by including her in the things we were planning.

A few days before Christmas Eve saw a snow storm move through the area. Uncle Cliff kept the fire going in the fireplace as we kept ourselves busy with video games, toys, and board games. Grandma, Aunt Eva, and Aunt Chrissy were busy in the kitchen getting things prepared for Christmas Eve. George took us for a sleigh ride by grasping ropes attached to our sleds and dragging us around the yard and hills. What a blast!

It was late that night when I came down to the kitchen for a drink. I could hear the adults talking in the family room. Why did they always talk about us when we weren't there?

"Do you think he's trying to intimidate her?" Uncle Cliff asked.

"No." It was Aunt Eva's voice. "I think he's poking around for information. It sounded like he was trying to get Kelly to admit she had the Gift. What he was going to do with that information is beyond me."

"You let him know not to bother her again, didn't you?" Granma asked.

"Oh, yes. In no uncertain terms," Aunt Eva said emphatically.

"What could he want with Kelly, though?" Aunt Chrissy asked.

"I'm not certain, but I think it has something to do with the upcoming equinox. A few of my sources have been saying that the hot topic being debated amongst the Gifters in the area."

"Is that a good thing or a bad thing?"

Aunt Eva chuckled. "I guess that depends on what side you're on."

"How are they doing with their studies, really?" Uncle Cliff asked.

"Excellent," Aunt Eva praised. "They're both learning quickly, handling way more than I could at their ages, and show an amazing amount of control and power when they team up. I'm very proud of them all."

"Is Alex showing signs of it, too?" Granma asked.

"No, but she's been great at helping them research out spells and techniques. It was Brandon and Kelly together that got her out of the mirror." Aunt Eva explained proudly. "Two inexperienced kids did what generations of experienced Gifters couldn't. Think about it."

There was a pause in the conversation. I got a couple of bottles of water from the fridge, grabbed a package of cookies, and turned around. Uncle Cliff stood in the archway.

"Eavesdropping again?" he asked pointedly.

"No," I replied with a grin. "Just came down for a drink and snacks. We're still up talking."

Uncle Cliff chuckled. "Abby in with you, too?" he asked. I could tell he was hoping I wasn't excluding his daughter.

"Abby, Brandon, Alex, and me. Jasper went to bed. The other kids are souuuuund asleep," I explained.

Uncle Cliff nodded. "Don't be up too late. The little ones are going to be going crazy in the morning."

I laughed. "We'll turn in soon."

The next day was Christmas Eve, and something strange happened. I sat quietly in the Family Room, reading a book. Alex and my cousins had gone to the lake to go ice skating. I'm not much for ice skating, so I chose to read an adventure book for a change. The women had gone to town for some last-minute shopping. I laughed. They hooked up a sleigh and a team of horses to get there.

Out of nowhere, Brandon came bursting through the back door.

"Kelly! Kelly! Come quick!" he hollered as he pounded through the house.

I looked up, startled. "What's up?"

"You gotta come quick!"

"What's wrong?" I asked, getting up from the chair.

"The ghosts are going crazy!"

"What?" I squinted. They already had their mid-monthly walk around the cemetery before everyone got there.

"I've never seen them like this!"

"Like what?"

"Come on! George is waiting for us!" he urged.

I ran with my cousin to the mudroom off the back door. I quickly dressed in a snowsuit, boots, warm hat, and gloves. Brandon still had his on. I followed Brandon out the door. Sure enough, George sat patiently in the driveway.

"Hurry, child!" he urged.

"What's going on?"

"No one knows, but I'll wager you'll be the only one who can find out!" he said urgently.

Securely on George's back, I hung on to a horn at the base of his neck as George made a quick ride out to the lake. I saw it before we landed. The mist was thick, thicker than usual. Dozens of apparitions wandered around the cemetery trying to get out of the gates, but the containment spell still held fast. Brandon and I slid to the ground as George landed. Alex and Abby came running over.

"You rode a dragon?" Abby asked incredulously. "Can I have a ride?"

"I don't know," I responded, still watching the cemetery. "Ask him."

"No," George said flatly. "Do you see what I see, Kelly?" George asked.

"Yes," I responded thoughtfully.

"What's happening?" Alex asked. "Is Mother causing trouble again?"

"Mother?" Abby asked.

"Not now, Abby," I waved at my cousin. "I don't think so, Alex. It looks... like... they're arguing with each other."

"Can ghosts argue?" Brandon scowled in confusion.

The four of us turned to George. He suddenly realized he was being watched. "What?" he asked.

"Can ghosts argue?" I asked.

"What are you asking me for?" he responded. "I've never been dead!"

I sighed and shivered. "Only one way to find out what this is all about." I looked at George. "If I'm not back in 20 minutes, come get me out of there."

"Aunt Eva's not going to like this," Abby warned.

"Aunt Eva's not here," I replied bravely, "And it's obvious that something serious is up."

"You act like you see this all the time," Abby remarked. "It's creepy."

"Every month with the new moon," Brandon replied like it was really old news.

"What?" Abby looked at her brother like he was crazy.

"I wanna go back to the house." Lizzie tugged on Abby's coat. "I'm scared."

"It's okay, Lizzie," Alex comforted the girl. "The ghosts can't get out of the cemetery."

I walked up to the gate of the cemetery. The wind was biting cold. It was worse near the gates. The activity inside the cemetery was like nothing I'd ever seen. Usually, one or two ghosts would walk around, rarely the same ones. Today, though, it seemed like all of them were up and out.

As soon as the gate opened, all activity in the cemetery stopped. Every ghost looked at me. I swallowed and tried to put on a brave and knowing attitude. One ghost raced across the cemetery at me. He stopped only a few inches from me with a threatening face and stance. I rolled my eyes.

"You can't harm me," I said. I waved my hand through his abdomen. "See?" I scanned around the others. "Where's Tessa?"

I stepped around the threatening ghost; it wouldn't be polite to just walk through him. Scanning the other ghosts, I didn't see her anywhere. I addressed at another ghost. "Where's Tessa?"

The ghost pointed to the tombstone.

"I know where she's buried, but where is she?"

Again, it pointed at the tombstone. Dawning hit me like a ton of bricks. "Are you telling me she found peace?" The ghost nodded. Wow! Getting Alex out of the mirror gave Tessa the peace she needed. No, that can't be right. George said these were the ones cursed to roam the earth for eternity. I resigned myself to what I was here for.

"Who wants to explain to me what's going on?" I asked, looking around.

The ghosts all stared back at me. No one moved.

"You're all up later than usual. It's not a new moon. The mist is thick. Something has you disturbed. What is it?" I asked again.

One ghost came up to me. He had an old 1800-style suit with high-top shoes. His ascot was slightly askew. I recognized this one.

"Edmund, isn't it?" I asked. The ghost nodded. "Can you tell me what's going on?" The ghost shrugged. "Can you try?" The ghost nodded.

Another ghost came racing over and began arguing with Edmund. The two went back and forth for a bit. Several times, they pointed at me. Would've been nice to know what was being said. Finally, Edmund waved the other ghost off. He approached me and nodded. I responded in kind, giving him permission and hoping it would not end my life. I'd been through this before and knew what to expect. Hopefully, Edmund used the same techniques Tessa did.

The images weren't as clear as with Tessa. I found myself in a garden looking at some beautiful flowers. Tiny creatures flitted from flower to flower and up to the birdbath. They looked like varying types of butterflies. They would swirl together and flit away or dip down into the flowers.

Everything grew dark. Lightning flashed, and the wind blew. I could hear tiny squeals. A vortex seemed to pull everything in one direction, towards shadows of trees.

The garden was back, but the butterflies were gone. Instead, I could see the imps. The imps were upset, flying around angrily. Many raced towards the woods.

Edmund withdrew and looked at me. I shook my head to let the dizziness of the transfer subside, then looked at Edmund.

"The butterflies. Did the imps sabotage them?"

Edmund shook his head.

"The imps took their place?"

Edmund nodded.

Hundreds of theories went through my head like a highway. Butterflies and imps. I sighed. "I need to think about this. Why is this causing issues amongst the ghosts?"

All the ghosts turned to one of the others. Her head hung as she was being viewed by everyone. I didn't recognize her. Her clothing was of an era very long ago, though; like 15 or 1600s; maybe earlier. I approached the ghost.

"Do you know what happened?" The ghost nodded. "Can you tell me?" The ghost shook her head. I sighed. "Is what happened written somewhere?" The ghost nodded. "Can you spell it for me?"

The ghost looked at me for a long time. I nodded encouragingly, using my finger to write letters in the air. S-P-E-L-L. The ghost looked at me. "F-E-Y." I repeated each letter she wrote. "Fey? Is that the topic or the author?" The ghost nodded. I rolled my eyes. "Is it the author?" The ghost shrugged. "Is it the topic?" The ghost nodded. "Is it something dangerous?" The ghost waggled her head from side to side. Dawning hit me at that moment. "Does this have anything to do with the Equinox?"

You would have thought I swore in Old English. The ruckus began again with the surrounding ghosts. They began arguing again. The wind kicked up. I looked towards the sky, closed my eyes, and sighed. "I'll take that as a yes," I breathed and moved towards the gate.

George was already there as I came out.

"I was about to get you," he said, looking me over. "Are you alright?"

"Yea," I said, closing the gate behind me. "Not a lot of answers, but a topic, at least."

"Which is?"

"Fey."

"Fey?" Brandon asked.

"As in fairies?" Abby asked.

The three of us looked at Abby in surprise. Abby looked back at us blankly.

"What?" she asked. "You didn't realize that fey and fairies are the same thing?"

"That's not really up your alley," Brandon asked.

"You wouldn't know what's up my alley," she taunted her brother.

"Either way, it's something we need to look into. It has something to do with the equinox." I sighed. This was getting stranger with each hint.

"Let's get you kids back to the house. It's cold and the little ones are shivering," George remarked. "Everyone on my back. You older ones hold the little ones."

"Oh, wow! I get to ride a dragon!" Abby jumped with excitement.

It took some coaxing to get Lizzie on George's back. I had to promise to hold her tight; cross my heart and hope to die. George was great at flying to keep the kids in place. It was a brief ride, but it got us back to the house pretty quickly. Uncle Cliff was on the porch, looking for us. He stepped down to help the little ones off George's back.

"What's up? I got up from my nap to find everyone gone!"

"Problems at the cemetery," I informed, handing Lizzie down to him.

"Oh?"

"Later."

The next two hours saw me, Brandon, Alex, and Abby in the basement library searching through books.

"Are we certain there's no old volumes floating around the house?" Alex asked, opening another book. "You know, like how we found the one that got me out of the mirror?"

"Not to our knowledge," I replied, flipping through to the table of contents in the one she had. "We checked under all the beds. I'll ask Jasper to look around."

"This is impossible," Brandon complained, dropping a book on the table. "There are so many topics!"

"OK. Let's try to break this down," Abby said, closing the book in front of her. "You're telling me that the ghost said there used to be lots of butterflies around, but after a lightning storm, there were only imps?"

"Right."

Abby rolled her eyes. "I don't believe any of this, you know," she retorted.

"Then why are you helping us?" Brandon snarled back.

"Because I don't want to be left out in the cold again!" Abby retorted angrily.

"Guys!" I softly defused the situation. "Brandon, let it go. It's not worth fighting about. She'll get to see it soon enough."

Brandon sighed. "Yea. I guess," he mumbled.

"We'll be fine."

"Ok," Abby returned to me. "Generally, according to legend, fairies look like butterflies, moths, or dragonflies to humans. Only very special humans can see them for what they really are."

"I can believe that. How do they turn into imps?"

"I don't know. I've read a bunch of stories and legends, but none of them said anything about them turning into imps."

"Maybe we're going about this the wrong way?" Alex said.

"Huh?"

"Maybe we need to look up legends about fairies and imps. If we know how one becomes the other, then maybe we'll know what spell to look for."

"She's got a point," Brandon shrugged.

I turned on the computer in the room. I smirked as Uncle Cliff came in while we tried to get online.

"What's going on down here?" he asked.

"We're trying to find out how fairies could become imps," Brandon informed his father.

"What?" Uncle Cliff scowled. Brandon nodded. "Have you asked Aunt Eva?"

"Yes," I replied. "Well, actually, we asked about what happened to the fairies in the yard. She didn't know."

Googling "legends about fairies and imps" returned several pages of resources, none of which explained how fairies could become imps.

"If imps are lesser demons, could the rift be a door to hell?" Alex asked fearfully.

"Possibly," Uncle Cliff murmured.

"I don't think so," I replied.

"Why?" Abby asked.

"Because the rift isn't closed all the way. I was out there. There are voices coming in through the rift. Panicked voices. The imps want me to open the rift. I don't know why."

"Come on, kids! Bedtime. Christmas tomorrow!" Granma yelled down the stairs.

"Ah well. We'll just have to put this off for another day," Alex shrugged, closing the book she had out. She pushed it back onto the shelf she took it off of and left a tag next to it to mark her spot. The others did the same.

We turned off the lights and hurried upstairs. Tomorrow may be Christmas, but tonight was stormy. The wind had already been whipping around. Jasper came in as we were coming upstairs. He held something in his arms.

"Whatcha got?" Brandon asked.

"Fox," Jasper replied. "It got attacked by an owl. He's in pretty bad shape."

"I'll help," I offered, taking the fox in a towel from the bathroom. His pretty brown and white fur was coated in snow and ice as his malnourished body shivered in my arms.

"He's pretty cold," Jasper said, taking off his snow clothes.

I rubbed the fox in my arms in an effort to warm him up as Abbey reached over to pet it. It settled down in my hold, trying hard to nuzzle closer to the warmth of my body.

"I remember him," Alex remarked, looking over my shoulder. "He's one of the kits from last summer. I remember the blaze on his nose."

I looked down at him. "Yea, I do, too. It's an odd pattern."

"No wonder he's so friendly." Brandon chuckled and stifled a yawn. "I'm going to bed."

"Me, too," Abby said. "Night."

"Go on, Alex. We won't be long," I encouraged. I knew she was tired.

I followed Jasper down to the nursery. We turned on a heating lamp over a large cage. I kept cuddling the smaller fox as Jasper got first aid supplies out to clean up the wounds that bled as he warmed. I held the fox still as Jasper cleaned wounds, stitched one large gash, and gave him an antibiotic shot. As Jasper checked the guy out, I brought a bowl of food over for him. He ate like he was starving.

"Ya know," I began, reaching for a heating blanket. "I always thought something wasn't right about this kit."

"What makes you say that?" Jasper asked, watching the fox eat.

"He's incredibly skinny for a fox this time of year, don't ya think?"

"Yes. He should have more fat on his bones, and judging by how he's eating, I'd guess he hasn't been able to find a meal in a while, but there's plenty of game out there. And his fur isn't silky like it should be. It's dry and brittle."

"Watch his eyes," I suggested. "Use the flashlight and watch his eyes. See if you see what I saw."

Jasper moved the light around and looked into the fox's eyes. It looked towards the light, but didn't stop eating. When the fox finished, Jasper had me hold him so he could check. Sure enough, the irises weren't adjusting to the light.

"He's blind," Jasper whispered. "How'd we miss that when he was little?"

"I don't know," I retorted exaggeratedly. "102 baby animals in here is all!"

Jasper chuckled. "I don't know what Eva's gonna want to do with him. We can't release him into the wild again. He'll die. I'm not sure how he's survived this long."

"I don't think he's completely blind," I said. "He reacted to the light and moved towards it. I think he can probably see shadows, or things nearby, maybe. How do you check an animal for eyesight?"

"I'll look it up. Let's put him to bed and get some sleep."

We put the fox in the cage with the heating blanket set to low and a stuffed animal. After turning out the lights, we shut the door. Immediately, I heard a yip, yip, yip repeatedly. Jasper shut the next door, but the yipping was still consistent.

"He doesn't want to be alone," I smirked.

"He's a fox. He'll get over it."

"Go to bed," I suggested. "I'll stay until he stops."

An hour later, the fox was still crying. He was determined; I'd give him that. Finally, I went back into the nursery. I pulled out a litter box and some litter, then grabbed the fox and headed up to bed. "You're going to get us both in trouble," I whispered to the fox that was about the size of a large house cat; quite small for a full-grown fox.

Once in my room, I shut the door and set up the litter box in the corner with a blanket on the floor nearby. I wrapped the fox in the blanket. Sleepily, I got changed, took my medicine, climbed into bed, and turned out the light on my nightstand. I laughed quietly when a weight hopped up on the bed and crawled under the covers with me. He curled up next to my legs, and we both fell asleep.

20 – A Wizard's Duel

I woke to the knocking on my door.

"Who's there?" Alex called.

The door cracked open. Abby poked her head in. "Are you guys up?" she asked.

"We are now," I mumbled. "What's wrong?"

"The flashing lights. Have you looked outside?"

"It's only the imps. Go back to sleep," Alex grumbled as she rolled over.

"I can't. I'm scared," Abby said sadly.

"Go get a blanket and some pillows," I said understandingly. The wind was whipping around outside, and I could hear the chants of the imps through the windows. They must have been enjoying this snow storm. "You can sleep on the floor. The fan blocks out the stuff going on outside."

Abby quickly did as I suggested and returned a few moments later with her blanket, quilt, and pillows. "Thanks," she smiled at me.

I smiled back sleepily. "I remember how scary these events can be. Just don't open a window."

"No problem!" Abby replied, getting comfortable on the floor.

I listened to the outside. What is it about snow storms that got the imps going? They didn't do this with lightning storms.

Excitement filled Christmas morning as we exchanged gifts and emptied stockings. It took the family over three hours to open all their presents. To my surprise, the fox stayed right near me.

"Why is there a fox in the house?" Aunt Eva asked firmly.

"He was lonely?" I replied. "He spent the night with me, and you'll be happy to know he used the litter box this morning."

"A housebroken fox," Grandma mused with a grin. "Imagine that!" She looked knowingly at Aunt Eva.

"There's a slight problem with him," Jasper mentioned. "He's blind."

"What?"

"Well, we think he's blind—kind of." Jasper explained our findings from the night before. "Either way, releasing him back into the wild when those wounds heal will make him a goner for sure."

"Hmmm. We'll have to figure out what to do. He can stay with Kelly in the meantime."

We all enjoyed the day. Brandon, Alex, Jasper, and I purposely stayed away from the library, enjoying movies, video games, board games, card games, and lots of good food all day long. A few of Aunt Eva's friends came over for dinner. Overall, it was a great day for the family. It felt good being a normal teenager for a change.

Abby spent the night on our floor again. Even though the activity in the woods stopped by mid-morning, she was having nightmares. I dug out an air mattress for her from the supply closet.

"What's going on?" Alex asked my cousin when she woke up for the third time during the night.

"I... I... I don't know," Abby said, tears falling from her eyes. "I keep having these nightmares!"

"What sort of nightmares?" I asked, sitting up in bed. The fox came out from under the covers and went over to check on Abby.

"Weird ones. With lightning and flashes of bright light. There's always a scream just before I wake up."

"What happens in the dream?" I asked.

"I'm not sure. It's me and another person, a guy. There's some kind of chanting, then the ground explodes when it's hit by lighting. There's a bright flash. The guy with me is gone and I scream, then I wake up."

"Have you had this dream before?" Alex asked.

"No."

"How many times have you had this dream?" I asked.

"Four or five times since we got here. This is the third time tonight."

"Is it always the same?"

"Yes," Abby replied, worry etched across her features and tears streaming down her face.

"And it's only been since you got here?" Alex asked. Abby nodded.

"Wait here," I said gently. I went down the hall and came back with a glass of water about five minutes later. "Here," I gave the glass to Abby. I took one of my purple pills out of the jar and gave it to my cousin. "Aunt Eva said these should keep the boogeyman away." We chuckled, but Abby took the pill anyway.

"What's it do?"

"It shuts down your brain so you can sleep," Alex explained simply. "In Kelly's case, it prevents any dreams from becoming reality."

"What?" Abby asked, putting the glass near her pillow.

"Before I came here, I used to have dreams; then when I woke up, I found out they really happened. Remember the pink and white curtains in my bedroom?" Abby nodded. "I changed them into green and white curtains in my sleep." Abby looked at me with a disbelieving scowl. "Yea, that's why there was a sudden change in the décor of my room." I chuckled. "There's been others, some more deadly than others."

"That's an understatement," Alex grumbled.

"Anyway, that little pill will keep the nightmares away. See ya in the morning," I told my cousin and hopped back into bed. "Come on, Rusty!" I held the covers up and the fox hopped right in underneath them.

Uncle Cliff took everyone sledding the next day, only it wasn't on a hill. He latched a couple of toboggan discs to the back of a snowmobile. He could pull four of the little guys or two of the older kids at a time. We had a blast! It was like George's trip, but faster. A few hours later we all came in coated from head to toe in snow with red-rimmed eyes and cold button noses. We got undressed in the mudroom and hung everything out to dry.

"Good timing!" Aunt Chrissy smiled. "Water's all ready for hot chocolate."

"Super!" Alex cried excitedly. "Hot chocolate and left-over pumpkin pie!"

"Yea!" Uncle Cliff joined in.

"Apple!" I cried as Rusty greeted me as I came in.

"He has been sitting at the window whining the entire time you've been out there."

Jasper checked the stitches on his side. "Not yet. Some of the wound is still open. Not until it's completely closed." He ruffled the fox's fur.

"You heard the vet, boy! No outside for a few more days." I hugged the fox. "Come on, Rusty," I called as I joined the rest of the family in the dining room.

"Rusty?" Aunt Eva questioned with raised brows.

"Well, he has to have a name!" I retorted. "I can't keep calling him 'fox,' and the name fits his fur!"

"Mmm, hmmm!" she crossed her arms. "And who's taking care of him while you're in school?"

I stopped for a moment. "You?" I replied with raised brows and a tiny voice.

"I think he needs a sanctuary," Aunt Eva stated gently. "With other fox."

"He'd still be a target," Jasper replied. "Bad eyesight."

"I know, I know. Law of the fittest," Aunt Eva grumbled, but didn't say anymore. Mom chuckled knowingly to herself across the table. "What?" Aunt Eva snapped out at her.

"Nothing," Mom quipped, but the smile never left her face.

Brandon, Jasper, Abby, Alex, and I all sat in the library looking at the books on the shelves. We had been over at least half of them.

"She said 'Fey', right?" Jasper asked.

"That's what she said. I know it's a topic, but she thought it might also be an author."

"I'm not seeing anything," Abby remarked from her area of the library.

"Me, either," Alex responded.

"All I'm finding are little kids' books about stories with fairies in them," Brandon replied.

"Looks like we'll need to look at Indexes," Jasper sighed. "Perhaps your aunt knows something."

"I've already asked her," I replied. "All she knows is that the rift and the imps have been here a really long time; like, generations."

"This is going to be a chore," Alex sighed.

I sighed, leaning up against the bookcase I was in front of. "Yup. Story of our lives," I remarked sadly. "Do we still have that album with the family photos and images?" I asked.

"Yea," Alex replied. "It's in the journals section. Why?"

"There were a bunch of ghosts I didn't recognize at this 'meeting,'" I said, moving over to that section and looking for the large photo album. "I want to see if they're in the book."

I found what I was looking for and moved the book to the table. Abby joined me to look at the photos. Many of them were really old. Some were tin-types. Before that were sketches and small paintings. Each one had a name, a brief bio, and birth and death dates.

"Are all these people buried in that cemetery?" Abby asked, looking at some of the weirder photos.

"No," Alex explained. "Some are in the city cemetery, a few were burned, and some we don't know what happened to them."

"Here's Edmund," Kelly pointed to the handsome man on one page.

Edmund Thaddeus Royer.
Son of Hannibal and Germaine Royer.
18 April 1828 – 5 June 1878.

"He died young," Jasper said.

"He was 50!" Abby retorted. "That's pretty old!"

Jasper chuckled. "It is when you're only 13. As an adult, that's not that old."

I kept moving backwards. The images had moved to sketches. I identified three others from the ghosts I had seen in the cemetery. Finally, I stopped. I pointed at a picture in the book. Dark eyes peered out under long dark bangs. The face was unmistakable.

"Her!" Kelly said. "She's the one who told me about Fey."

"Faith Margaret Portworth," Alex read. "Hung for witchcraft. Daughter of Robere and Gwendolyne Portworth. 16 February 1596 – 12 October 1628."

"Witchcraft?" Abby exclaimed.

"To many people, The Gift seems like witchcraft. We can do a lot of things they can't. It makes people nervous and scared," I explained, still looking at the picture.

"You sound like you're casting spells and making potions!" Abby laughed. "That's ridiculous!"

Alex, Jasper, Brandon, and I just stared at Abby. Uncle Cliff had given Abby an overview of The Gift because she'd need to understand it if one of her children was born with it. It was clear, however, that many of the finer points of it missed their mark. Brandon turned and floated a bookmark from the desk to the book, placing it neatly on the page.

"We do," he said flatly to his sister's stunned expression.

"Faith. Faith. Faith," I murmured over and over. "Could she have been called 'Fey'?"

"On it!" Jasper remarked, heading to the Journals.

"I'll check from the bottom," Alex volunteered.

"What's such a big deal about fairies, anyway?" Abby asked, disgruntled.

"That's what we're trying to find out," I replied, closing the photo album. I handed it to Jasper to put it back. "Something about the fairies, the imps, and the Equinox coming up has the ghosts in an uproar, but what?"

"Dinner!" Aunt Eva's voice yelled down the stairs. All five of us groaned. The adults in this house had the worst timing!

I sighed. "We'll have to pick this up again later."

"After practice," Brandon muttered.

I chuckled at my cousin and patted his back. "Yup."

Practice was different tonight. Aunt Eva had the whole family out on the front lawn. Uncle Cliff had lit some lawn torches to keep the imps away.

"Ok," Aunt Eva explained with a grin. "We're going to go through a few exercises, then we're going to have a wizard's duel."

"A what?" Brandon asked.

Aunt Eva smiled. "You and Kelly are just about at the same point in your lessons."

"No, she's ahead of me," Brandon defended.

"Not by much," Aunt Eva comforted. "So, we're going to run through a few spells that you already know. Once I think they're coming along rather smoothly, you two are going to fling them at each other and defend yourselves."

"What about us?" Devin asked. "Why are we here?"

"You are going to be the judges," Aunt Eva explained. "You'll decide who did which spell better, who was sloppy, and who wins."

"Brandon," Lizzy said matter-of-factly.

"You have to watch them first!" Eddie pushed his sister.

"Hey!" she pushed back.

"Not now!" Uncle Cliff stopped them.

Aunt Eva brought out a target on a stand. "This is your target for practice," she said, placing it about ten feet away towards the yard. George came and settled in the field behind it. "You don't want to stay there!" Aunt Eva laughed.

"Why not?" George asked.

"Stray spells coming your way!"

"I'm moving!" George replied quickly. He hopped over towards the house alongside the others.

"A dragon," Abby muttered. "I still can't believe it." George just chuckled.

The rest of the family watched as Aunt Eva threw minor spells at the two students, having them raise a shield to protect themselves from the spell. At first, both of us got hit a lot. Luckily, no one sustained any major injuries. Once we got to the point she couldn't hit us anymore, we moved towards the target.

"OK, Brandon. Let's see your firebolt. Hit the target," Aunt Eva instructed.

Brandon looked at the target in the field. "It'll burn."

Aunt Eva chuckled. "It'll be fine. Fire away!"

Brandon concentrated a bit, then flung his hand towards the target. The bolt missed it. He threw another one. Another miss.

"Stop looking away from the target," Aunt Eva instructed.

"I am looking at the target," Brandon insisted.

"You're closing your eyes just before you let go of the cast," I pointed out. "Stop being afraid of what it's going to do. Watch your target. Like kicking a soccer ball."

Brandon watched the target. He threw another bolt at it, hitting it squarely in the middle. To everyone's amazement, the flame flickered out quickly, leaving no damage to the target.

"Magical target," Aunt Eva chuckled. Brandon threw three more, each one hitting somewhere on the target. "OK, Kelly. Your turn. Same one."

I hit the target first try. I threw three more, adding more power to the last one so it knocked over the target.

"Well done!" Eva praised us. She waved her hand and stood the target back up. "OK. Same procedure. Frost."

The practice continued until we had practiced an instant missile, an entanglement, and a push spell. Once Aunt Eva was satisfied, she removed the target, then moved us away from the group for safety. She placed a slight spell on each of us. It left me feeling tingly.

"That's to minimize any damage," she smiled.

"But you said we wouldn't get hurt," Brandon scowled.

"Never said that," Aunt Eva smiled at the boy, "But, of course, I know you two. Competition at its best. I just don't want either of you to get seriously injured. Now, back-to-back."

"Good luck," I said to Brandon as I turned my back to him.

"You, too?" Brandon questioned.

"Walk twenty paces," Aunt Eva instructed, backing up herself. The combatants walked out 20 paces each. "Now, when I say 'go,' turn and begin the battle. Think about your first spell and remember: you're cousins. You love each other."

Aunt Eva backed away another 10 feet and waited, letting the tension rise. "Go!" she called out.

I whirled around to get hit with a snowball right in the face. Brandon laughed. I whirled my hand towards him, tossing a firebolt. It exploded on Brandon's shield. A missile of energy came at me, exploding on my shield. Brandon tried the firebolt this time. I ran to the side, dodging the bolt, and threw an instant missile at Brandon. He countered it, sending a push spell at me. I resisted it.

In turn, I cast grease all over the ground around him. I followed that with a push spell. Brandon slipped and slid as he tried to resist the spell, eventually landing on his rump. He looked up angrily, cast a flaming sphere in front of me.

The sphere was so large it blocked my view of Brandon. I had to move around the five-foot burning entity to find my target. As I came around, a force of energy came at me, hitting me square in the chest. I doubled over, feeling incredibly weak.

Angry eyes looked at my cousin, lifting him up and up and up. Eventually, he was ten feet in the air. Brandon countered the spell, dissolving the force and cast a spell that would set him on the ground softly. His shield went up just as I unleashed a barrage of small fire balls.

Brandon cast something. He was murmuring while keeping his shield up. He cast a push spell at me. I flew through the air as the push spell knocked me over. I tumbled about three feet. Getting back on my feet, I cast an acidic arrow at him. It was more of a bolt, but the name was cool. It hit him square in his shield. Suddenly, I began wriggled from something tickling my ribs. I couldn't see what it was.

"Stop!" I commanded, but it continued. I tried wiggling away from whatever it was, but it stayed next to me. "Stop!" I laughed, all the while feeling unseen fingers tickling me mercilessly. "No!" I cried out, trying to fight the thing away. The more I moved, the more it came towards me. Eventually, I fell over in a fit of laughter, still trying to get away from the tickling.

"Halt!" Brandon called out.

The tickling stopped. I lay on the ground exhausted, dragging in huge gulps of air. Oddly, I was still giggling a little.

Brandon dissipated the spell. With a big grin, he ran over to me. He leaned over me with his hands on his knees.

"You okay?" he asked.

"Y... Y... Yea," I stuttered, trying to catch my breath. "That... that... that was cruel!"

"That was brilliant!" Aunt Eva smiled proudly. "An unseen servant. The perfect distraction for an enemy. In a dangerous circumstance, your enemy is more concerned with the invisible attacker, then you can get in a crippling blow. Nicely done, Brandon."

I hoisted myself out of the snow and patted Brandon on the shoulder. "Good job."

"Thanks," Brandon grinned. "I knew I couldn't beat you otherwise."

We walked back towards the group. Everyone clapped for us.

"That was awesome!" Devin cried out.

"So cool!" Abby agreed. His disbelieving eyes had turned to admiration.

"I've never seen it done like that," Alex grinned. "But he beat your butt!"

"Yea," I smiled at my cousin. "He did good."

"So, folks. Anything sloppy?" Aunt Eva asked.

"Greasy stuff on the snow," Lizzy wrinkled her nose. "It smells."

Aunt Eva chuckled.

"I saw a few stray bullets," Uncle Cliff mentioned. "They need to focus on their targets."

"I thought it was wonderful!" Mom smiled. "I haven't seen that since you and Dad went at it when you were 13."

"And he took it easy on me!" Aunt Eva laughed. "That's why I knew these two would be okay. They're at the same level of experience."

"Although, I did see a few spells that weren't on the menu," George mentioned.

"That's okay. They used their imagination." Aunt Eva looked over at the group. "Better spells?"

"Brandon did that push thingy good," Eddie chimed in.

"Yes, he did," Aunt Eva agreed.

"Actually," George said proudly. "They both did well. Spells were mostly under control. I didn't see too many misses. They remembered who they were fighting and kept damage counts to a minimum. Both offense and defense came off well. They're coming along nicely."

"Thank you, George," Aunt Eva smiled. "Ok, so who won?"

No one said a word. I burst out laughing. "Brandon won! I landed on the ground laughing my head off! If I'd been an enemy, he could have decapitated me!"

Brandon smiled up at me. I had never seen him so happy. I also saw a bit more confidence in him.

"Thanks," he muttered.

"Next time, though, I'll whip your butt!" I warned playfully.

"Bring it on!"

21 – I Made a New Friend

The day after, we said goodbye to Grandma, Uncle Cliff, Aunt Chrissy, and the cousins. The house suddenly seemed empty. Brandon, Alex, and I helped with laundry and clean up, putting everything back where it belonged. Rusty had taken to taking naps in my room on the blanket I left for him near the heat.

Alex and I started doing rounds with Jasper, looking for injured animals and throwing hay, suet, and other foods out for the wild animals. At one point, we looked up when George's shadow flew overhead. We stared in horror as a large deer hung from George's paws.

"What?" Jasper said, looking at them. "He's gotta eat, too!"

"Somehow, that's not what I thought about when I thought about Grandpa eating dinner," Alex said in a small voice.

"Me, either," I cleared the croak in my throat.

It was two days later when Brandon came up with a great idea.

"I was thinking about our imp problem," he said one afternoon.

"What about it?"

"Well, you know how we got some information from the ghosts?"

"Yea."

"What if we asked the imps what they know?"

Alex and I exchanged stunned glances, then looked at Brandon with admiration. Neither of us had ever thought of that.

"Why not?" Brandon asked. "If the ghosts can tell us things, and the imps have been here that long, one of them has to speak English!"

Brandon and I pulled on three layers of clothes and grabbed the keys to the snowmobile. Aunt Eva pulled on just as many and took the other snow mobile keys. She wasn't about the let us attempt this alone. George was already waiting for us near the woods. What was he, a mind reader?

"Are you absolutely certain you want to try this?" George replied. "I don't think it's safe."

"We're not going into the woods, just to the edge. The imps won't come out past the shadows during the day," I explained.

"And between the two of us, we can keep a shield up enough that they can't get to us," Brandon added.

"I don't like it," George said. He looked at Aunt Eva. "Talk some sense into these kids, will ya?"

"They actually talked sense into me, George," Aunt Eva laughed. "They're right. In order to fix this, we need answers, and the ghosts aren't helping."

"We did find out who the girl was that actually caused the problem," Brandon told Aunt Eva. "She's in the history book. Her name is Faith Porter. It just doesn't say what she did or when."

"The dates were really old," I replied, gathering courage. "She was nearly back to the start of the timeline."

My eyes never left the woods. I could feel hundreds of eyes on us. "Ready, Brandon?"

"Ready," he replied, much braver than he felt.

"What is the plan?" Aunt Eva asked.

I quickly explained the plan to Aunt Eva and George. "Keep an eye on us. If we look like we're falling under a spell or if we walk into the woods, come get us out." I remembered all too well my last visit to the imps.

Brandon and I removed the finger covers on our fingertip gloves. We linked hands so that our fingers could touch each other and walked over to the edge of the woods. We stepped between two trees and stopped. On guard, we peered into the woods. I expected the imps to jump on us, but instead, they seemed to stay away.

"Come talk to us," Brandon cried out. "We want to talk to you!"

No reply.

"We want to help," I called out.

Nothing.

I let out a sigh. "All right. If you want to stay here like you are, then we'll leave!" I turned when a dozen imps surrounded us almost immediately. Each of them screeching at us in some strange language. Their eyes were wild, their claws scraping the air towards me, and their wings flapping fast.

"You hit the mark," Brandon mumbled with a smirk. "Now, how do we understand them?"

"Keep the shield up," I whispered to Brandon. "Whoa! Whoa!" I motioned with my free hand. "We can't understand a word you're saying! You guys can speak our language. You did it before. I need one of you to speak with me."

A large imp came forward. She wasn't exactly an imp, more of a person, but she was pretty, for an imp. She pointed to Brandon.

"You'll speak to him?" I asked. The imp shook her head. I scowled thoughtfully. The imp made a motion of one hand going through the other's fingers. "You'll speak through him?" I questioned warily. The imp nodded. "Are you going to hurt him?" No. "Are you going to possess him?" No.

"Let's try it," Brandon replied. "George has our back if something happens."

"It's going to mean dropping the shield," I whispered.

"Yea, I know. Just remember, we don't go any further."

I nodded to the imp. She flew forward and sat on Brandon's shoulder as the shield dropped. She giggled as she nuzzled up to him.

"Ewww!" Brandon scowled.

"Forgive him," I replied to the imp with a small smile on my lips. "He's still quite young."

"I know." The voice that came from Brandon was a slight bit higher than Brandon's own voice. It was definitely feminine. "I am Intrid."

"A pleasure to meet you, Intrid," I replied with a polite nod. "I'm Kelly."

"I know. We have been watching you for a long time. You are strong enough to help us."

"Help you how?" I asked.

"Repair the door."

"Repair the door? Has the rift always been there?"

"No."

"How did the rift open?"

"We aren't sure how it opened. There was a storm one day. Great rumblings and lightning. It was a magic storm. The lightning struck the door, and the rift opened. It sucked us into this world and brought others into ours."

"How long did it take?"

"Seconds," Intrid replied. "Then the door closed, but not completely. It is as if something is stuck."

"How long ago did this happen?"

"Many, many years ago."

"About 500 years ago?"

"No, not that long. 300 maybe? We can't tell time here."

"Was anyone near the rift when it happened?"

"Yes. A young lady was near the woods. She was doing something with a book."

"Do you recall the words she said?"

"No. She was looking surprised when we came through."

"Did you see the title of the book?"

"No. Once she realized something was wrong, she screeched and ran."

I thought for a moment. "Was there anyone else here besides the girl?"

Some excitement went on with the other imps. They began arguing again.

"Yes," Intrid replied. "They say another human went into our world when the door opened. I, personally, don't recall."

"How many others are in the area that can help?"

Intrid smirked. "There are five others like you, not counting Eva. None are strong enough to complete this task, but you and Brandon are."

I nodded. "Do you have any other information we can use to help you with the rift?"

"I've told you all I know. You must help us go home."

"I'll do my best," I promised. "I can't guarantee it, but I'll do my best."

"Fair enough."

Intrid flitted away, leaving Brandon to himself again. The imps followed her. I held Brandon up as he swayed, his head dizzy from the interaction.

"You okay?" Concern laced my voice.

"Yea. I was just a little dizzy when she let me go," he smiled up at her. "I'm alright now."

We returned to George and Aunt Eva. "Mission accomplished." We relayed the information Intrid gave us. Aunt Eva mulled the information over.

"This doesn't look like it will give us any more information than we already have." I sagged.

"Actually, it does," Brandon replied.

"What?" I asked.

"Could Faith have been trying a transport spell?" he asked.

"You mean like a teleport thing?" Aunt Eva asked.

"Yea. Was she trying to teleport her friend from the woods to the house and got caught in the equinox?"

My eyes widened. I suddenly remembered the spell Brandon was talking about. It clearly had a warning on it about circumstances not to use it under.

"Get on," I urged, hopping onto the snowmobile.

"Where are you going?" Aunt Eva asked.

"To the cemetery!" I yelled over the motor. I took off with Brandon holding tight around my waist.

The activity in the cemetery had quelled a bit, but it was still active. I marched into the gate to the same reaction as before. Everything stopped.

"Where's Faith?" I asked them. They all turned to a ghost sitting on a tombstone, weeping. I walked over to her. "Faith, were you trying to do the Transpondent spell that night?"

The ghost's face snapped up to me, surprised.

"You were, weren't you?" I replied with understanding. "It went wrong, didn't it?" The ghost nodded. "Instead of sending whomever was with you where you wanted, it opened the rift." Again, the ghost nodded. "Who was with you?"

The ghost looked down.

"Was it a brother or sister?" She shook her head. "One of your parents?" Again, she shook her head. "A friend?" No. I thought for a moment. "Was it your boyfriend?" Affirmative. Oh, this would not work out well at all. "OK. I'll see what I can do."

I returned to the gate. As I opened it, the ghosts started bickering again. "Oh, for Pete's sake! Go take a rest!" I yelled at them. The ghosts simply stared at me in surprise.

"Did you get the answer?" Brandon asked.

"Yep. We've got work to do."

It was New Year's Eve. Brandon, Jasper, Alex, and I huddled over a spell book in the library.

"This is a very complicated spell," I said, looking it over. "It's no wonder Faith had trouble with it. We're going to need Aunt Eva to help with this one."

"I'll go get her," Brandon jumped up and disappeared upstairs. The rest of us made notes of the ingredients we were going to need. Aunt Eva was going to need to put in an order.

Aunt Eva looked over the spell. Her brows rose as she read the intricate instructions. She let out a low whistle.

"What have you figured out?" she asked us, sitting down at the table.

"Well, you remember you said that certain circumstances can lend energy to the spells?" I asked.

"Yes. Positions of the sun, moon, stars, all can aid or hinder your spells. What about it?"

"We figured Faith was trying to send her boyfriend somewhere," Alex replied. "Probably to show off or something."

"But she was doing it during an Equinox," Brandon chimed in. "It probably would make it look mysterious or something. The energy from the equinox became too powerful for her, turned into lightning, struck the ground, and opened the rift."

"The vortex that caused sucked her boyfriend into the rift with the fairies, and tossed the imps out here." Jasper finished.

"The issues we're running into are (1) how to repeat the spell just as she did, and (2) what is the name of her boyfriend," I added.

"She won't tell you?"

"She's not telling me anything! I think she's just so racked up with guilt and shame that she won't do anything to help the situation."

Aunt Eva sighed. "You'll need to see if we have a journal from her. She'll have mentioned a boyfriend in there somewhere. As for repeating the spell exactly as she did, that's going to be impossible."

"Wait a minute! Maybe not!" Alex's eyes went wide.

"Huh?" Brandon and I snapped up.

"Abby!" Alex said, pointing at me. "Abby was having a nightmare. She was the girl, and there was a boy. The lightning hit the ground. The boy was gone, and she screamed, waking up. Remember?"

I palmed my forehead. "I never put two and two together! Someone was giving Abby the answer!"

"Faith!" Brandon cried excitedly.

"No, it wouldn't be the ghosts," Aunt Eva said. "They're suspended in time and space. They can't affect any other area but the cemetery. But if Abby was dreaming about the event, someone somewhere is sending you the answer. Best get your cousin on the phone."

"But not right now," Jasper grinned, looking at his watch. "It's quarter to 12."

Giddily, we all ran upstairs to watch the countdown of the new year on television. After wishing everyone a happy new year, Jasper lit off some fireworks in the yard. By one, everyone wandered to bed.

22 – The Traitor with the Gift

With the new year came new classes for the second semester. Most of our schedules were the same, but Alex and I had a new class: Photography I. Our art class finished just before the winter break, and now this class started. On the first day, Alex and I sat in the back of the classroom, waiting for the teacher to start class. I was reading a book from the library, trying to understand how to do a spell.

"Hey," Alex whispered next to me. "How many others did Intrid say there were in the area?"

"Huh? Oh, five, not counting Aunt Eva or us," I whispered back.

"I think one just walked in the room," Alex nodded towards the door.

I snapped up to see a tall young man with jet black hair combed to the side, a pasty complexion, and sharp blue eyes standing by the first desk talking to the red-haired guy sitting there. He had a squared jaw, and his shoulders were broad—football player broad. He glanced around the room, taking in the students, when he met eyes with me. I immediately put my head down to break the connection.

"Could be," I murmured. "Aunt Eva didn't say who they were."

"You're about to find out," Alex whispered.

"Huh?"

"He's coming this way."

With my heart in my throat, I looked up over the table as the young man in question slid into the chair opposite me. I swallowed hard, pulling the book I was reading up to my chest. I hated meeting new people. He glanced at both of us with a grin.

"So, we finally get to meet," he began. "I'm Cal Venzana."

"Alex," Alex introduced timidly, with a small grin.

I met Cal's expectant gaze. "Kelly," I replied softer than Alex. Man, this guy was cute!

"Hey, man!" another young man sat next to Cal. "She could pass for your sister!" This young man wasn't as tall or buff as Cal was, but he wasn't skinny, either. His mousy brown hair was in a shag down to his shoulders. His brown eyes sparkled as he glanced over at Alex. His face was oval with a narrow jaw. I took this opportunity to close my book and slip it into my backpack.

"If I had a sister," Cal came back quickly. "Girls, this is Max Jesser. Max, this is Alex and Kelly."

"It's a pleasure, ladies," Max smiled widely with a flirtatious voice. "What are we doing?"

The teacher cleared his throat loudly to get everyone's attention. "If you're done flirting, Mr. Jesser," he announced, "I'd like to get started?"

Max blushed brightly. "Um, sure, Mr. Cowan. Go right ahead."

"Thank you."

It was pretty obvious that Max knew our teacher fairly well.

"Good afternoon, ladies and gentlemen. I'm Mr. Cowan, and this is Photography I. If you're looking for an easy grade, this is not your class. If you are an over-achiever, this is not your class. You will need a digital

Single Lens Reflex camera with a flash, built in or added, to complete the assignments. I recommend a 35-millimeter lens, but a 50 or 75 will also do. It will simply make the actual taking of the images a little harder. You will need a computer!" Most of the kids laughed. "I know. Silly to say in this day and age, however, you will need a computer with internet access. You will have a disc in the back of your book to install the software from. Those of you who don't have a DVD or CD player on your computer, please see me. I have SD cards with the software as well. You will display your assignments using the Flickr website. We'll be going over how to access that at a later date.

"That being said, if I have scared you or you feel this isn't your class, you are free to leave and report to counseling to reassign your class."

Mr. Cowen waited. I watched three people gather their things and leave the classroom. Mr. Cowen nodded to each good-naturedly. When the last person left, he returned to the class.

"There's always a few who get frightened away. Too bad. You'll learn a lot in this class," he shook his head sadly. "Alright. Mr. Brady," he called a blonde-haired student up close to him. "Please pass these out on that side of the classroom?" He handed the student a stack of thin books. He took the other stack and began walking through the classroom, handing out books. It didn't take long. There were only eighteen of us left. Alex and I instantly began flipping through the book itself when we received ours.

"Let's see," Mr. Cowen began looking around the classroom. "Amanda, why don't you move to this table here," he motioned. "John, over there, please." He looked like he was trying to balance out the class. He wandered over to our table and peered at the two gentlemen, then at us. "Max, can I trust you to behave yourself if I leave you at this table?"

Max looked sheepish. "Well, gee, I dunno!" Max teased the teacher.

Cal's fist nearly knocked his friend off his seat as it collided with his shoulder. Max looked back angrily. I didn't miss the message. Cal's eyes went sideways to motion towards me and Alex. Max must have gotten the message.

"Yes, sir," Max replied. "I'll be good."

"If you're not, I'm moving you!" Mr. Cowen warned, "And that's a promise, not a threat."

Max chuckled. "Yes, sir."

"Alright, folks. The people at your table will be your team. You'll have individual assignments and team assignments. Be sure to share your phone number with each other. You're gonna need it!

"Let's dive right in. Open to Chapter 1."

The rest of the class was going over the different parts of the camera, how to set the speed and aperture, and how to determine what is a good picture.

"Your assignment for tonight is to get your hands on your camera, go through it with this book, identify all the parts, and take a few photos. Nothing big. Point and click. Whatever you feel like. Most cameras have an auto function that will automatically focus on the subject. You can use that for this assignment. Just get the feel for the camera. Read through Chapter 1 and answer the questions at the end of the chapter."

The bell rang just as he finished up.

"See you tomorrow!" Mr. Cowen called above the din of students gathering their things and heading out the door.

"Where do you go next?" Cal asked.

I looked up nervously. "French," I replied softly. "Why?"

"I'll walk you. I have to go that way for math."

"That's ok. Alex and I know the way," I replied. I glanced at Alex, who rolled her eyes, then cocked her head to the side as she looked at me. Cal didn't get the message, anyway. He and Max joined us walking down the hall.

"So, word is you're new in the area," Cal mentioned.

"Not really," Kelly began. "I've been here since June."

"Okay. Kinda new," Cal grinned. "Where ya from?"

"Illinois. You?"

"Born and raised here," Cal laughed. "Never get to go anywhere. I'm not staying here, though. I can't wait to get out of this ho-dunk town for the city."

"You graduating soon?"

"Next year," Cal said. "I'm trying to decide which college I want to attend."

"I suppose that depends on what you want to study." Would he go away already? He was making me nervous.

"Yea. Where do you live? I've never seen you around town."

"Up the mountain," I tried to dodge the question. "I live with my aunt."

Cal stopped in the middle of the hallway. "Wait. You live with Eva?"

"You know my aunt?" I squinted, trying to determine Cal's motives.

"I've known Eva all my life. She and my mother are good friends." Cal looked at Max a moment, then shook his head as if he was going to say something and decided not to. "That's pretty cool! Mom said Eva was getting company for the summer, but she didn't mention it was you."

"No big deal. Just me." I paused and glanced at Alex. "And Alex."

"And Brandon," Alex added.

"And Jasper," I grinning as the list was getting longer.

"And your mom," Alex noted.

"Yup. That's the group." Cal and Max laughed at the way we presented it.

"You're lucky," Cal began down the hall again. "It's just me, my mom, and my dad. My house is boring!"

"I'll attest to that!" Max interjected. "Unless I'm there. Then the fun begins!"

"Get real, dork!" Cal teased his friend. "When you're there, trouble begins!" Max just laughed off the insult.

We turned towards our classroom. The guys waved and wished us a good night.

"I think he's into you," Alex smiled.

"What? No way!" I retorted. "I'm just trying to figure out what he really wants."

"Not everyone has a secret agenda!" Alex chastised me.

I rolled my eyes. "Yea. Sure."

We slid into our seats and watched as Mr. Broward wrote conjugated irregular verbs on the blackboard. Alex leaned over and whispered, "You don't suppose he's related, do you?" She glanced over at our teacher.

I shrugged. "Anything's possible."

I brought Cal up at dinner that night. "Why didn't you tell me there were other teens with the Gift?" I asked Aunt Eva.

"Huh?" Aunt Eva looked up suddenly.

"There's a guy in my photography class, Cal something, that says his mom and you are friends."

"Cal Venzano's in your class?" Aunt Eva asked brightly. "I suppose that shouldn't surprise me. Yes, Cal is my friend Yvette's son. Nice young man. I work with him from time to time. Why?"

I shrugged. "Is he trustworthy?"

"I seem to think so. Why?" Aunt Eva put her fork down. "Did he say something wrong today?"

"No, but he came and sat at our table without even knowing us."

Aunt Eva chuckled. "Kelly, not everyone has an ulterior motive."

"That's what I said!" Alex exclaimed.

"Cal has been known as The Greeter since he was 10. He'll walk up to anyone he doesn't know and introduce himself."

"That's exactly what he did," Alex smirked.

"Who are the others?" I asked.

"Is Teddy one?" Brandon asked.

"Teddy?"

"Yea. He's in the grade above me, but we have gym together. He looks so much like me; people think we're brothers."

"Oh, yeah. Theodore. He's going by Teddy now?" Aunt Eva grinned. "Yes. Teddy is one. He hasn't started showing signs yet." She turned back toward me. "There's also Kaylyn

Welsh. She'll be a year ahead of you, but I'm pretty sure she's being homeschooled."

"She has the gift, too?" Brandon asked.

"Yes," Aunt Eva replied, "But she has more intelligence and less ability. You two have both. Cal has a strong area, but the rest are a little weaker. Most Gifters are like that. To find Gifters like you two, who can do it all, is really rare."

"But you do it all," Alex mentioned.

"Not really. I'm good at the magic, but not at the alchemy."

"Alchemy?" Brandon asked.

"Potion making," I smirked. "In other words, she can cook up a five-course meal but can't make a simple healing potion."

The rest of the table laughed. "Nobody's perfect," Mom teased.

Aunt Eva shrugged as she laughed. "So, back to Cal. What about him has you worried?"

"He just kinda came over and started talking to us," I said nervously. "Wanted to know where we lived, and how long we'd been here."

"You!" Alex pointed out. "He wanted to know how long *you'd* been here. I could have been a spot on the wall!"

"Could not!"

Aunt Eva smirked and looked at my mother with raised eyebrows. "Really?"

"I think he thinks Kelly's cute," Alex announced.

"Ewww!" Brandon cried.

"He does not!" I countered.

"We'll see. He's safe, at any rate; but don't go discussing what goes on here—especially the imp issue."

"Heck, no!" I sounded horrified.

Alex looked up from her homework thoughtfully. "Didn't you say Intrid said there were five other people in the area that had the Gift?"

"Yes."

"You have Mr. Broward, Cal, the boy Brandon mentioned..."

"Teddy," Brandon remarked from across the table.

Alex nodded. "and that homeschooled girl. That's 4. If each of them, less Mr. Broward - although he still could - had at least 1 parent with the Gift, that would make 8. Intrid said 5."

"Well," I thought about it a moment. "I'm going on the assumption that the imps only tried five, besides us. It's possible Mr. Broward is here by himself. He's old, so his parents may live somewhere else; and we're dealing with genetics, so I guess it's possible for the Gift to skip a generation."

"That would still make six. Who are the other ones?" Alex questioned.

"Maybe Intrid meant that they only talked to five. I got the impression there were several of us in the area," Brandon replied.

"And some may not be trustworthy," I added.

Alex sagged. "How do we know?" she asked worriedly.

"It's easy," Brandon replied. "If they're friends with Aunt Eva, then they must be okay. If she's warning people, like Mr. Broward, then they're not."

I glanced at my cousin with a smirk. "You know, for a 10-year-old, you're pretty intuitive."

Brandon scowled. "Is that a good thing?"

Alex and I laughed. "Yes, Brandon," Alex comforted the boy. "That's a very good thing. Wish I was as good."

"You've got an excuse," I teased my friend.

"Really?" Alex didn't seem sure.

"You've been trapped in a mirror for more than a hundred years," Brandon remarked as he went back to his homework.

Jasper poked his head in the library about an hour later. "Rounds," he commented.

"Finally!" Alex slammed her book shut. "I'm sick of algebra problems!"

I laughed. "Yea. I know what you mean. Mrs. Anderson must think that math is the only high school subject."

"Hey, let's take the camera!" Alex brightened. "Maybe we can get some shots for class."

"It's getting dark," Jasper warned. "It'll be tough getting some good shots."

"Did the sun go down yet?" I asked.

"Not yet. It's heading for the horizon."

"Great!" I jumped up, ran up to the study, and grasped the camera Aunt Eva said we could use for class. Quickly, I darted up to the attic and opened the door to the west-side balcony. The attic housed four other rooms: Jasper's, two guest rooms, and a storage room. For an attic, it was incredibly warm and inviting instead of dusty and scary.

I aimed the camera towards the setting sun. I tried a few different settings and caught a beautiful sunset. Happily, I closed the door, ran down the stairs, and met everyone in the mudroom bundling up.

"Where'd you go?" Alex scowled.

"To the attic. See?" I showed Alex the pictures I took.

"That's so cool!" Brandon cried out. "Look at the aura around the sun."

"Cool blue giving way to pink, orange, and purple," Jasper mentioned. "Yup. Another bitter day tomorrow."

"You going into meteorology now?" Alex teased him.

"Naw," Jasper blushed. "My grandfather was really into it and very good at it. He taught me everything I know about it."

We started out to the snowmobiles.

"Can I ask a sensitive question?" I looked at Jasper.

"You can ask," Jasper replied, pulling out the keys. He tossed one to me. "Doesn't mean I'll answer."

"What happened that you had to leave home and come live with Aunt Eva?"

Jasper paused at the side of the snowmobile. He wet his lips nervously. Even Alex seemed uncomfortable. It was clear the girl knew the answer.

"Family problems," Jasper replied lowly.

"Kinda figured that one," I replied softly.

Jasper took a deep breath. "My father is an alcoholic. He beat up my mother and me on a fairly regular basis. I fought back a few years ago. Nearly knocked him through the living room wall. The battle was pretty fierce. He threw me out of the house that night with nothing but the clothes on my back. I went straight to the police. With the bruises

on me, and then on my mother when they got there, my
father got arrested. He's serving eight years in prison for
several counts."

"But that would leave you and your mother,"
Brandon scowled. "Couldn't you live with her?"

Jasper turned his head away, but not before I caught
the pained expression on his face. He didn't reply after that.

"Jasper's mother lives in the convalescent home in
Hearts Bluff," Alex murmured. "The... damage was
extensive." A catch in her voice told me that Alex was near
tears.

"Oh, wow!" I blew out. "Jasper, I'm so sorry! I didn't
know!"

Jasper put a hand on my shoulder. "It's ok. You
probably should have known by now. That's where I go on
Wednesdays and Sundays. I go visit my mother. She's really
weak, but she's alive. I don't associate with my father."

"Can't blame you there," Brandon agreed.

"Come on," Jasper tried to brighten a bit. "The light
should be just right for Alex to capture the barn just after
sunset."

Sure enough, the lighting was perfect. The red and
white barn had a rangy glow bouncing off it. Alex had just
enough time to catch it on the camera before the sun set
completely. She seemed pretty pleased with the shot. Our
entire group oohed and aahed over it.

"That looks better than my sunset!" I complemented.
Alex just blushed.

"Alright. Let's get some work done before it gets too
cold," Jasper suggested. Brandon was already shivering.
"Kel, why don't you and Brandon take the southern end? I'll

take Alex to the northern end. We'll meet back in the middle."

"Got it!" I nodded and put the camera in the storage compartment.

"Why can't I go with Jasper?" Brandon grumbled.

"Cause," I said, starting the motor. As soon as Brandon grasped my waist, I darted across the lane towards the southern end of the property. We had a pretty good search pattern set up, so she started towards the beginning.

"Cause why?" Brandon scowled when the engine was soft enough to talk again.

"'Cause I think he wanted some alone time with Alex," I picked up the conversation.

"Huh?" Brandon didn't understand the statement.

"Never mind," I chuckled. "You'll understand in about three years. Let's see if we can find anything. I'd hate for injured animals to freeze to death."

I took the route slowly as we scouted the area for injured or weakened animals. It was harder to see in the dark, so Brandon pulled out a high-powered flashlight to peer into the trees and hills. I turned to go parallel with the woods, seeing menacing shadows inside that I knew enough to stay away from. The imps had left us alone since our talk with Intrid. This was something much more menacing.

"What's that?" Brandon pointed north, near the woods.

A shadow was outside the woods. There was a commotion going on as the bipedal creature was swinging and twisting, as if trying to fight something off.

"I don't know," I scowled, "But let's find out!"

I gunned the engine and took off over the snow. The snowmobile was flying up a little on some of the minor hills made by the snow. The wind in my face was hurting my cheeks. As we got closer, the flashlight caught sight of a person being attacked by the imps. He was trying to throw some magic spell, but the imps were overpowering him.

"Slide up, Brandon," I yelled. I skidded the snowmobile up near the man. One imp tried to attack me. I flicked it off with a minor spell, then muttered an incantation. I waved my hand to the side. A strong wind emanated, blowing the imps back towards the trees and knocking the person over.

"Get on!" I ordered. "Hurry!"

The person wasted no time. He quickly got up and jumped behind Brandon. I turned the snowmobile towards home and went as fast as I safely could to get away from the imps. Pulling around back, I turned off the engine. The stranger got off the mobile, still trying to catch his breath. Brandon hopped off after him. I turned to see who was on our property. My face hardened as Cal's face came back from the parka.

"Cal?" I asked with a scowl.

"Hi, Kel," he said sheepishly.

High-pitched chatter reached my ears before the imps came into view.

"Into the house! Fast!" Brandon pushed the guy.

Cal didn't need to be told twice. He raced for the back door with Brandon hot on his heels.

"Brandon!" I called. The boy turned to look at me. "I need you!"

Brandon sighed and came back as the imps came around the house. I erected a barrier that stopped them. They pounded on the invisible force field.

"Where is Intrid?" I asked. The imps stopped and looked at me. "I want to speak with Intrid!" I demanded. It took nearly four or five minutes before the imp showed up in front of me.

"May I speak with you?" I asked the imp politely. The imp turned towards Brandon.

Brandon sighed and nodded. Once again, I let down the shield, and the imp settled on Brandon's shoulder.

"Good evening, Kelly; Brandon. How may I help you?" Intrid began.

"The man the others attacked by the woods," I began. "What was he doing?"

Intrid conferred with other imps. They all began chattering at once. Finally, she put up her hand. "The others found him near the portal," she reported. "A shadow was next to him. He was pressing something against the portal. They drove him off."

I nodded. "Thank you. Ask them to maintain vigilance. I fear someone is going to try to destroy the portal. We can't let that happen."

"Agreed," Intrid nodded and flew off. The imps followed her.

I waited until Brandon's dizziness subsided. We went into the house to find Aunt Eva and Cal sitting at the table chatting amicably. I took off my coat, then stormed into the kitchen.

"What were you doing near our woods?" I demanded angrily.

"Huh?" Cal started.

"Kelly!" Aunt Eva chastised, obviously disturbed by this outburst.

"N... Nothin!" Cal denied.

Mom came in from the family room. "What's all the noise about?"

"Not now, Mom!" I snapped back and returned to Cal. "You were in our woods. The bugs attacked you, and I saved your butt!" I argued back at him. "What were you doing?"

"You were near the woods, Cal?" Aunt Eva questioned worriedly.

"Yea, thanks for that," Cal replied sheepishly towards me.

"What. Were. You. Doing?" I pressured, leaning on the table and towards him. My eyes were burning, I knew.

Cal turned to Aunt Eva. "Is this the same timid girl I have photography with?" he asked. "Couldn't hardly get three words from her this afternoon."

"Answer the question, Cal," Aunt Eva nodded towards me.

"Um, well, nothing really. Trying to get photographs for class."

"Where's your camera?" Brandon asked.

"I must have dropped it in the woods," the boy feigned.

I looked at Brandon. He nodded and pulled his coat and boots back on.

"Where are you going?" Aunt Eva questioned.

"To check out his claim," Brandon replied, "with company, of course. I think he's lying."

Aunt Eva looked at Cal. "Calvin Thomas Venzana, I want the truth and the whole truth! Don't make me drag it out of you."

Calvin looked terrified. He took a deep breath and bowed his head. "I was looking at the rift. I thought it would be cool getting that glow coming out of the rocks for the photography class."

"Who was with you?" I asked.

Cal startled. "What? No one was with me."

"Hey, Brandon," I called. "Come'ere."

"Yea? What?" Brandon asked, confused, but moved to my side.

I held out my hand, palm up, and looked pointedly at my cousin. Brandon grinned and took my hand.

"Kel-ly," Aunt Eva warned.

I muttered a few words, reached out with my free hand, and touched Cal's forehead with my finger. The boy instantly went stiff as a board. His eyes were vacant as he stared straight ahead. Aunt Eva's hand went to her mouth.

"Kelly, where'd you learn that?"

"In a book in the library. I'm just not strong enough to do it alone yet." I turned towards Cal. "Cal, why were you in our woods? Why were you near the rift?"

"Imps," came Cal's monotone voice. "Must destroy. I went to inspect the rift. How deep. How wide. How strong."

"Who wants to know about the rift? Who wants it destroyed?" My voice was getting harder.

"Him."

"Him who? Give me a name!"

"Broward." The name stunned Aunt Eva, but it only confirmed what I had been suspecting all along. "He believes the imps are going to take over. Destroy the rift, destroy the imps. Says imps are coming through."

"Really!" Aunt Eva sounded exasperated.

"Invasion Conspiracy," Brandon frowned.

"Who else was with you?" I continued the interrogation.

"No one was with me. I was alone. Better to get into the woods unnoticed."

"Intrid said there was a shadow with him," I said to Aunt Eva.

"Cal, did Mr. Broward give you anything? A charm, a stone, something small?"

"Yes." Cal's voice was soft.

"What did he give you?" I questioned.

"A piece of star."

"A rock?" Brandon asked.

"May I have it?" Aunt Eva held out her hand. Cal's hand reached into the breast pocket of his shirt mechanically and pulled out a flat, broken triangle. It looked like the piece of a Christmas ornament. It was glittery and about two inches long. Aunt Eva looked it over.

"What's it do?" I looked at the piece in Aunt Eva's hand curiously.

"It's a channel," Aunt Eva explained. "It allows a shadow of Rolf to join the holder no matter where he or she is. He's not really here, but those with the insight can see the shadow."

"That's what Intrid said. She said there was a shadow with him, and they put something up against the rift."

"Could it be his camera?" Brandon asked. "I mean, he might be telling the truth about taking pictures of the rift."

"What could he learn from that?" I questioned.

"Depends on what comes out in the image," Aunt Eva replied. "Finish this, then we'll send Brandon out with George to look for the camera."

I turned back to Cal. "You are to tell Broward that you found the rift, but it was dead. There is no light coming from the rift. You don't know anything more. If he asks you to come out here again, tell him to do his own dirty work! Understood?"

"Rift is dead. No light. Nothing more. Do your own dirty work." Cal repeated the instructions in a dead tone.

"Where's his car?" Brandon scowled.

"How did you get here?" I asked the boy.

"Left car by road, in the culvet."

"Explains why we didn't see it," I remarked.

"Culvet?" Brandon asked.

"It's a tiny cul-de-sac or circle along a street that is only big enough for a single car and hidden by bushes or trees. In our case, trees," I explained. I touched Cal's head again, then dropped Brandon's hand. "Camera."

"Got it!" Brandon ran for the door and slammed it behind him. I could hear him yelling for George.

Cal came to holding his head. "Oh, wow!" he muttered. "What did you hit me with?"

"You don't want to know," I glared with my arms crossed. "Just know you don't want to mess with me."

Cal shook his head. "Then I guess you don't want to go to the winter dance with me?"

"No," I answered without hesitating. "I don't date traitors."

"What?" Cal asked, confused.

"Aunt Eva, you got this?" I asked, irritated. "I need to finish my run."

"I've got it," Aunt Eva nodded. "You go ahead." She looked at the confused boy in front of her. "Cal, I'm extremely disappointed."

I returned about an hour later with Jasper and Alex. Cal was gone. My mother looked up at us when we came in. She was just putting dishes away.

"Where's Cal?" I asked softly.

"He went home," Mom replied just as softly. "You really rattled him."

"Good! He deserved it."

"Where's Aunt Eva and Brandon?" Alex asked.

"Eva's in her study. Brandon said something about looking up something in the library." Mom shook her head. "That boy studies more than anyone else I know. Most boys his age would rather play video games."

I smirked as I stared off into space. It was only now I was realizing how different we were because of the Gift; I mean, how many kids our age go looking up history and magic? Nodding, I went towards the study. I could hear my mother behind me.

"Any new occupants?"

"Nope. Was a clean run," Jasper replied. "Actually, I'm glad. I suspect anything..." His voice died away as I knocked on the door.

"Come in."

Aunt Eva was staring at the star piece on her desk when I entered. She had a concerned look on her face. She glanced up and smiled.

"What happened?" I asked.

"Cal left after Brandon got back. He was telling the truth about the camera. Brandon found it about 20 feet from the rift. Oddly, the imps left him alone this trip."

"'Cause they know we're trying to help."

"Possibly. I checked the images. The only thing showing up in the image is green light. Absolutely nothing else. I deleted the images."

I nodded. "Odd, considering green is not one of the colors coming from the rift. So, what's got you so worried about the star piece?"

Aunt Eva looked down. "The type of magic used to create it is very dark. To use it, the person needs to put part of their soul into the spell. Kind of like losing a piece of your heart when someone or something you love dies." I nodded. I'd heard Mom use that term. "My concern is that it's a star piece."

"So?"

"How many points are on a star?"

"Humans typically use five, but it could be four or six." I glanced at the broken piece of the star. "Wait! Are you thinking there's four more of those?"

Aunt Eva chuckled sadly. "You catch on quick, lady! Yes, I think there could possibly be up to four more; based on the angles of this one. My concern isn't for the channels. It's for Rolf."

"Why? He's trying to destroy what we're trying to save."

Aunt Eva smiled sadly. "Rolf wasn't always like this. He's actually a very nice, kind man. He used to have a heart of gold."

"You liked him, didn't you?" It was written all over my aunt's whimsical face.

Aunt Eva laughed. "Not like that. The only man I really loved is long gone."

"Oh." I wanted to ask more, but now wasn't the time. "So, what happened to Mr. Broward?"

"I'm not sure. I know he met with the Magistrate, and shortly after that, his personality started to change. Almost a split personality; like it was him and someone else in his body."

"Like Tessa?"

"Yes. It's a common effect of meeting someone with that much power." Aunt Eva shook her head. "Our friendship thinned a lot after that. It was like talking to Dr. Jekyll and Mr. Hyde."

I swallowed. "I'm sorry." It was all I could say. "So, what do we do now?" "Now, young lady, you will not try spells you haven't been tutored in. If you want to learn a spell, ask me!" Aunt Eva became firm. "The one you pulled on Cal could have turned deadly very quickly."

"But it looks so simple in the book. The instructions are really well written."

"But as you said, you're not strong enough to do it on your own. For homework, I want you to research the dangers associated with that spell. You'll find it in the back of the book you learned it from."

I sagged. "Yes, ma'am."

"Really, Kelly. I'm very pleased with your progress and your powers, but you have to understand the dangers that go with it. Some results can be reversed, but some can't. For every spell you want to learn, there are possible repercussions. Check with me first!"

"Then why can we look through the spell books?" I asked. "I mean, I thought we're supposed to learn this stuff."

"You are!" Aunt Eva chuckled. "I was the same way you are. Those spells are awesome! There are so many things that we can do! But think about the transportation spell that Faith used. It was only supposed to move a person from one area to another, not send him to another plane of existence."

With a stunned expression, I sat back a moment. Wow! I hadn't thought of that. The circumstances poor Faith used the spell in completely changed it. I nodded, finally understanding what my aunt was getting at.

"Ok. I'll make a list!" I smirked.

Aunt Eva chuckled. "Have you searched for Faith's spell?"

"Yes. We've narrowed it down to three. We just need the hint which one it was."

"Good. Keep looking."

"I know, I know. We're running out of time!" I got up chuckling and headed for the door. I stopped and looked at the floor for a while before I turned back. "Aunt Eva?"

"Yes, sweetheart,"

"What do I do about Cal?"

"What about Cal?" Aunt Eva asked.

"I mean, he now knows I can use the gift."

"Better than he can," Aunt Eva smirked.

"But I can't trust him now," I leaned on the wall, "and I still have class with him. He's on my team."

Aunt Eva smiled warmly. "I think you and Cal should sit down and have a heart-to-heart talk. Cal's not the bad guy. He just got pulled in. And you were pretty harsh calling him a traitor."

"Well, he is! He's supposed to be your friend, yet he trespasses on your property and is working for someone who wants to damage that property."

Aunt Eva smiled wisely. "Talk to him, Kelly."

I sagged. "Maybe; I'll think about it." I turned and left the office. Behind me, I heard Aunt Eva chuckling and muttering something about teens.

23 – Shanghaied in the Parlor

I watched Alex getting ready for the winter dance. It was casual, so she picked out a skirt and a nice top. Mom had helped her put on some makeup. I chuckled to myself. Alex was so giddy! I saw a bit of what got her stuck in the mirror as Alex checked herself on all sides. Max had asked her to the dance. Since she hadn't had a date in 150 years, she said yes.

"Come on, Kelly!" Alex pleaded yet again. "It'll be fun!"

"That's ok. I'll be fine here," I refused yet again. "Besides, I don't know how to dance."

"Neither do I," Alex revealed. "Well, not like they do today. When I was a teen—gosh, I sound like my grandmother! Back then, I knew how to dance. Father taught me."

"Maybe they'll play a waltz or something," I encouraged, not expecting it to happen.

"Cal might be there," Alex dropped hopefully. "Maybe you and he can talk things out."

"Not happening," I retorted darkly. I returned to my book, not missing the concerned look Alex gave Mom.

Reality is Cal had tried to talk to me. Twice before Photography he tried to pull me aside. I wasn't having anything to do with it. He was a traitor. I'll work with him for class assignments, but that's all.

"Kel, we need to talk," he said softly next to me.

"Go away!" came my response.

"Please! Just talk!"

"Not here, not now."

That was the first time. I was still pissed off at him. The second time, the conversation went similarly.

"Kelly," Cal began.

"No."

Cal sighed. "This is getting us nowhere."

"That's fine. You're my partner for class. That's all! I wasn't looking for another friend, and now you've made sure that isn't happening."

I shut him down in the cafeteria, too. Too many ears that could hear the topic. I was still mad. What irritated me more was that Aunt Eva wasn't. She excused his decisions as if he had been shanghaied or something.

The doorbell downstairs rang. Alex got jittery as she picked up a small purse. She dropped her wallet and her phone into it, then looked up nervously.

"You're going to be fine," Mom calmed the girl. "Just be yourself."

"Ok. I'm just a little scared, though."

"Why?" Mom asked with a raised brow.

"It's the first time since I came out of the mirror that I'm going somewhere without Kelly."

Mom laughed and hugged the girl. I was trying to hide a grin, too. "You are not Kelly's sidekick. You are a bright, intelligent, strong young lady. You can stand on your own two feet. And if things go wrong, just call. We'll come get you."

"Jasper will be there, too," I reminded her. "He asked Hannah Shuster to go with him."

"That's where he disappeared to!" Mom mused with an interested smile.

"We took care of the animals early," I noted.

"Alex!" Aunt Eva's voice came up the stairs.

I grinned at Alex's deer-in-the-headlights expression. "Go on!" I urged her. "Max is waiting. I'll still be up when you get home."

Alex bounced out of the room. I could hear her going down the stairs. I could only imagine the look on Max's face. He was going to be stunned.

"You can still go, ya know," Mom mentioned as she folded Alex's jeans.

"There will be other dances, Mom," I said in a voice that was much older than I was.

"And there will be other spell books," Mom countered.

I held up my book to show her the title. *The Dragon's Sword.* "Not a spell book. Aunt Eva thought I'd like this series."

"You're sure?"

"Yup."

"Kelly!" Aunt Eva's voice called upstairs. "Can you come down, please?"

I rolled my eyes with a sigh. Another one trying to get me to go to the dance. Ugh! "Coming!" I called and marked my place in the book.

My frustrated eyes met my mother's as I passed her and bounced down the stairs. "You wanted..." My voice died off, and a knot sank in my stomach as I stopped on the stairs. I could feel the dark expression cross my face. Cal stood in the living room; his hands deep in the pockets of his pants. Aunt Eva stood at the archway.

"Come on down," Aunt Eva instructed.

"Why is *he* here?" My voice was hard. I came down the last few steps slowly and stood in front of Aunt Eva.

"Do you recall my request to you the night you found him?" she asked.

"Yes," I still eyed the young man distrustfully.

"And have you?"

"No."

"Why?"

"Because school is not the place to be discussing it. There's too many ears who could hear the conversation."

"If you'd let me...." Cal began.

Aunt Eva held up her hand. Cal immediately stopped. Aunt Eva motioned to the living room. "There are no ears here that don't know what is going on. You now have the privilege of speaking with Cal on the subject."

I closed my eyes and sagged. This wasn't happening! Still, I nodded submissively and entered the living room. I noticed Aunt Eva left the room.

"Can I get you anything? A drink or something?" I asked to be polite, but my voice was glum. Still, I'd get shot by both my mother and my aunt if I wasn't a polite hostess, even if I didn't ask him here.

"No, thanks. I want to talk about that night. We need to talk it out."

"No, we don't," I replied.

"Um, yea, we do." Cal smirked. "For starters, the rest of the class knows you're really pissed at me and want to know why, and I can't tell them."

"Oh." It was all I could say.

"Small towns. People pick up on things quickly. The gossip is probably worse than in the big cities."

I dropped into an armchair and waved towards the couch next to me. "Sorry about that."

Cal sat on the edge of the cushion. He rested his elbows on his knees. "Look, I'm sorry I trespassed." He scowled. "I'm not even sure why I did it. I mean, Broward asked me if I could check on it. I didn't even know the rift was there, but he knew exactly where it was."

"He what?" I snapped up. Cal suddenly had my full attention.

"Yea. It's like he scouted it out before. He gave me exact locations, trail markers, and distances. Almost as if he'd been there time and time again."

My mind raced through scene after scene. Too many times at dusk or during the early night, I'd seen shadows around the woods. The darkness made it impossible to identify them. Several had been staring out of the woods. Had Mr. Broward been searching our woods?

"He may have," I drawled slowly.

Cal shook his head. "He said he hadn't been here since he was a kid, but he knew about it then. Said something about the imps coming through a portal and the longer it's open, the more will come through."

"Are the imps going beyond the property?" I asked. I didn't recall seeing any when I'd gone into town, but Intrid knew which Gifters in town were possibly strong enough to close the rift.

"Not that I know of."

"What did you tell him when he asked for the details of the rift?"

"That's the weird thing. I couldn't remember any details of the rift. I told him I found a crevice and there was nothing there." A wave a pride went through me which I tried desperately to hide.

"And the imps?"

Cal shook his head. "I remember being in the woods and running from them as I was being attacked by them. Next thing I knew, you came cruising over on a snowmobile. How you knew I was there, I'll never know."

"I was doing rounds looking for injured animals," I revealed. "We go around every night or two to rescue them."

"Sweet!" Cal seemed impressed.

"It's Jasper's pet project. I just help."

"What did you do to get rid of the imps?" Cal was watching me expectantly. I hesitated, eyeing him suspiciously. "Look, I already know Eva is training you. She said so."

I released a heavy sigh. "Alright. I used a wind spell to blow them back. When we got back to the house and I sent you inside, I talked with them to find out what you were doing."

"You can talk to the imps?" Cal seemed surprised.

"Only when Brandon is here. One of them can talk to me through Brandon. It leaves him with a whale of a headache. It's how we know the history of the rift."

"You... wait! You found out where it came from?" Cal asked, surprised.

"There's a lot about me and Brandon you don't know. I'd prefer to leave it that way," I replied defensively.

"You can't just stop now!" Cal exclaimed.

"Yea. I can," I confirmed firmly. "If you're going to be aiding Broward, I'm not telling you anything."

"What if I told you I'm not aiding Broward? He asked me to do him that favor, that's it. When he asked me to do another one, I told him to do it himself." Cal scowled. "I'm still not sure why I said that. He's not that bad of a guy."

I knew exactly why he had said that. "Still," I replied. "Broward has been harassing me all year, trying to find out what I know. I've managed to play dumb up to now. You were serving someone who clearly is doing something against my family. I don't know that I can trust you."

"What do I need to prove to you I would never to do anything that would harm Eva?"

I shook my head. "I don't know." It was true. I didn't know what he could do to gain my trust. It had been broken. That's the thing about trust. Once it's broken, it's really hard to rebuild.

Aunt Eva came in with a tray in her hand. On it were some cookies and three cups of hot cocoa. She placed it down on the coffee table.

"So, how's it going?" she asked.

"It's not nice to eavesdrop," I smirked, repeating the line Uncle Cliff told me again and again. Aunt Eva laughed heartily.

"That obvious?"

"A bit," Cal smirked. He took a cup of cocoa. "Thanks."

"I'm going to go out on a limb here," Aunt Eva said, taking a cup from the tray and sitting in the armchair opposite the couch. "The biggest problem is that neither of you knows the other. In Kelly's case, she comes from a bigger city where she wasn't always the popular kid."

I dipped my head to look at my hands. "That's an understatement," I muttered.

"She stuck out, was considered an outsider, and had very few friends. She's been betrayed several times and, therefore, is less likely to trust. You weren't exactly on her acquaintance's list when you pulled this stunt, Cal. It's going to be very difficult for you to gain her trust now." Cal sighed and nodded.

"Kelly, Cal understands what it means to be the odd man out." It was Cal's turn to look at his hands; but Aunt Eva went on. "That's one reason he goes out of his way to introduce himself to everyone. He doesn't want anyone to feel left out and alone. As Cal's powers came to the surface, he experienced much of the same things you did. As a result, many of the people he thought were his friends turned their backs on him. He was considered odd; much like you were. Cal has a good heart, as do you.

"You are both in the same boat here. You can use each other for protection and support..."

"I have support," I interrupted. "I have you and Alex and Brandon and Jasper and Mom."

"Yes. And while I understand where you stand, Brandon has yet to get that far. At ten years old, his experience with social standings is extremely low. He's not going to be able to help you with your peers. Cal's been where you are now. He can help you out. He knows that the Gift's powers are not to be talked about or demonstrated in public."

"He was helping Broward," I repeated.

"Have you never made a poor decision?" Aunt Eva asked knowingly. I shrank down. "How about the last time you didn't take your medicine?" I shrank down a little farther. "Mm-hmmm. A very charismatic teacher simply took Cal in. Rolf can be very persuasive. He knows better now. I think you should give him one more chance; especially since he drove all the way out here just to talk to you."

I glanced up at Aunt Eva with pleading eyes before turning toward Cal. I stared at him for a while. He stared back with a worried expression on his face. He was waiting for me. It was all in my ballpark. Finally, I sighed and nodded.

"Alright. One more chance, but you'd better watch out if you try to cross my family again."

Cal smiled. "She's feisty!" he grinned at Aunt Eva. "I'm gonna like her."

"Just watch your back," Aunt Eva warned him. "Her abilities exceed yours by years!"

Cal's face went slack. "Really?" he croaked.

"Really," Aunt Eva nodded. "She has more power in her little finger than you have in your whole body! She makes your spells look like child's play."

Cal stared at me, stunned. "Wow!" He recovered pretty quickly, though. Cal rubbed his hands together. "So," he began awkwardly. "There's still time. You want to go to the dance?"

I shook my head. "No, but you can go."

Cal shrugged. "Ok. What do you want to do?"

I looked at Aunt Eva for help. Aunt Eva just raised her eyebrows and smiled. I closed my eyes and sagged. So much for reading. Obviously, Cal wanted to spend more time with me.

"Well, Brandon's got some video games in the family room. I guess we could play those."

"Sure! Sounds like fun."

So *not* the way I wanted to spend the night. I grabbed the last mug of cocoa and a couple of cookies. "Thanks, Aunt Eva," I said as I led Cal towards the family room.

Brandon joined us at the game console. We had a great time racing cars, playing RPGs, and solving puzzles. I was surprised Cal didn't mind having Brandon around. In fact, they got along really well. Around 11, Brandon fell asleep on the couch. I shooed him off to bed. A few minutes later, Alex came in from the dance with Max. They joined us at the game console. Around 12, Jasper poked his head in to say goodnight. He grinned at Cal and nodded. I wondered what that meant. It was nearly one in the morning when Cal mentioned he should get going.

"Yea, I suppose I should, too," Max looked at his watch. He got up to leave. Alex walked him to the door to say good night.

"Thanks," Cal said softly. He reached for my hand, but must have thought better of it. Instead, he shoved his hands into his pockets.

"For what?"

"A second chance? A fun night? Both," he explained.

"Why are you so adamant about me giving you a chance?" I asked him. "Most people don't give me the time of day."

"Their loss." Cal gave me a sly grin, getting up from the couch. "Think about it. You might figure it out. I'll see ya Monday."

"Yea. I guess so." I walked Cal to the back door where he parked his car. He bundled up with his coat, said goodnight, and walked out to the car. I listened as his car and Max's left the driveway.

Alex came into the kitchen as I stared out the window. "So, how'd your night go?" she asked with an inquisitive grin.

I shrugged, confusion still raging in my brain. "I'm trying to figure out why Cal is so bent on becoming friends with me."

Alex grinned. "Ever think that maybe he likes you?"

"He doesn't even know me!" I rolled my eyes. "We've had five classes together, and besides the discussion tonight, haven't really said six words to each other. How can he possibly like me?" Besides, I was still hesitant where he was concerned. He might have Aunt Eva fooled, but I was still on guard.

"I don't know," Alex sang. "Max told me you're all Cal has talked about since he met you."

"So?"

"So..." Alex was trying to tell me something. It wasn't registering. I shook my head. "Girl, we have got to get your head out of your spell books once in a while!" she cried, exasperated. "The guy thinks you're hot!"

"What?" I exclaimed. "No way!"

"Yes, way!" Alex grinned ear to ear, obviously satisfied with the bomb she just dropped.

"That's not possible."

"Oh, yes, it is!" Alex leaned on the counter. "And from what Max says, Cal's not the only one watching you. You've been quite the topic at the lunch tables."

I groaned. This wasn't good. Then I thought about Jasper. What did he know? "And what are you going to do?" I turned the tables.

"About what?"

"Well, now you've got two guys interested in you."

Alex scowled. "Two?"

I nodded. "I'm guessing Max wants to be a bit more than friends, but I've noticed Jasper's been trying to pair up with you more as well."

"Jasper?"

This time, I was the one who grinned. "Tell me you haven't noticed."

Alex's eyes went wide. "I haven't. Oh, my gosh!"

"Ladies," Mom came into the room in her bathrobe. "As much as girl talk about guys is a great thing, it's nearly 1:30 in the morning. Go to bed!"

We all laughed. I grabbed a couple of bottles of water from the fridge and followed Alex upstairs. I wanted to hear about her night. Yup. We're going to be up for at least another hour.

Two days later, Alex came up to our room with a book in her hand. "Hey, look at this."

I looked up from my desk and my homework. The book in Alex's hands was so old the binding was coming apart. The old brown tome was dusty and faded with browning pages.

"What is it?"

"Not what it appears. Look," Alex handed me the book.

"The Guide to Astrophysics?" I questioned. "Not usually your topic."

"Yea. I thought it might give us a clue about the Syzygy and the increase in energy."

I opened the book gingerly. This thing was so fragile, I didn't want to break it. Odd. The first three pages were glued to the cover. Three more followed; all blank. As I turned the third page, my jaw dropped. The center of the book had been glued together and cut out. An extremely old diary stared back at me from the opening.

24 – Some Really Old Information

"Do you think it's Faith's?" I whispered in awe, speculation in my voice.

"I don't know. I was afraid to take it out," Alex replied. She had a worried tremble in her voice.

With a deep breath, I carefully extracted the smaller book from the larger enclosure. The book felt gritty with dust and age. I placed the larger book on the corner of my desk. I laid the smaller book in the center of the desk so I wouldn't drop it. Carefully, I turned the cover. Faded, swirling handwriting met my eyes. I could barely make it out.

"Bingo!" I whispered excitedly.

"The Journal of
Faith S. Portworth
1596 - "

I turned another page. It was blank. A date in 1612 started on the next page. The first couple of entries were Faith talking about the gift and how scared she was to have it. In the third entry, she talked about how the gift was like witchcraft, but it didn't have the evil influences. Still, she had to keep things quiet. Luckily, the homestead let her do that.

"Wow! Her handwriting is worse than my mother's!" Alex exclaimed, looking over my shoulder.

"Yea. If I hadn't read your mother's diary, I'd never be able to figure this one out," I agreed. "See how the Fs look like Ss? The Gs look like Js, and the Ps look like Bs with a smaller bottom circle. It's similar to some of the older spell books in the library."

"Her spelling is atrocious!"

"No, words have changed spellings, and meanings, since the 1600s."

We continued through the diary. They were the typical girl entries. Who she crushed on that week. The community feasts. Things the local chief said at the tribal meeting. Problems learning to cook. Disagreements with her mother. Nothing that struck a chord about what was going on. We continued turning pages.

"What if we started from the back?" Alex suggested. "We might get closer to what we're looking for."

"I'm looking for a progression," I replied. "Like in your mother's diary, she states the spells she learned in order. I'm hoping she did something like that as well. Although she was already 16 when she started this, so she may have already learned several spells."

"Here!" Alex pointed at the book. "Father taught me a new gift today. It is supposed to make water good to drink."

"Easy spell," I muttered. "It's one of the first ones I learned. She's just learning it at 16?"

"17," Alex pointed out. "Look at the date. And she's calling it a gift."

I kept skimming entries. Some I couldn't get the whole idea because the ink was so faded. Faith finally listed another 'gift' she called *o'tahkomatpokoniksi.*

"What is that?" Alex asked.

"I'm not sure," I squinted. "The description sounds like the flaming ball that Brandon used in our duel. It's a favorite of ours."

"Maybe Jasper would know."

"We can ask." I kept looking through the book. The names of the spells were different, but the descriptions I knew well. "Here!" I cried, pointing to an entry.

"What?"

"It's blurry and fading. She learned a spell that could transport a person from one location to another nearby. She's calling it *á'póót stápoot opáa't*. I'm sure I'm slaughtering these words. Anyway. What she's describing, if I'm reading it right, is the transpondent spell I had asked her about. She was trying it with her father and places in the barn."

"Ok. But who did she use it on?" Alex asked.

I grinned. "Next entry. *I met a nice young man at the trading post today. He's new to the area. His name is Wohali Lightfoot. He's from an area south of here. I love his green eyes! It's like he's always smiling. Father asked him to come to dinner.*"

"New crush?"

I looked at the entry. "Yup. Let's keep going. Her next entry is talking about practicing with her father and how she thinks her gift is getting stronger. The one after that is dinner with Wohali at the family home." I turned the page. "Another visit from Wohali. Here!

"'*I'm in major trouble now. Wohali was asking me about the Gift. I tried to explain it to him, but he wasn't quite understanding it. After showing him a few minor skills, I asked if he wanted to see my latest gift. He said yes. We went out towards the woods so I could show him by distance. I was only going to move him across the yard. It was getting dark because of the eclipse. I read the words from my text, then a streak of lightning came crashing down into the woods. A huge wind seemed to swoop everything around me towards the woods. I heard Wohali yell, but I was being held in place by a tree. I looked around and around, but I couldn't find Wohali. An orange and yellow glow was coming from the woods. I went to check it out. It was a narrow hole in the rocks by the mountain. There are no fireflies around, and the fairies have gone. I could hear yelling behind the light, but I couldn't understand it. Suddenly, dozens of bugs were clawing at me. I ran for home calling Papa. He said he didn't understand what happened."*

"Oh, my gosh! She caused it!"

"We knew that," I smirked. "Oh, boy! Look at this one. *'I've been in hiding for two weeks now. Mother and Father have told the authorities that I have gone to visit a cousin. I don't know why Father insists I stay in the basement. It's very cold and damp.'*"

"Look at the next page." Alex pointed to the right side. *"'The authorities searched the house today. Somehow, they did not get down here. It's only a matter of time before they do. It's been four weeks since Wohali's disappearance. Everyone is looking for him, and now they're looking for me.'"*

"Look at the date," I pointed.

"6 October 1618. Wait. When did she die?"

"Shortly after that, if I remember right. And that's the last entry. I'm guessing they found her, tried her for Wohali's disappearance, and hung her for witchcraft."

"Wohali Lightfoot," Alex mumbled over. "Could he have been Native American?"

"More than likely."

Aunt Eva's voice yelled upstairs that dinner was ready. I smirked, thinking a moment as I carefully closed the book, and thought my reply to my aunt.

"Come on, Rusty," I called the fox from my bed.

As we came down for dinner, Aunt Eva looked suspiciously at me. "Trying the messaging spell?"

"Did I do it right?" I asked. "Seemed harmless enough."

"It is, and yes, you did it right," Aunt Eva grinned mischievously as she handed me a bowl of vegetables. "Alex, would you get drinks, please?"

"Yes, ma'am," she replied. Mom was setting silverware at the table. Brandon and Jasper came in from the bathroom. The group sat down for dinner.

"We found Faith's journal," Alex mentioned to the others.

"And?" Aunt Eva asked with interest.

"Well, we discovered the man she was showing off to was named Wohali Lightfoot."

"Sounds like an Indian name," Mom remarked thoughtfully. "But I don't think it's Blackfoot."

"Sounds like a combination to me," said Jasper. "Lightfoot is generally an English translation. Wohali, hmmm, could be Paiute or Navajo, maybe Shoshone." Jasper always amazed me with the number of random things he knew.

"The words she used for the spells were really different, too," I mentioned. "I couldn't pronounce them right."

"They were probably in Blackfoot," Aunt Eva replied, taking a bite of her vegetables. "Remember, our family started there. I'm willing to bet most of her education was of the Blackfoot variety."

"But she could write in English," Alex scowled. "How is that?"

"She may have had both educations. One parent may have been Blackfoot and one English. Remember, there were plenty of people here long before Lewis and Clark discovered this part of the world," Aunt Eva pointed out. "Just because your history books don't list this as a country, it was."

"Historical point of view," I nodded. "Mr. Jorgesson warned us about that."

"He's a smart teacher," Mom smiled.

January continued as usual. Cal continued to try to gain my trust, but I still wasn't sure about him. He, Max, Alex, and I had a photography project we needed to work on, so we were together quite a bit. Several times, Cal would treat me to a shake at the ice cream parlor in town.

February came in windy and cold. Jasper and I were doing most of the runs ourselves and finding more animals in distress. Brandon and Alex manned the nursery while we were out finding the poor things. They were on heating duty. We lost a few animals due to exposure, but we saved more than we lost.

It was the beginning of March when Brandon announced a bombshell to our theories.

"Look at this!" Brandon said, putting a piece of paper in front of me and Alex. We were at the kitchen table having an after-school snack.

"What is it?" I asked. The paper was a series of circles and rings with names pointing to them.

"I understand Jupiter and Mars," Alex pointed at the paper.

"I was talking with my science teacher today during lunch," Brandon began. "He was talking about the upcoming eclipse and what was making it so special."

"Go on!" Alex encouraged. Aunt Eva came in from the other room to listen.

"Mr. Warren said that from a celestial point of view, this particular eclipse is unheard of. Not only will the sun, moon, and Earth be in line, so will Jupiter, Mars, Mercury, Titon from Saturn's rotation, and three other stars just outside our solar system. That's ten celestial bodies all lined up in a row!"

"That's incredibly rare," Aunt Eva said thoughtfully. Her eyes met mine. "And dangerous. That explains why the magical pull is already starting."

"I still haven't figured out which transportation spell she was using."

"We can compare the diary to the spells," Aunt Eva mentioned uneasily. "Hopefully, it'll shed some light on the subject."

"I hope so. There's three different spells it could be," I sighed. "I don't want to use the wrong one. I'll be dead before we have another chance at this."

It was several hours later when Aunt Eva began comparing the journal to the spells. We had all four books laid out across the table.

"This one doesn't list that it transports to a specific location," Aunt Eva pointed to one book. "We can eliminate that one."

"What's this name?" I pointed to the one in the journal Faith had written. *á'póót stápoot opáa't.*

"Jasper?" Aunt Eva asked.

Jasper looked over the name in the book. "Hmmm. It's Blackfoot," he deduced. "Move. There. Place. If I had to guess, it's supposed to be *move to a place.*"

"This one," Aunt Eva pointed to a page. "It'll be this one."

"Why?" I asked, looking at the two spells open.

"She's talking about moving a person or thing to a location. This other spell requires a teleport circle to land at, which means she'd have to draw another circle wherever she was. The circles anchor themselves. This spell," she pointed to the one she chose, "is a standard transportation spell; also known as a transpondent. It can be done from anywhere to anywhere, within range, and doesn't need an anchor.

"Also, if you look at the dates at the top," Jasper pointed, "the second spell wasn't around in Faith's time."

"That doesn't mean anything," Aunt Eva corrected him. "The spell may have been taught. That's just the date someone finally wrote it down."

"Oh. Sorry."

"Good try," Aunt Eva smiled. She pushed one open book towards me. "Start going over each step of this spell with a fine-tooth comb," she instructed. "We need to have pronunciation exact. In fact, if I recall you saying so, get

Abby on the phone and go over the language of the spell. See if she can remember how it was pronounced."

Brandon interrupted us as he came pounding down the stairs at top speed. "Aunt Eva! Aunt Eva!" he cried as he came down.

"Whoa! Brandon, calm down! What's wrong?" Aunt Eva laid a hand on the boy's arm.

"There's that Broward guy upstairs," Brandon breathed hard. "He wants to talk to you. Aunt Marie is with him now."

Aunt Eva took a deep breath. "Ok. Let's see what this is about." She turned back towards me. "Start looking it over. That ritual is going to be difficult to duplicate."

The four of us watched Aunt Eva gracefully ascend the stairs. We waited until she was upstairs and we could hear her going down the hall.

"So," Alex said wonderingly, "Do we stay down here and review the spell, or do we go up and listen?"

"I've got animals to take care of," Jasper bowed out and headed towards the nursery.

"We weren't told to stay here," Brandon grinned.

"Aunt Eva doesn't like us eavesdropping," I said, looking at the spell book. Quickly, I dropped a bookmark in the book and closed it. "Let's go."

AUNT EVA

I entered the living room where Marie and Rolf were catching up. Rolf was extolling Kelly's wonderful progress in French.

"She's a natural," he smiled at Marie.

"I like to think so, but I'm her mother," Marie countered. "I'm partial."

"Evening, Rolf," I greeted at the archway.

The man stood as I entered the room. He gave me an appreciative assessment. Glad I can still turn a head. "Evening, Eva," he nodded. "I, um, need to speak with you."

"Regarding?"

Rolf looked over at Marie hesitantly.

"She's well familiar with everything," I chuckled.

"I'll go start lunches for tomorrow." Marie made the excuse to get out of the room. We waited politely for her to leave the room.

"So, what brings you by?"

"The upcoming eclipse."

"What about it? We have some time before that." I motioned towards the seat he had vacated and got comfortable in the armchair opposite him.

"I'm sure you're already aware the eclipse is increasing the magical pull in the atmosphere."

"That's not unusual in an eclipse, Rolf."

"No, it's not. But it is enough to destroy the rift and the imps."

I sat back and studied the man. "Why are you so concerned about the rift, Rolf?"

"Those imps are a nuisance and dangerous. Our people have been trying to get rid of them for generations. It's the only viable option."

"Have the imps been bothering you? My family has been living with the imps for centuries," I countered. "And yes, they can be a nuisance, but they are no more dangerous than a mosquito if you give them their space."

"They are dangerous to the rest of us, then. Perhaps because they live on your land, they're more tame."

"Tame?" I laughed. "I would call them anything but tame!"

"But you said..." Rolf seemed confused.

"I said they aren't dangerous if you give them space, Rolf. I never said they were tame!"

"All the more, then," Rolf nodded. "That rift needs to be destroyed."

"That rift is on my property, and I will decide what happens to it," I stated firmly. "You will stay away from it."

"Eva, listen to reason!"

"No, Rolf. You listen to reason. How you know about the rift I don't know, nor do I care. However, if I find you so much as 30 feet inside my property line, I will have you arrested for trespassing. You will leave it *alone.* Do I make myself clear?"

Rolf sighed. "Not going to hear me out, then?"

"I believe I understand your intentions quite well," I replied politely.

"You haven't changed." He shook his head.

"I haven't needed to. In fact, I've gotten better. Thank you for expressing your concern."

"They'll be the end of us all," he warned, getting up.

"Rolf, if they haven't destroyed us in however many centuries that they've been here, they're not about to do it now."

Rolf looked me in the eye with a disappointed expression. "As you wish. Sorry to trouble you. Have a good evening."

"You as well," I replied and walked him to the door.

I watched him enter his car from the window next to the door. As he drove away, he was watching the woods. Nothing seemed amiss there, however.

I smirked as I heard the kids shushing each other as they went back downstairs. Well, at least they knew what Rolf's intentions were.

25 – The Battle of the Equinox

With less than two weeks to go, I studied the spell more than my homework. I managed to get Abby on the phone, but she couldn't remember the way things were pronounced. She was just glad the nightmare hadn't followed her home.

Mr. Broward hadn't stopped either. He was still trying to get the low-down on me.

"Kelly," he asked after class was dismissed one day. "May I ask you something?"

I paused putting my books in my backpack. "Yes, sir?"

"What do you know about the imps at your house?"

"Imps, sir? What imps?" I feigned.

"Come on, now," he sighed. "I'm not that stupid. You're living with Eva. You know about the imps, and I'll bet you know about The Gift."

I shrugged. "I'm sorry, sir, I..."

"She doesn't know what you're talking about."

My attention snapped to the door. Cal stood in it, glaring at Mr. Broward. He stepped into the room.

"I've already told you, she looks like Eva, but she hasn't shown any signs," Cal defended me. "I've been over there."

"She would still know what's happening!" Broward insisted.

"Apparently not," Cal replied, then turned to me. "Ready to go?"

"Yes," I looked up gratefully. Alex and I followed Cal out the door with a good night to our teacher. "Thank you," I whispered as we moved down the hallway.

"No problem," Cal shrugged.

"How'd you know he was going to pursue that?" Alex asked him.

"I didn't," Cal revealed as we approached our lockers. "Jasper couldn't meet you tonight, so he asked me to meet you at class. Something about Broward giving you trouble. I can see what he's talking about."

"If Jasper isn't here, how're we getting home?" Alex looked worriedly at me, closing her locker.

"I'm taking you," Cal replied. "I told Jasper not to worry. I'd make sure you girls got home safely."

I rolled my eyes. White knight. "I appreciate the ride," I said kindly.

"Still not going to forgive me?" Cal smirked.

"I'm still giving you the chance you asked for," I replied congenially. Alex rolled her eyes. "What?"

"Nothing!" Alex brushed off with a snap.

Cal chuckled. "Come on. Max is meeting me at my locker."

Cal and Max did indeed escort us home. Max made the ride home very entertaining. I hadn't laughed so hard in months! The boys came in to say hello to Aunt Eva.

"Thank you, Cal, Max. Want something to eat?" Aunt Eva offered.

"No, thank you," Cal replied. "We have another assignment we need to go work on. It's due tomorrow."

"I am so not looking forward to this," Max grumbled. "Night, ladies." He gave Alex a hug and slumped his way towards the door.

Cal laughed. "Wuss!" he teased his friend. "Night."

I waited until the boys left. "What happened to Jasper?" she asked, sitting down to some cookies. "He always drives us home, even on the days he goes to his mother."

"The home rushed his mother to the hospital this afternoon. She's had a seizure. Jasper drove in to see what was going on."

"Oh, no!" Alex suddenly looked up, worried. "Wait. What about Brandon?"

With that question, Mom drove into the driveway with Brandon in the passenger seat. The two came in laughing over something that had happened in Brandon's classroom that day. He became serious, though, when he saw Aunt Eva.

"We may have a problem," he said solemnly.

"Nothing we can't handle. What's the problem?" Aunt Eva replied, dipping a chocolate chip cookie into a glass of milk.

"My teacher started talking weird during class," Brandon replied.

"Weird? Weird how?"

"He stopped what he was teaching, held the back of his chair, and started spouting things about aliens, Aquarius, and some really strange words. None of us could make them out. Then he was silent for a few minutes, shook his head, and continued the lesson like nothing had happened."

Aunt Eva stared at Brandon. Brandon's teacher didn't have the Gift, so she wasn't sure how this tied in. The plunk of her cookie dropping into her milk disrupted the silence. Everyone was looking to her for the answers.

"That is strange," Aunt Eva replied slowly, taking a spoon to dig out the cookie. "Did he remember doing any of that?"

"No. I asked him after class. He had no clue."

"Could it be the imps?" Alex asked.

"No. No, it's something else. We'll need to stay on guard."

"The magical pull is getting stronger," I stated. "I've been feeling it in my chest. Like it's trying to get me to perform some kind of magic without telling me what it is."

"Never give in to that feeling," Aunt Eva warned.

I shook my head. "I'm not," I reassured my aunt, "but it's really difficult not to."

"I know," Aunt Eva replied kindly. "I'm feeling it, too."

The day of the equinox finally arrived. Aunt Eva called our schools to let them know we would be home that day. Alex, Brandon, and I planned all morning, setting up a checklist of what we needed and the order everything needed to be done. The counter-spell to the one Faith cast was much more complicated than the original. It was one of those rituals where we'd be able to read the spell as we went, but the sequences had to be done at the right times.

"I've got the rosemary," Alex said, placing a baggie on the table.

"Mince," Brandon replied.

"Water." I placed a small jar on the table.

"Wand." Alex pulled one from a drawer. "Wow! This is old!" She placed the cedar wand with intricate carvings on the table.

"Bowl!" Brandon found a bowl and mortar in one of the cupboards. He left the mortar in the closet.

"A metal rod," I said, going down the list. It was a thin skewer that was already on the table.

"Rose petals." Brandon moved the plastic container of petals to the table.

"Head lamps," Alex said, laying four headbands with lights on them. "It's going to be dark. Hard to read that way." I giggled.

Anxiously, I went down the list one more time. I didn't want to miss anything. "Ready," I said. "Let's get ready. Brandon, we're going to need that mortar, too."

Aunt Eva watched carefully as I poured a bit of water into the bowl. I added the mince and rosemary, smashing it together with the mortar. The rose petals came next, smashing them in as well. The wand laid over the bowl and I repeated the strange words as best I could. I must have said them right, because the mixture bubbled. I dipped the top of the rod into the mixture and let it dry. Now to wait for the right time to go to the rift. Curiously, I glanced up at Aunt Eva. A proud gleam sparkled in her eyes as I nodded with a thin smile. Boy, was I nervous! My hands were still shaking. I'd never done anything this big before. Deep breath. You and Brandon can do anything together, I reminded myself.

Aunt Eva placed a gentle hand on my shoulder to calm me. "I'm so proud of you. Look how far you've come from last summer! You're not that squeaky, frightened child anymore. You're standing up for what's right, telling boys off, and performing complicated magic. I'm so proud of the woman you're becoming."

I stared at Aunt Eva with tears in my eyes. No one had ever praised me like that before. I wet my lips nervously. Aunt Eva laughed and hugged me.

"I need to find Rusty," I whispered. My voice was still shaking. "I don't want him outside while this is happening."

"Go on. We'll need to head out in about a half hour."

Aunt Eva drove us towards the woods in the truck as the time got closer. The moon was already starting to cover the sun. George was waiting for us near the woods. We all got out and got things ready. Brandon ran up to the rift and set the rod, then came back. I poured drops of the mixture at varying points between us and the rift.

"It's weird," Brandon said, shaking his head.

"What's weird?" I asked.

"How quiet it is in there."

"The imps there?"

"Yea, but nothing is moving. They're just clinging to the trees and watching."

"Let's hope we do this right, then," I muttered. "I sensed some unusual quiet in the cemetery as well."

Intrid came flying up to us. She landed on Brandon's shoulder.

"We wish you well," she said. "Regardless of the outcome, we know you've done your best."

"Thank you for your support," I said to her. "I appreciate your friendship."

"As do I." She floated away into the woods. Brandon shook his head as I smiled sympathetically.

"Why can't she do that to you?" he asked with a scowl.

"I don't know. Maybe your brain is easier to infiltrate, or maybe it's not as complex as mine yet, or maybe she thinks you're cute. I really don't know." I laughed as Brandon's face scrunched up in disgust.

As the light was getting dimmer, I turned on my headlamp. Brandon did the same. Aunt Eva and George waited near the car. Alex peered out the back window and nodded encouragingly. Brandon and I set up a music stand and the book about ten feet from the woods.

"We could start now," Brandon suggested, taking my hand.

"No. The instructions say to wait until the sun is completely covered." I pointed to the spot on the page. "We've got another 5 minutes. I'm betting that's one place where Faith went wrong." Inside, my stomach churned. My anxiety was getting to me. I had to breathe deep to stay in control.

Out of nowhere, a figure came from our left, taking my mind off my anxiety. A black cape covered the body as it raced towards the woods. Bright blue lightning bolts were flashing towards the rift.

I shot out an air burst, knocking the person over. The hood fell from his head, revealing Mr. Broward. He got to his feet, throwing a fireball at us. Brandon's shield stopped it. I sent it back, barely missing him.

Aunt Eva cast a spell from behind us, dragging him away from the woods. He fought against it and threw a lightning bolt at Aunt Eva; eventually breaking free of the spell and returning to his trajectory. I intervened again, freezing him in place. He wrestled with ice.

Broward threw an acid blob towards me. I ducked and hit him with a lightning bolt. Broward tumbled from the force. He turned with angry eyes and tried to hit me with something else. My shield held.

"We have to start!" Brandon urged, looking at the moon falling into place.

"Trees, cage him!" I ordered angrily. To everyone else's surprise, the trees nearby arched over, creating a cage around Broward with their branches. Roots came out of the ground to twist around his ankles. He could barely see out between the leaves and the wood. Aunt Eva cast a ward on the cage so Broward couldn't get out.

I began the incantation, holding Brandon's hand and reading carefully from the book on the stand. The wind whipped up, blowing everything around. Brandon grabbed the book. Holding tight to Brandon, I tried to ignore the wind. Lightning began flashing overhead as clouds rolled in. Oddly, the clouds were only over the woods. I wet my lips nervously as I continued, making the necessary gestures with both my hand and the wand. Holding onto Brandon meant I often had to switch. The wind was getting stronger, trying to drag us towards the rift.

I called out the last line of the spell above the wind. Whirlwinds formed around us, one breaking the cage around Broward and dragging him towards the rift. I saw him clawing at the ground to get away as Brandon and I tried to resist the wind. George immediately landed on him, securing him to the ground under one claw.

Unfortunately, we weren't staying put. Aunt Eva was holding onto the shaking truck while Alex hid inside. My shield was weakening. Brandon was clutching me for security. I grasped the book off the music stand. Just as the shield broke and the two of us began a slow drag towards the rift, another body plowed into us, knocking us to the ground.

"Stay down," the ragged voice came as another spell was cast.

Lighting was flashing. Thunder was rumbling. Trees were cracking. Ground was shaking. Dust, dirt, leaves, and debris were flying around like a tornado. Looking up, I spotted a streak of lightning strike the rod. The rift blew open and a yellow-orange light flooded the dark. I could barely make out what happened through the dirt and leaves. Then suddenly, all was quiet. The wind stopped and all the debris hit the ground. The moon slowly moved away from the sun, letting the Earthly light back onto the scene.

The figure above me rose slowly to his knees, making certain it was safe before letting me up.

"Are you alright?" he asked with concern.

"Cal?" I asked, getting to my knees.

"Yea. Are you alright? Brandon?"

"Yes. Brandon?"

"All good," Brandon smiled. "Look!"

Sitting on the ground, Cal, Brandon, and I looked around. Hundreds of fairies of all styles and colors were flying around us, celebrating. Several came down and nodded to us before flying off to areas of the property.

"How beautiful!" I mused.

"Yea," Cal agreed, getting up. He held out a hand for me and helped me up. "Good work," he complimented.

I swayed a bit, feeling light-headed and weak, and grabbed onto Cal's arm. Cal chuckled as he wrapped his other arm around me.

"Perhaps we should get you back to the house," Cal suggested. "That spell took a lot out of you." I nodded. He carefully led me to the truck.

"May day!" Brandon called, running towards a figure lying prone on the ground near the edge of the now damaged woods. Aunt Eva ran over as well. They turned the figure over to find a groggy young man. His reddish face was pale, and his eyes were confused. The clothing he had on was from another era altogether. His hair was dark, and his body was extremely thin.

"Wh... where be I?" he asked hoarsely.

"You're with friends," Aunt Eva replied, helping him up. "Let's take you to the house and see how you're faring."

"What should I do with the vermin?" George asked, still holding an angry Broward to the ground.

Aunt Eva sighed. "Let him up, George. He'll have his own interrogation to answer to."

George sighed begrudgingly. "Very well." He made us laugh when he murmured something about missing out on a good snack.

Aunt Eva directed everyone to the back of the truck. George said goodbye and flew off towards his cave.

"Was that... a dragon?" Broward asked.

"Can we do a mind wipe?" I asked, glaring at Broward. "Please? I don't like George's life being in danger because of *him*." Mr. Broward spun towards me, a stunned look on his face.

"We'll see what we're going to do about Rolf later. Let's get back to the house and do a health check on everyone." Aunt Eva was helping Wohali into the truck bed. Cal quickly jumped to help her.

I looked over at the woods. "Thank you, trees!" I shouted.

To everyone's surprise, the trees started swaying back and forth in response. I just smiled.

Mom was ready in the kitchen when we returned. She had hot chocolate, coffee, and tea ready and the first aid kit on the kitchen table. She immediately grasped me in a huge hug.

"Are you alright? Anything hurt?" she asked, noting a few scratches on my face and arms.

"I'm fine," I tried to reassure my mother.

"Here, Marie," Aunt Eva said, helping the young man into the kitchen. "I think he needs your help more."

"You lied to me!" Broward yelled at Aunt Eva.

"Excuse me?"

"You said she didn't have any magic!"

"I never said that. I said she didn't understand what you were asking, which, at the time, she didn't."

"And you kept up the ruse?" he glared at me.

My face hardened as I glared at him. "I did what I had to in order to keep my family safe," I replied darkly. "And if that meant pretending I didn't know what you wanted, that's what it meant."

"And a dragon? You have a dragon?" he exclaimed.

"I told you before that I was going to call the police if you trespassed again," Aunt Eva replied. "Shall I?"

A knock at the front door stopped us all. Everyone looked at each other, stunned, trying to figure out silently who it could be. The knock came again. Alex went down the hall to answer the door.

"Good afternoon, Miss. Is Eva at home?" an old but recognizable voice came through the door. I exchanged worried glances with Brandon.

"Y... yes, sir. Would you like to come in?" she asked politely. I noticed he wasn't throwing around any powerful light. "Aunt Eva?" she called.

Aunt Eva entered the hallway. She nodded politely. "Magistrate. Won't you come in? Can I get you something to drink?"

"No, no! Thank you, but I would like to see those marvelous youngsters."

"Of course. This way."

Cal and I rose to our feet when the Magistrate came into the room. He paused as he looked at the group in the room.

"I'll take this one into the family room to rest," Mom remarked nervously. "Come along, Hali. Let's get you settled with some soup."

"Yes, ma'am," the young man replied, standing shakily. "I still und'rstandeth not what hath happened. Wh'ren is Faith?"

"Later," Mom comforted. "Alex, can you get me some soup from the stove?"

"Yes, ma'am," Alex replied and went to do as directed.

"Well, now," the magistrate nodded, looking about. "We have our two heroes, Calvin, and Rolf. What an interesting gathering!"

"Magistrate, there is something very abnormal going on here. She is deliberately hiding..."

"Oh, stuff it, Rolf!" the magistrate grumbled at him. My eyes danced as I covered my mouth. "She is doing exactly what she should be!" He turned and approached me and Brandon, who watched him worriedly. Brandon stepped in front of me protectively. The magistrate laughed heartily. "Yes, Brandon, one day you may need to do that, but not today. I came to congratulate you both on a job well done. The imps are gone, the fairies have returned to the valley, and the rift is closed. It was a very difficult spell to cast, and you did it wonderfully."

I let out a breath I didn't know I was holding. "Thank you, sir," I replied shyly.

"Thank you," Brandon followed my lead.

"I can't wait to see what you'll be capable of in a few years. Yes, yes, the Seth Drinel. I never thought I'd live to see the day."

"The Seth Drinel?" Rolf asked, wide-eyed. "Are you for real?"

The magistrate looked over his shoulder. "Rolf, these two children have more power in their little fingers than you will ever see in your lifetime. Leave them be and you might live to a ripe old age. Interfere and you'll have more than me to answer to."

"Y... y... yes, sir," he quipped out, still staring at me and Brandon in disbelief.

"Now, for you two," he returned to us. "Learn as much as you can and train hard. Your strength will come with practice."

"But not above being children first," Aunt Eva stepped in. "Their mental health is just as important as their Gifting lessons."

The magistrate laughed. "Yes, of course. You're right, Eva. So, tell me, what things do you like to do?" My mouth dropped open. He was acting like a long-lost grandfather.

"I like soccer," Brandon replied uncertainly. "And video games, and helping with the animals."

At that point, Rusty came running up the stairs with Jasper. He ran straight to me and pawed to be picked up. I chuckled and picked up the fox.

"I have a variety of interests," I replied politely. "Art, reading,..."

"Caring for the animals as well, I see," the magistrate patted Rusty's head. "And the trees seem to like you. Well done." He looked at Calvin. "And you, Mr. Verazano? How do you fit into this rosy picture?"

"Me? Um, I'm just a friend."

"That's good. These two are going to need good friends. Keep it up."

He began looking at me again. "Eva, perhaps Kelly should spend some of her summer with Rhoda."

"Rhoda? The druid?" Eva asked, surprised.

"Yes. Yes. Kelly will need guidance in that area," he turned to Aunt Eva with a teasing gleam in his eyes, "which is so not your department."

Aunt Eva laughed. "No, sir, it is not. I'll contact Rhoda and see what she thinks."

Alex had returned to the room and stood to the side. She jumped when the magistrate turned to her. "And you, Miss Reed?"

"Me?" Alex's knees shook.

"Yes, miss," he approached her slowly, leaning heavily on his staff. "Are you content here?"

"Yes, sir."

"Would you rather return to your own time?"

"No, sir. I like it here. I have a family here."

"Yes, you do. And you make a wonderful anchor for Kelly and Brandon. I'm pleased with your progress as well. Should you decide you'd rather return to your time, simply let Eva know and I shall arrange it." Alex nodded. "Well, I will be off. Oh, let me take that young man with me," he mentioned to Aunt Eva. "He will not survive long here. Too much damage from the other realm."

"If you think that best," Aunt Eva nodded. "I didn't think he was going to last long."

"Yes. I believe that would be wise."

"I'll fetch him," she smiled sadly and left for the family room.

"Excuse me?" Brandon asked.

"Yes, son?" the magistrate turned towards him.

"I don't know what this Seth Dr... whatever... is, but I get the feeling it's pretty powerful." The magistrate nodded. "Will we become as powerful as you?"

The magistrate chuckled. "Son, if you pay attention to Eva and practice well, even my powers will be dim next to yours. Learn well and remember to stay in control."

"Yes, sir," Brandon nodded, smiling.

"Rolf," the magistrate barked.

"Yes, sir?"

"I meant what I said. Leave those two alone and stop trying to take over everything. Learn to work as a team instead of an individual."

Mr. Broward didn't reply. He glared at the old man.

"Be careful," the old man said with a sparkle in his eye. "Your face might freeze that way."

Alex, Brandon, Cal, and I burst out laughing. We had often heard that phrase, but never towards an adult. Mr. Broward just continued to glare.

Aunt Eva and Mom returned with Wahali. They slowly walked him and the magistrate out to the front lawn. They returned a few minutes later. Inside, while the others sat at the table, I simply remained standing, cuddling Rusty and staring at Mr. Broward, who stared back. It was almost a contest.

Cal came up behind me and wrapped an arm around my waist. "Come on," he whispered. "He isn't worth it." I stood firm.

"Alright!" Aunt Eva smiled, returning from the front door. "Pizza for dinner?"

"Yea!" we replied.

"Care to stay for dinner, Rolf?"

"I don't think so," he said coolly.

"Then let's go to my office and talk. Marie, would you?"

"The usual?" she asked.

"Whatever they want!" Aunt Eva smiled proudly. "It's their celebration."

"Cal? Are you staying?"

"If I may, please?" he smiled at me. I nodded. After all, he saved my life.

26 – The Seth Drinel

Brandon and Alex ran into the family room to relax. I led Cal to the living room. I sat on the couch, dropping Rusty next to me. Cal settled in on the other side of me.

"So, why did you come?" I asked Cal.

"I knew the equinox was going to do something, but I didn't know what," Cal replied. "He kept asking me things about it, and I didn't trust him to leave the rift alone, so I came out and hid in the woods to watch. When I saw you were getting caught up in the repercussions, I knocked you down and put up my shield. It was enough to keep the three of us tied to the ground."

"That's when Brandon cast the entangle spell," I said. "It made the roots go over us."

"That's what I was feeling!" Cal smiled. "Good thinking."

"Thank you," I murmured and gave Cal a shy smile. "I don't know what would have happened."

"Brandon probably would have cast the entangle spell anyway and saved the day," Cal blushed. "I didn't think of that one."

"Me, either."

"So, have I gained your trust yet?" Cal asked nervously.

I dipped my head shyly. "You're getting there."

Cal smiled. "Sweet. So, um, can I convince you to go to prom with me?"

I let out a laugh. "Yes, Cal, I'll go to prom with you. Really? You didn't have to save my life for that answer."

"With you, who knows? I'm still trying to get on your good side."

My fingers fidgeting in my lap. "I suppose I've been a bit harsh. Sorry. I don't trust easily."

"I understand, but some of us are trustworthy."

"And Max?"

Cal chuckled. "Max is just a daredevil. There isn't a mean bone in his body."

"Does he know about all this?"

"Oh, yeah. We've been friends since, what, fifth grade? He's seen some things I can do. He says it makes him nervous, but he accepts it and helps hide it."

"Good. I'd hate to have to take him out or something."

"So, the Seth Drinel, huh? That's mighty impressive."

"Still don't know what it means."

Cal's eyes sparkled. "It means that you will rise to be the most powerful Gifters of all time," he told her. "You will not only keep the Gifters safe, but the world. Some say the Seth Drinel will replace the magistrate."

"What? How? Aunt Eva says he's been around for centuries!"

"Yea, I know. I don't know all the answers. I'd surmise that once you're finished training with Eva, you'll go train with the magistrate. I don't know of anyone stronger than Eva who could train you except him.

"Funny," he smirked. "The Seth Drinel has been prophesied for centuries. Always a pair: a male and a female. I just never thought I'd live to see it. I mean, the way they worded the prophecy, you'd think they were talking about 2525."

My mouth thinned into a straight line. "I don't know about all this."

Cal nudged me with his shoulder. "You don't have to worry about it now. Just keep being you."

We looked up as Mr. Broward headed towards the door. He paused and looked at me. His hard features softened.

"Well done, Kelly. Have a good evening. I'll see you in class tomorrow."

"Yes, sir," I replied. "Thank you."

"I do have a question," Aunt Eva interrupted them after Rolf left.

"Shoot," I replied to my aunt.

"What was with the order to the trees? When did you learn that?"

I squirmed. "Oh. Um, well, I guess last summer in the orchard. I couldn't reach some of the fruit on the cherry tree and my levitation wasn't pulling the fruit off, so I looked at the tree and wished it would bring the bough to me, only I said it out loud. To my surprise, the boughs came down to my height so I could reach them."

"And you've kept that up?"

"Every now and again. I found I enjoy talking to the trees. It brings me comfort somehow."

"Not only Gifting, but Druidism as well. That explains why the animals like you so much," Aunt Eva mused. "The magistrate is right, Kelly. You are a very complex Gifter; and we're only beginning to scratch the surface of your talents. Job well done," she smiled at me.

Alex and I headed out into the yard later that evening. We looked around, but didn't see George flying about.

"Think he's already eaten dinner?" Alex asked.

"I don't know," I replied distastefully. "I don't know how often he eats."

"His cave?"

"Sure. Let's take the ATV, though. After this afternoon, I don't want to walk that far."

After picking up the key from the rack in the mudroom, I started up the ATV in the garage. Alex climbed up behind me.

"Hey!" Brandon cried, bursting out the back door. "Where're ya going?"

"To find George!" I cried. "We'll be back soon."

I hit the gas and drove the vehicle up towards the cave as far as I could. We had to climb the rest of the way up.

"Are you okay with the power you have?" Alex asked out of nowhere.

"Huh?"

"You know, the magic power you have inside. Are you okay with that?"

I thought for a moment as we climbed the path. "I guess so. Don't really see where I have a choice. Why?"

Alex looked at the sky. "I remember when you came. You were frightened and quiet. You looked like you wanted to cry yourself to sleep most nights, but you didn't want to appear weak."

"Childish would be a better description."

"Alright, childish. That first week was scary, and I was in the mirror!" Alex smiled. "I'll never forget the look on your face, or Eva's, at the eight butcher's knives peeking out of your wall."

I shivered. "Yea. That was a scary one. I wish I could figure out what triggered it."

"I don't know. I just remember Eva's face going white. She almost looked like a ghost. But you've come a long way in a short time."

"You'd know. How many Gifters did you see trained?"

"I've lost count. I guess I'm just wondering if you want to go back to the way you were last summer, or if you're happy the way you are?"

I thought for a moment. "It's hard to say," I mused. "When I came last summer, I didn't know anything about the Gift or the magic or talking with nature. Clues about mirror prisons or talking with ghosts or imps or dragons were non-existent." I sighed. "It was nice being ignorant of all this, but the magic is within me, and whether I like it or not, it's who I am. I don't think I could go back to the city and live like I used to."

"You've gained more confidence, that's for sure," Alex smiled at me. "I guess it's what parents call development. You know, how you change as you get older."

"I guess." I kicked a stone over the ledge. "I'm still scared, though."

"You wouldn't know it to watch you."

I sniffed. "Just watch me around Cal. I'm so afraid of trusting him. I don't know how to act or what to say or what I should do."

Alex let out a laugh! "Girl, that's just learning. The advice over the years has always been to be yourself. Every parent I've seen gave that advice to their son or daughter. Aunt Marie gave it to me at the Winter Dance. Remember?" She bumped my shoulder with hers. "Just be you. He's already smitten."

"Smitten?" I laughed at my friend. "We definitely have to modernize your vocabulary!!"

We came around onto the platform laughing. Peering into the cave, we found it was empty. I looked out into the darkening sky for any sign George was around. Nothing.

"George!" I called. "George?"

A flash of fire in the distance told me George had heard. We waited only a few moments before the majestic dragon landed on the plateau. He sauntered towards his cave, turned around, and got comfortable.

"Now," he said, looking at us. "To what do I owe the pleasure of your company?"

"Well, first, I wanted to thank you for your help this afternoon," I said. "Couldn't have done it without you."

"My pleasure. I'm quite pleased at your success."

"Me, too."

"I noticed the magistrate visit. He didn't cause any trouble, did he?"

"No. He actually came to congratulate us. Weird."

"He even gave me the option of returning to my time period," Alex told him. "But I like it here. I don't think I could go back."

"It would be difficult," George nodded at his granddaughter. "With all that you know now, you would be very frustrated returning to that time period."

"Which brings me to the other reason we came up," I squinted.

"Continue," George encouraged.

"We wanted to know if you would want to return to your human form."

George pulled his head back and looked sharply at me. "Why?"

"Well, we found the right spell to close the rift. I suppose with a little research, we could find the right spell to turn you back."

"Don't you like having a dragon?"

"I love having a dragon!" I cried. "But you might like to be human again."

"And I'd like to know my grandfather," Alex squirmed.

George chuckled. "Child, you don't need me in human form to get to know me. I'm the same whether man or dragon. The form might be different, and some intricacies have changed, but I am still the same person."

"That's good to know," Alex smiled and hugged George. George's head came down to hug her closer to him.

"I'm very proud of the young lady you've become, Alexandria. If you need anything, you know you can call on me or Eva, right?"

"Yes."

"Good."

"So, what do you think?" I asked.

"Kelly, while my becoming a dragon wasn't my choice, I have made peace with it. I also know that if I were to return to human form, age would catch up with me rapidly. I might only survive a few years, if that. This way, I still have several hundred years to go. I am content as a dragon."

"As you wish," I nodded with a grin. "I just thought I would give you the opportunity."

"Opportunity appreciated. Now, I think you two should go to the cemetery."

"The cemetery? Why?"

"The activity there hasn't settled down. I think you're wanted."

"But it isn't a new moon," Alex said, looking up into the sky. "Wait, where's the moon?"

"On the side of the earth." I pointed at the horizon. "Remember? It was present during the day."

"Oh, yeah."

"Come on," I sighed. "Let's go see what's going on. Night, George."

"Good night, darlings," the dragon wished.

The lights of the ATV shone off the mist of the cemetery. I climbed off and headed towards the gate. "You want to come in?"

"I... don't know."

"Come on. They can't hurt you."

"O... Kay?" Alex followed me into the cemetery.

As usual, all activity stopped when I entered the gate. Also, as usual, Frederick came to scare me. I rolled my eyes and walked around as Alex let out a slight whimper.

"Really, Fred; that is so last summer," I muttered. "So! What's going on?"

Oddly, most of the ghosts were looking at me, hopefully this time. They parted as Faith came forward. She smiled warmly as she approached. She curtsied with a polite nod.

"You're welcome," I replied. "The rift is closed, and Wahali is with the magistrate. The other realm wasn't very good to him, and the magistrate felt he could recover better with him." Once again, Faith nodded. She turned and floated off, melding with her tombstone.

Another ghost came forward; one I hadn't seen in a while. I smiled at her.

"Alex, I think this one wants to see you," I pulled my friend from quivering behind me.

"What?"

Alex stared at her mother's ghost. Her eyes widened at the figure before her. The features and hair looked exactly like Alex described to me, but the eyes were blank. The woman looked Alex over. An icy hand reached up and stroked her cheek. I thought I saw a tear slip from one eye, but ghosts couldn't cry, could they? Then again, water from rocks supposedly couldn't burn either.

Tessa's hands reached around Alex's head. Alex pulled back.

"It's ok. She's just going to show you something," I comforted, laying an understanding hand on Alex's arm. "It won't hurt. And I'm right here."

After a few moments, Tessa let Alex go. She turned and floated back to her burial spot. Like Faith, she melted into the tombstone.

I glanced around the cemetery. The mist was thinning. Most of the ghosts had disappeared. All had quieted down.

"Let's get home. I think it's later than we thought," I suggested. Alex just nodded.

"What did she show you?" I asked as Alex closed the gate.

"Nothing. She said she loved me and that she was happy you got me out of the mirror. She said she was sorry for what she did. I told her you were helping me and that I was doing well at school and stuff. She seemed happy."

"I don't think we'll be seeing her or Faith anymore."

"I don't think so either." Alex looked at the cemetery. "I never thought I'd see her again."

"And now that you have?"

"I don't know. I feel sad."

"Well, I guess, on one hand, I understand. Kind of like me and my dad. On the other hand, if she hadn't put you in the mirror, we'd have never met."

Alex smiled at me. "Yea. I guess it was a good thing, after all."

"Come on, let's go home."

I maneuvered the ATV across the property I'd come to know so well. Inadvertently, I glanced over towards the woods as we neared the house. Quickly, I pulled the ATV to a halt.

"What?" Alex asked, looking in the direction I was.

"Look at the woods."

"What about them?"

"Do you see a shadow?"

"No."

"There's a shadow, about the size of a tall man, standing near the woods, looking in our direction. I've seen it several times before. It just stands there staring."

"How can you see that in the dark?"

"I don't know, but I'm sure it's not a good sign."

"Perhaps we should tell Aunt Eva," Alex suggested.

"You know I will." I pushed the vehicle towards home. Apparently, the rift was only the beginning.

About The Author

Jan is the mother of four, a lovable cat, and a cuddly dog. Seven grandchildren call her "Nana." She has a vivid imagination and loves to weave adventures. The more outlandish the adventure, the better she likes it. Much of her story creating has been put to good use setting up Dungeons and Dragons quests for her children and their friends.

Jan started writing at thirteen as a way to cope with life's stress. Over the years, she has continued to learn about writing and has honed her skills. She enjoys encouraging young writers to continue writing and explore their imaginations.

Jan loves to read with favorite genres being fantasy (go figure) and sci-fi. She dabbles in art and computers, enjoys cake decorating, and collects vinyl and porcelain dolls.

Want to send Jan a letter or picture? You can write to Jan at contact@janmhill.com. She'd love to hear from you!